BOHEMIA NIGHTS

by

Lucy Lakestone

VELVET PETAL PRESS

Florida

Published by Velvet Petal Press, Florida

Learn more about the author at LucyLakestone.com

Cover design by Sky Diary Productions

Original photo by 4pmphoto@gmail.com, DepositPhotos

Paperback ISBN: 978-1-943134-10-6

Kindle ISBN: 978-1-943134-11-3

First edition

PART 1

I knew within five minutes of meeting Duncan Flyte that he was an incorrigible man-whore.

I'd seen him in person once before, but from afar, when he interviewed people for his video blog at the fair. A video blog that I couldn't help watching. There was something about his buttery voice, that touch of Scottish accent, the intimacy of his tone, the sparkle in his pale blue eyes as he addressed the lens. The broad shoulders, the roguish cut of his reddish-brown hair, the hint of beard and the dimples didn't hurt, either. When I was working on one of my paper sculptures, luxuriating in his confidential tone and humor in the stillness of my studio apartment late at night, he seemed like the boyfriend I'd never had.

And then I had to go ahead and meet him for real, in the glittering two-story lobby of the Chamberlain Theater after the premiere of *Midsummer at Midnight*. I saw the way he enthralled the women, moving just inside their personal space, coaxing them into giggling and confessing their secrets for the camera. My celebrity crush almost immediately began to wither, but I hadn't succeeded in banishing it entirely before he caught me.

I was standing in a corner with my friends, including costumer Penelope, who was breathlessly watching Jace, the playwright and star, talk to the press.

Carrying a small but fancy-looking digital SLR camera mounted with extra gear, Duncan went for Penelope first, as the guys always did, until he saw that my glamorous friend was hopelessly distracted by Jace. Then he skipped past Cali and Sloane, as they were obviously inseparable from their boyfriends.

That left me, forever single and in no mood for the wiles of a heartbreaker who would normally never give me the time of day. He might have gone for another victim, but most of the women in the theater were fluttering to Jace like a cloud of migrating butterflies.

To give Duncan credit, he shone the full light of his sunny charm on me, even if I was the last cupcake left on the buffet — the one nobody wanted, too tall, too carrot-topped, too gawky and, at this point, entirely too cynical. I took a big gulp of my second glass of budget red wine and watched him approach.

"Hello, beautiful," he said, and only that alluring hint of Scotland kept me from kicking him in the shins.

OK. Maybe I was being just a *tad* hostile. Maybe I wasn't judging the guy fairly. Maybe I was profiling.

It was easy to relent when he stood next to me, smiling, smelling of fresh soap and spice and man, managing to be taller than me. Height was always an endearing trait in a man, given my size. I was no basketball player, but I had dwarfed my rare dates on more than one occasion.

So he didn't make me want to shrink. That was nice, even

if I wanted to kick him for calling me beautiful. He was clearly a natural-born liar.

"Hello, Duncan," I replied to his greeting, my tone dry.

His eyebrows flew upward. "Ah, you know me, then? How lucky for me." Despite his flirty words, I could see the question wiggling its way across his forehead: *Do I really know her? Did I do some evil thing to her in the past?*

Or maybe I was profiling again.

"I've seen your vlog," I admitted. More like watched it every night for the past month, catching up on all his past episodes, but he didn't need to know that.

"Have you, now? It's good to know somebody watches me."

"Me and your six hundred thousand channel subscribers, you mean?"

Duncan laughed. "Oh, they all got free hamsters for signing up. You're my first real fan." My friends elbowed one another and drifted out of range as he set up his camera on a tripod and stood next to me, holding a microphone.

"Maybe I hate your videos," I suggested, but I couldn't stop my mouth from quirking up at the corner. His good humor was contagious.

"Aw, that would be impossible," he said with a grin. "Somebody has to like me. You're the first!" Duncan held the mike up to my mouth with obvious enjoyment. His eyes flicked to my lips, prompting me to lick them out of nervousness, and then he looked at them again with interest before catching my gaze with his. Suddenly I was hot all over. "Now, will you let me interview you? What's your name?"

"Thea McKay."

"Ah, you see, it's destiny. My first real fan is a fair Scottish lass, and I'm from Scotland!"

"I'm an American mongrel, with more Ireland than Scot-land," I said. "So really I'm from Florida and Kansas."

"We can overlook those flaws," Duncan declared.

"I have plenty of flaws, but that's not one of them."

"Perhaps I can find more flaws upon *close examination,*" he said suggestively.

"Like that's going to happen," I said, though to my dismay, I suddenly pictured a much more intimate interview. I scram-bled to change the subject. "Are you really from Scotland?"

Duncan put a hand over his heart in mock dismay. "You wound me! Of course! Though I came here when I was twelve, so I've grown out of my kilt. Just don't ask what I'm wearing under my jeans."

My face heated even as I barked out a laugh.

"So what did you think of the play, Ms. McKay?" Duncan went on.

"It was quirky and funny and romantic. I think Shake-speare would have liked it."

"But it took some balls to rewrite Shakespeare, don't you think?" The way he said it, it sounded like *baws.*

"Jace wasn't wearing a kilt, so it was hard to tell."

Duncan's jaw dropped open for a split second, and then he smiled. "Oh, you are a naughty lass, aren't you?"

"No!" Great, now I had Duncan thinking I had a dirty mind, which I did, but he didn't need to know that, either. Plus, I'd potentially insulted Penelope's boyfriend on camera. "I mean, Jace had the *talent* to do it right. It was a great adap-tation. I've always liked 'A Midsummer Night's Dream,' because it's more like a fairy tale than any of Shakespeare's plays."

"You like fairy tales, then?"

"Love them."

"You know," Duncan said in a low, inviting tone, "you can find handsome princes in real life."

"I prefer handsome princes who don't screw me over." *Shit.* Did I say that out loud? One-point-five glasses of wine, and all my filters were gone. I took another sip for courage.

"Oh, darlin'," he said. "Tell me about the prince who screwed you over. I'll challenge him to a duel."

"Pistols or swords?"

"How violent you are," he remarked, even though he was the one who'd brought up duels. "Are you a theater person?"

"I'm more of an art person," I said.

"Oh, a starving artist. That explains the cheekbones."

I scowled. It's true I'd been skipping meals lately due to work and stress, but it was unkind of him to make note of it.

"I thought you couldn't be too rich or too thin," I shot back.

"You're perfect just the way you are, cheekbones and curves and all," he crooned in his butterscotch voice. He took in the way I filled out my V-neck T-shirt and short denim skirt in a glance. "I think you should love your curves as much as I do."

Wait a minute. Had he just called me scrawny *and* fat in the span of a minute?

He winked at the camera, reminding me that I wasn't the only one hearing his insults. My body flushed hot. I rubbed the back of my ring with my thumb, the ring my mother had given me, and tried to look cool.

Duncan touched my shoulder, and I shrugged him off, even as my body lit up like a pinball machine. My fight or flight instinct kicked in. Or should that be flight or Flyte? Because his teasing triggered my temper and my desire to hide, even as my body couldn't ignore the spark in his touch.

"Your eyes are turning the most fascinating shade of sapphire," he said. "Please don't be offended. I'm just trying to tell you you're beautiful, darlin'. Are you rich, too? If so, I might have to ask you to marry me."

"And I might have to say no."

"How could you turn me down?" he implored. "You being my only real fan?"

"Given my extreme wealth, I have half a dozen men in kilts waiting for me at home." I turned to the camera with a grim smile. "He's all yours, ladies."

As I turned on the low heel of my sandals, tearing myself away from his magnetic pull, I heard Duncan laughing.

"Now there goes a spark plug from her red curls right down to her toes!" he said to his audience. "What do you think, friends? Can I possibly let her have the last word?"

I made sure *he* wouldn't. I pushed past the fans and the actors celebrating opening night and set my empty glass on a table on the way out. I couldn't get out of the theater fast enough.

In the balmy summer evening, amid the drunken revelers of downtown Bohemia, I walked quickly toward the Junction Box to meet my friends for an after-show drink. The more space I put between myself and the theater, the more I thought about my encounter with Duncan Flyte. I couldn't shake the feeling I would come to regret it. Not only was he an accomplished flirt, he was completely obnoxious. He pissed me off. And that wasn't the most annoying thing about him.

I was fucking *attracted* to him.

～

CALI'S CALL Saturday afternoon was a welcome interruption. I was at my computer, neck-deep in graphics for a tedious construction company website, about to stab myself with my dullest pair of scissors. I pulled off my headphones and answered my cell.

"So, fun opening night, right?" she asked. A gregarious photographer, Cali sometimes seemed like the glue who held our group of friends together. I'd met her when I painted the sign on her gallery window as part of the work I sometimes did for my dad's business. That was shortly after I moved back to Florida from Wichita about six months ago.

"Loved the play. The drinks were fun, too," I said. "Ez's band sounded great."

"Yeah, their trials and tribulations did something for their sound," Cali agreed. "And how did you like meeting Duncan Flyte?"

"Flyte is the perfect name for him. Flighty, all right."

"You watch his vlog, don't you?"

"You know I do. Or did. What are you getting at?"

"Did you see the video he posted today?" she asked.

"Um, no." I closed some windows so I could get to my browser and open the video site. My connection lagged, and my nerves started to tingle. "What?"

"Oh, Thea." Cali's voice was somewhere between a giggle and a lament.

"Damn it. What did he do?"

"You'll see. I'll let you watch it. Call me back later if you want."

She hung up, and I put down the phone in a daze as I found Duncan's channel. The video was featured at the top of the page: "Midsummer at Midnight: Your Correspondent in Love!" The thumbnail showed him grinning with his microphone as I stood next to him, giving him the side-eye. If the shot was of anyone else, it would have been hilarious.

Fuck fuck fuck. The butterflies in my tummy started doing somersaults. I was glad I'd skipped lunch.

I blew the player up to full screen. In slow motion, I moved my hand forward with the mouse until the cursor hovered over the "play" button, gritted my teeth and clicked.

The vlog started with its usual guitar lick and title, *Flyte Night,* over a fast montage of Duncan doing silly things. Then it transitioned to an external shot of the Chamberlain Theater in downtown Bohemia. Next was a rapid succession of lobby shots and quick, funny questions and answers from Duncan and his interviewees.

"All that drama!" Duncan said finally, addressing the camera. The crowd milled behind him, and, high above, the sparkling modern chandeliers lent dazzle to the theater's lobby.

"We've had an incredible night — or should I say *Flyte Night?* — here at Bohemia's Chamberlain Theater," he continued, "where the debut of Jace Edison's *Midsummer at Midnight* was greeted with acclaim and the raging hormones of any number of lovely female fans. And they *were* lovely." In that subtle accent, *lovely* rolled off his tongue like some kind of caramel confection. "But what I really want to talk to you about, my friends, is the fan I found tonight. Her name is Thea, and she's a beautiful Scottish lass, or at least has a touch of Scotland in her Irish veins. Nobody's perfect," he joked. "But she simply *delighted* in giving me shit."

I almost spewed my fizzy water all over the screen.

"And for that reason," Duncan continued with a wry expression, "I think I'm in love. Please, my friends, judge for yourself."

The son of a bitch was *mocking* me. The image spun into our interview, of which he cut nothing. Usually this lack of editing was part of the charm of *Flyte Night,* as you got a real sense of people, but the last thing I wanted was anyone getting a real sense of me. With my friends, I was nice. Capable of happiness. Deceptively optimistic. Even, until lately, a morning person.

In Duncan's interview, I was a sarcastic bitch.

Which was, more and more, the real me. Maybe life had made me this way, but he brought out my worst.

His last shot from the interview was me walking away from the camera, and then the image flipped again to show Duncan in front of the lens with his mike, waxing rhapsodic, tongue firmly planted in cheek. "Tell me, my friends, is she not perfect for me? Her hair as bright as a Florida orange? Her eyes as blue as the Bohemia Beach waves? Let me know in the comments, and I'll update you on my courtship in the next *Flyte Night!*"

"Oh, no," I said out loud. The comments were always the worst part of any online video. I didn't want to look. I really, really didn't want to look.

I scrolled down and looked.

She's perfect for you if you want a witch!

Duncan SWEETIE come see me and forget that girl. She's not good enough for you.

Keep after her. She obviously needs a big strapping Scottish boy between her legs . . .

Shaking, I closed my eyes and rolled my chair away from

the computer. When I opened them again after a few cleansing breaths, I took in the airy space that was my apartment and reminded myself that they weren't here, those people. They hadn't invaded my privacy, not really. They didn't know me.

I lived here alone, in a roomy third-floor studio in what had once been an art-deco ice plant on the edge of Bohemia's industrial district, right along the railroad tracks. Bohemia had never been that industrial, but nearby, what had formerly been a furniture factory, a couple of warehouses and a citrus packing plant were rapidly being turned into apartments and condos. My friends Ez and Gary lived in a similar pad down the street, a loft twice as big, with plenty of room for Gary's pottery wheel and drums and Ez's grand piano.

I was OK with living here alone. Happy about it, really. When I'd come back to Bohemia after living most of my life in Wichita with my mom, I'd had to stay with my dad to save a little money. Those first few months had been fraught with stress and argument. This place had been my way out. I got an introductory price, and I was barely making it.

My dad still pressured me to agree to take over his sign-painting and graphics business every time I saw him, especially on the two or three days a week I worked out of his office, but I wanted my own clients and my own time. I wanted to make art. This place, if I could afford it when the rent went up, would let me do it.

There was enough space for a double bed, above which flew a flock of white origami birds; a dresser; an art and work space including a big L-shaped desk; thrift-store living room furniture; and a 1950s chrome-legged dining set Sloane had given me after she moved in with Alex. There was also a closet, a bathroom and a cozy kitchen. Big windows along the southwest wall gave me great light. It was peaceful here. I went out and met my friends on occasion, and the rest of the time, I could work and fantasize about the perfect boyfriend without actually obtaining an annoying real one. There was no one to stress me out.

At least, not until Duncan Flyte broke the fourth wall and decided to make me the target of his dubious humor — the humor I'd enjoyed so much before I met him.

I got up and walked away from the computer. I spent too much time in front of it anyway. I drifted over to my work table, covered with tools, paper cutouts and pop-up art, my secret obsession. I opened a folded piece of red cardstock, and a blossoming tree in contrasting colors burst upward from the white interior. I was delighted at the elaborate cutouts and layers I'd created, the petals and branches and trunk, but I was still striving to find the thing that would make my sculptures different. I wanted to capture the same magic I felt when I got my first pop-up book as a kid, only make it interesting enough to intrigue a grown-up. I wanted to get into a gallery or an event like the Regional Show at the art museum, if I was ever good enough. But there were so many artists doing so many things that were so much more spectacular. How could I ever be good enough?

I put my soul into these projects for hours at the end of my work day. I was sleepless. Restless. Desperate. And yet happy in the act of creation. I tried to tell myself that was all that mattered, but part of me wanted more. I wanted someone to acknowledge my work. I just didn't know if I'd ever strike upon a concept worth showing anyone.

Damn Duncan Flyte. He had demolished my focus.

That racket from the street wasn't helping, either. A car

stereo cranked up to eleven played alternative rock. I wandered over to the windows and looked down into the parking lot. Another moving truck was parked just outside of the reach of the big oak tree. This must be the renter for No. 10, the last empty unit, across the hall from mine. A coterie of five or six strapping young men were taking boxes and furniture out of the rented truck. Now why couldn't I meet someone like that? Someone normal? Though I knew if I found one of them attractive enough to give up my hermit habits, he was probably out of my league.

I leaned my face against the glass, daydreaming, until I heard a boisterous laugh. I stood up straight, not believing my eyes. A man with ruddy hair and a scruff of beard had emerged from the truck, carrying stereo speakers, clearly amused with life.

Surely he was helping someone else move in.

Surely Duncan Flyte was not moving into my building.

There's no way. An absurd coincidence. He's helping a friend. Get real.

Unobserved, I watched them go back and forth and listened to the chatter in the hallway. I repeated my self-assurances as he and the other guys hauled stuff and joked with one another.

Duncan might be an ass, but he looked damn good in shorts and a tight T-shirt. Tall. Brawny. With a great laugh and the nicest smile. Too bad he wasn't nice in real life.

Finally, their job done, the guys scattered. Duncan and one of the guys drove off in the rental truck. He was gone. He wasn't moving in. I sighed in relief, even as I snuffed the little ember of disappointment that flared in the part of my brain devoted to frivolous pleasures.

I refilled my fizzy water and got back to work until a loud

car stereo bugged me again, just as I'd been thinking about how pleasantly quiet this place was. I returned to the window.

Getting out of a compact SUV the color of a deep blue ocean was Duncan Flyte, all by himself, heading into the building. To visit a friend, of course. Right?

Creeping panic turned my veins to rivers of ice water, and then I heard a noise in the hall. I dashed to the door to look through the peephole.

Duncan Flyte, every sweaty, manly inch of him, was unlocking the door across the hall. As he stepped inside and prepared to close it, he glanced up at my door, a quizzical expression in his eyes.

I ducked. As if he could see me peeking through the peephole. Absurd.

It was much worse. Duncan Flyte had seen into my brain. He'd invaded my sanctum, and not just virtually. He was now my freaking neighbor.

FOREWARNED IS FOREARMED. Why else would I watch Duncan's vlog? I wanted to be ready for his next move.

That's what I told myself Sunday evening when I called up his latest video on my laptop. I'd made myself comfy on the couch in my sleep shorts and tank top, after a dinner of buttered popcorn, hoping I could watch calmly, without fear.

It hadn't worked.

When Duncan wasn't out and about interviewing people, he usually filmed his video blog in the late afternoon or evening. He didn't post every day, but when he did, it was generally online by 8 p.m. It was sad how well I knew his schedule.

"Spring is when a young man's thoughts turn to love, or so we're told," Duncan said to his camera in his trademark cheeky delivery. "But today is the first official day of summer. And since it's felt like summer in Bohemia for at least two months, I'm not going to let the season stop me. As you know, I'm on a quest to track down the lovely Thea, whom I met at a divertingly educational play on Friday." A link to the previous video popped up in the window as he spoke. "Unfortunately, I've been a little too busy moving to look very hard." He waved behind him, indicating a wall of boxes, and I sighed in relief.

"But I did have a couple of hours today to go hunting for her, and it turns out that she spends at least some of her time painting signs. So I went to look into the windows of her office, peeper that I am, and you'll never guess who I met."

Oh, shit. Now the video showed a point-of-view shot of Duncan entering my dad's sign and graphics business. The good thing was that I hadn't been working in the office today. The bad thing? My dad was. He often worked on Sundays, catching up on the books.

"Who did you say you were again?" my father asked as Duncan held out the camera so both of them were in the shot. Milton McKay's silver-shot brown hair was cut short, and his golf shirt wasn't particularly clean. It hung loosely on his thin frame, over his well-worn khakis. At least he wasn't covered with paint today. Under his black-framed glasses, his tanned face was creased with annoyance, as usual. Like me, he was tall, but Duncan still had him beat by an inch or two.

"I'm Duncan Flyte, of the *Flyte Night* show."

"I've never heard of that. What network is it on?" It took a lot for me to feel pity for my gruff father, but I pitied him at this moment. He had no idea what he was dealing with.

"We're part of Duncan Flyte International Productions," Duncan plowed on. "I'm looking for Thea. Do you know where I can find her?"

"Did she put you up to this?"

"Yes, sir, in a way she did, by being so sweet when we met at the theater Saturday night."

My father laughed. "Sweet? Are you sure you have the right gal?"

Gee, thanks, Dad.

"Yes. It was love at first sight," Duncan rhapsodized in a way that made it clear it was anything but.

I wanted to melt into the cushions of my couch and merge with the molecules of spilled beer and cookie crumbs.

"I don't interfere with her love life," my dad said. "I'm kind of surprised she has one."

Thanks again, Dad!

"She's not here today, anyway," my father continued. "She should be here tomorrow if you want to stop by."

"Thank you so much, sir. You seem like a very understanding boss."

"I'm not just her boss. I'm her father."

"You are?" Duncan's eyes lit up, and he turned to the camera and wiggled his eyebrows. *Oh, no.* "Do you mind if I call you Dad?"

"That seems a little premature, but if you need a father figure, feel free." My father was not without his own reservoir of sarcasm.

"Thanks, Dad! I'll see you tomorrow. Unless you'll give me a tour of Thea's desk?"

"I think I'll let her do that. I have work to do now." It was my dad's turn to face the camera. "But if anyone needs a sign painted the old-fashioned, high-quality way, or any kind of graphic design, come on down to McKay Signs and Graphics in Bohemia, and we'll fix you up!"

"That'll be five thousand dollars," Duncan said without missing a beat.

"What?"

"Advertising fee."

"You might want to leave now, son," my dad said, his tone darker.

"OK, Daddy-o. Can't wait till next time."

The image spun back to Duncan sitting in his apartment. "Now wasn't he a fine, upstanding example of fatherhood? I would expect nothing less of the father of my soul mate." His mien grew serious, and he moved closer to the camera. "Thea, I know you're watching. You are my one true fan, after all. Don't break my heart, love. Send me an email. Or some chocolates. Or someone to unpack all these boxes. I'll see you tomorrow, sweetheart!"

The video already had three hundred and forty-two comments. I closed the computer so I wouldn't be tempted to torment myself with them.

I didn't even remember the twenty seconds it must have taken me to get up, leave my apartment, cross the hall and bang on his door. When the echo of the last thump penetrated my haze of fury, it occurred to me that this, perhaps, wasn't my wisest strategy.

I was about to turn around and flee when the door opened, and there was Duncan, in boxers and nothing else. His eyes widened slightly.

"Well, that was fast," he deadpanned.

"It's one thing to make my life a living hell, but keep my father out of it!"

Duncan crossed his arms over his disturbingly muscular chest and leaned against the doorjamb. "I don't see the problem. He got a commercial out of it. And what are you doing here, anyway? Stalking me?"

"Look who's talking!"

"Look who's stalking." He grinned and looked me over, and I was suddenly conscious of the shortness of my shorts and the thinness of my sleep tank over my braless breasts — and of Duncan, far too close. *Those dimples. That chest, dusted with fine, reddish-gold hair. Those muscle-carved arms . . .*

"You need to stop this right now," I said, trying to rally. *Damn. Those legs. They're like tree trunks. Well-shaped tree trunks.*

"Seriously, darlin'." He hadn't missed my wandering eyes, and his smile broadened. "This is more than I expected. Would you like to come in?"

"Why would I do that?"

Duncan shrugged. "You tracked me down to my apartment. Isn't that what you want?"

"You asshole," I said. "I live here!"

His eyebrows rose in sardonic distress, and he looked around. "Uh, I don't think so, love."

"Not *here,* you idiot. Across the hall."

Duncan uncrossed his arms and stood up straight, a new spark in his eyes. *"Really?* Could I possibly be so lucky? Will you wait a moment while I get my camera?"

My mouth dropped open. *What have I done?*

I didn't give myself time to think about it. I was across the hall and slamming my door faster than Duncan could call out, "Darlin'! Wait!"

AFTER STAYING up until 2 a.m. working on a new pop-up sculpture, trying to forget my foolish foray across the hall, I still got up at 7. The morning-person archetype was built into my genes. I always got up early; the problem was, these days, I didn't have enough sleep to do so without pain.

I put on lightweight tan pants and a sleeveless pale orange blouse and tied up my red curls in defense against the heat, then left my apartment as quietly as I could, hoping I wouldn't run into my inconvenient new neighbor. I cranked up my car's air-conditioning for the short drive. I walked sometimes, but in the caldron of summer, my mom's old white Honda Civic was both an island of cool and a shield from late-day thunderstorms. And besides, it reminded me of her. The car still evoked her comforting presence, and it helped me start the day.

I parked downtown, walked to Sugar Shack for a peanut-covered doughnut and an iced coffee and ran into Ez.

"Hey, how's that Melodeon site working out?" I asked her. Cali and I had done the photos and graphics for her company's website.

"Looks slick," Ez said, standing with me on the sidewalk outside while we sipped our coffees and enjoyed our doughnuts. The bangs of her mod haircut half-hid her eyes. "My boss loves me right now. It makes it easier to sneak out a little early to practice with the band."

"You sounded great on Friday."

"We're doing OK, I think. Sorry I couldn't go to opening night. Cali sent me a link to that Duncan guy's vlog. That was hilarious."

"She did not!"

Ez shrugged and smiled. "He's pretty hot. Why not go along with it? I thought you were Miss 'Just Go With Your Feelings.' "

"That only applies when it's someone else's feelings," I scoffed. "And besides, the only thing I feel for him right now is loathing."

"Last night's vlog was pushing the envelope, I admit," Ez said.

"You saw that, too?" I felt the tingle of a nascent headache.

"Cali sent the link to all of us. I mean, Sloane and Pen and me. He has, like, a billion followers. You know we're not the only ones who saw it."

"I know, I know. It's just so humiliating." I took another sip of coffee and polished off my doughnut.

"I say, get him in the sack, have your way with him, and ignore him if it doesn't work out."

"There is nothing to 'work out,' and besides, it will be hard to ignore him."

She raised her eyebrows. "Is he following you around?"

"I hope not. It's worse. He moved in across the hall from me."

Ez let out a hoot of laughter. "On *purpose?*"

"No. He seemed as surprised as I was."

"You talked to him about it?"

"I — I may have gone across the hall to yell at him last night."

"Oh, this is going to be good. You thought you were immune, didn't you?" Ez laughed again. "I'll see you later. Maybe online?" She grinned and headed for her car.

I grimaced and walked in the other direction, toward my dad's sign shop, which was a block off Bohemia's main street on the edge of downtown. There were still a few utilitarian businesses in this part of town, despite the boom in galleries, shops, restaurants and clubs in the heart of Bohemia. An ancient two-story hardware store was next door, and a marine shop and a restaurant supply store were across the street. On a day this hot, I wished I were headed across the lagoon, over the causeway to Bohemia Beach, but I had to pay the bills somehow.

The shop was a squat, stucco affair with a couple of cabbage palms and a bird-of-paradise to the left of the door. A big display window on the right was almost covered with hand-painted lettering.

The door jingled as I entered. I greeted Connie behind the reception counter with a smile before heading to the back. To one side was an office where two full-time graphics guys created and finalized designs, adjoining a printer room. On the other side was my dad's office. My workspace was in the middle. It used to be a place for my dad to discuss projects with clients and sometimes still was. The square table and its chairs had been shifted aside to make room for my desk, which also shared the space with a couple of filing cabinets and shelves full of graphic-art books. Posters of the firm's work filled the walls.

I quietly sat at my desk and started up the computer, hoping my dad, on the phone in his office with his back to the door, wouldn't notice my arrival. But it wasn't that big of a space, and within a minute, he'd come out to greet me, his outfit almost the same as it had been on last night's video.

"Who the hell was that guy who came into my store yesterday?"

"Good morning to you, too, Dad," I said, sipping my iced coffee as my design software loaded.

"Don't be a smart-ass. Are you dating that guy?"

"Absolutely not."

"He seems to think you're engaged or something."

"It's all part of his shtick. Did you take your blood pressure medicine?"

"Irrelevant."

"Do you have anything other than the new Martin's Groves logo for me?" I asked, trying to distract him.

"You concentrate on working up a few concepts for that. I've got a sign to do this afternoon over in Bohemia Beach."

"I thought I'd do something cute with an orange or two."

"It better have an orange on it," he said, managing to make his agreement sound like an argument. "That's the last orange grove we've got around here, I think."

"Uh-huh." He was spoiling for a fight, and I wasn't going to give it to him.

He hovered for a moment. "You're wearing your mom's ring, I see."

"She gave it to me. Before . . . "

"Right. I know. That's good. She used to talk about that ring like it was something magical. She was always sort of crazy like that," he said almost wistfully. He rubbed his hand over his face, went back into his office and closed the door.

His words and abrupt departure stunned me for a moment.

Nothing shut up my dad as fast as bringing up my mother's death. He'd barely talked to her for two decades; I wondered why he seemed so emotionally bent about her now.

It's not like I wasn't. I still thought of her every day. I rubbed the ring, a solid silver band etched with a woven knot pattern. At the head, a circle contained a deeply carved Celtic knot of three linked spirals. When she'd given it to me, I'd told her I was sorry. Sorry she and Dad broke up. Sorry she was sick.

"It's the key to time travel," she'd whispered in my ear, as she had so many times. "Don't forget. You can go back and visit me."

"I won't forget," I'd whispered back.

Seated at my barren desk, I pressed my thumb hard against the Celtic knot and pulled it away, seeing the pattern in my skin, watching it fade. So strange that my father mentioned magic. That's just the sort of thing my mom would say. The time-travel idea was silly, a way for her to reassure me, but could the ring still hold a secret?

I wished I could travel back in time and make things right between my parents. I had no notions of finding love myself. I had seen how it broke people. I loved fairy tales, sure, but I didn't believe in them.

My father left the office a few minutes later, mumbling about a meeting, and I turned to my work. Over the next couple of hours of sketching on the computer, I came up with three concepts. My favorite was a vintage-style smiling orange peeking up from the corner of a crate with "Martin's Groves" stenciled on the wooden planks.

A jingle woke me from my graphics trance, and I looked through the window of the interior door to see my worst nightmare in the lobby — Duncan Flyte with a camera.

"No, no, no," I murmured. I could sneak out the back door. But then, that would be the chicken's way out.

It was too late, anyway. He'd seen me. I was plucked.

"Go on back," I heard Connie say, and the interior door opened. Duncan stood in the doorway. His physicality was palpable; he seemed to fill the small room. He wore loose Army-green pants and a button-up white linen shirt with rolled-up sleeves that showed off his muscular arms. His face broke into a smile — *those dimples!* — when he saw me. I wanted to believe his delight was real, but how could I? A guy like that was always "on," always performing.

"I was hoping I'd find you in," he said as he planted his tripod. "You left too early this morning for me to catch you at home."

"You were monitoring my departure?"

"I heard you curse when you dropped your keys."

"That was before coffee." I looked him over. He was adorably rumpled. "Did you just get up?"

"I slept in," he said as he swiftly set up his camera. "I do a lot of my work at night. Which you would have known if you'd chosen to sleep in with me."

"As if!" I stood awkwardly and crossed my arms. "Duncan, may I make a request?"

"Anything, love."

"You've had your fun. It's time for this charade to be over. Go find yourself another prop."

"But someone else wouldn't be nearly as alluring as you," he said as he blithely fiddled with settings on his camera and made sure his microphone was plugged in.

"Get out."

"But Dad gave me permission to be here." He moved to get in front of the camera with me.

"Turn that thing off. And stop calling him Dad!"

"You call him Dad, don't you, darlin'?" He continued our conversation in front of the lens. "But you didn't get your looks from him. Is your mother as pretty as you are?"

"My mother is dead," I said flatly.

After a microsecond of hesitation, his eyes softened. "I'm

sorry, darlin'. You're so beautiful, sometimes I don't know what I'm saying before I say it."

Somewhere deep inside me, a heart string twanged. *My God.* I actually almost believed him — something about him — some tiny note of sincerity in what was clearly just another fabulous lie.

I took another tack. "Duncan, please. This isn't fun for me. You don't mean it. Why don't you just move on?"

"Because I don't want to. And my fans don't want me to, do you, friends?" he asked the camera.

"Are they really your friends, Duncan?"

"Of course. But just friends. Otherwise, it would get weird," he joked.

"They're like me. Just friends. So go on and find another friend, OK?"

"Not like you!" He was more emphatic now, and he moved closer. He seemed to fill up every cubic inch of space around me. "You're my divine ginger angel, you are."

I swallowed, trying not to notice his gravitational pull. "If I were your divine — whatever — you would not be torturing me like this. You would leave me alone."

"Ah." He rubbed the thin beard on his chin with an extra dollop of fake introspection for the camera. "You do have a point there. I don't want to torment my one true fan. My true love. I propose a compromise."

"There can be no compromise. I just told you to get lost."

"Ah, but there can be," he said. "I will pause in my attentions."

"Pause?" I asked with trepidation.

"Yes, pause. I will refrain from featuring you in my show every night, except for the briefest mention, for a whole week."

"How about forever?"

"I'll do it for a week," he went on as if I hadn't spoken, "if you will spend every night with me for that week."

"Every *night*? All night?" *Sex every night? What? I mean, tempting, if I were — but hell no!*

"I meant every *evening*," he said with a wicked laugh. "But now that you mention it, yes, every night would be better." I shook my head violently as he continued. "I want to convince you of my sincerity. And if, at the end of the week, you still want me to get lost, then I will wander off like a spurned knight and find another war to fight."

"I'm not spending every evening with you for a week."

"You mean every night."

"You said you meant evening!"

"But you said night, and those are the terms. Look, you don't have to *compromise* yourself. Unless you want to." He grinned again, leaning even closer, and I wanted to smack him. Or maybe kiss him. No, *no*, smack him.

"What would these evenings involve?"

"*Nights*. Totally up to you."

I scowled at him, and he waited patiently. In my mind, I pictured the video he'd edit later, with a clock superimposed under my face.

"I don't know about this," I said finally. "I don't know if I can trust you."

"Ouch. Do you hear that?" He glanced at the camera again, then back at me. "These folks can tell you I'm good for any bet I make. Every dare I've done on every collab. I'm a man of honor."

It was my turn to laugh. "We could spend every night together not talking and not touching, on opposite sides of a room, and I could still tell you to go to hell at the end of the week, and you will?"

"You can tell me to go to hell anytime, darlin'," Duncan said, brimming with amusement.

"And if I agree to this deal, you won't put any of our, um — "

"Dates?"

"Not dates! Um, hangouts on camera?"

He nodded. "As much as it pains me to say so, I would agree to those terms."

A week to get him out of my life. A week to get my privacy back. It could be worse.

"OK," I said in a small voice, sneaking a glance at the camera as if it was a person watching me.

Except it was six hundred thousand persons, give or take.

"Excellent!" Duncan said. "Seal it with a kiss?"

"Go to hell and get out of my office!"

He grinned and blew me a kiss on camera, wiggled his eyebrows at the lens and shut it off.

"Now, that wasn't so bad, was it?" Duncan asked, moving so close to me that I could feel his breath, minty and warm.

"You don't actually expect to do this, right? That speech was just your clever way out?" I asked, though my id was gleefully putting on lingerie and imagining what a night with this man would be like. My superego informed my id that I would be wearing a suit of armor lined with ice packs.

"Of course we're going to do this." He leaned in and whispered in my ear. "I told you, I never go back on a bet." He smiled, and for a moment, the intensity in his pale blue eyes stole my breath away. "I can't wait. See you at 7."

"You can't mean you want to start tonight?" I called after him as he whirled out the door.

"Seven!" he shouted on his way out.

I felt sick. I'd never even tried Internet dating. Spending seven nights with a video star who would no doubt tell the world about every minute we were together was a hell of a way to start.

HE KNOCKED on my door at 7:05.

I knew it was him. I'd decided that he would have to come to me. I wasn't about to look eager.

That said, I'd been a tumble of mixed feelings and rationalizations all day. I'd Googled him to find out as much as I could, though the confessional nature of his videos meant that I already knew most of what I found in my research. He was twenty-five, a couple of years older than me. There were shots of him at video blogger conventions and stuff, and more of him at parties and other events, usually with his camera.

He'd already posted his video of us making the deal, and my friends had called me in turn, with divergent advice. Given they all had boyfriends, it was telling.

Sloane: "Unless you like them pushy, push him away. If you like a guy to take charge, well, he's pretty cute."

Ez: "You kept saying you wanted a boyfriend. You've got one for a week. Use him and lose him. Easy in, easy out."

Cali: "I wouldn't touch him with a ten-foot pole. Too intense for me. Too desperate for an audience. If you ignore him, he'll give up. If that's what you want, I mean."

Penelope, a renowned serial dater, was last to call.

"You have to be ready to deal with fame, *his* fame, but he's scrumptious," she said. She would know, given her hot actor boyfriend, whom she'd met during the production of *Midsummer at Midnight.*

"It's not like this is any kind of real relationship, though. This is a stunt for his blog, and at the end of the week, it's over," I said as I put on a little makeup, a rarity for me. Even if this situation was completely contrived, I wanted to look and feel good. Though I was dressing down in jeans and a T-shirt — my preferred mode — to make a point.

"Maybe it's not real now, but who knows what could happen? He really seems interested in you."

"It's all an act," I scoffed. "Plus, he's completely obnoxious."

"I don't know," Penelope said. "There's something in his voice when he talks to you. In his eyes. I think there's more going on there."

"Even if there was, say, sexual interest" — just saying the phrase made my face turn hot — "he is so out of my league."

"Now why would you say that? You're really pretty, Thea. I'd kill for that red hair."

"Yeah, but you didn't get called Carrot Top throughout your entire school career." And so much worse, but I didn't want to get into that on the phone.

"No, I had different issues," she said drily. It was hard to imagine what they were. She was the most glamorous of all of us, with her pink-streaked blond hair and retro pinup wardrobe.

"Look, this is just impossible. Can you imagine me with an extrovert like that? A famous vlogger? Someone that cute?" Crap, I was saying too much.

"And why not? Buck up, buttercup. You're hot, and he's hot for you."

"I'm not hot," I said, "and the hottest a guy's ever been for me was when I spilled soup on one in my waitressing days. I don't want to set myself up for disappointment."

Penelope chuckled. "So you *are* interested?"

"I didn't say — "

"Yes, you did. You're interested. And guess what? Setting yourself up for disappointment is what it's all about. No risk, no kiss. When was the last time you had a date?"

I didn't say anything.

"Oh, boy," she said. "Last boyfriend?"

"There was this guy when I was in art school, but he was — let's just say he was no good for me. Handsome guys are poison."

"Unless they're perfect for you. I can hear your pain," Penelope said, "but you can't judge every guy from that experience. Give this guy a chance. What are you wearing?"

At Pen's urging, I changed, a little. I still wore the jeans and sandals, but I switched to a tight black knit V-neck T-shirt. The thin fabric allowed a hint of my black bra to show through, and my cleavage made a rare appearance. It was only a hint of sex, but it sure felt provocative to me. I almost never dressed to provoke, and usually I wore a tank under this top. I opted for reddish-orange lipstick to match my cloud of curly hair. With my dark-blue eyes, the contrasts made me look as pale as moonlight. Duncan was getting a redheaded vampire tonight.

I smirked at the idea.

And then, remembering his scent and the sensation of his broad-shouldered body next to mine, I imagined sinking my teeth into his neck, tasting his skin.

Or other parts of him.

I shook my head and tried to get my brain into the right zone to handle this bizarre situation. The way I saw it, I could freeze him out, ignore him and tell him to go to hell at the end of the week. No harm, no foul — except for a serious waste of my time.

Or I could be friendly and cool and, again, cut him loose at the end of the week.

Or — and this would require courage I wasn't sure I had — I could take a chance. I could play along with his courtship, if it continued off-camera, and take advantage of being thrown together with a man who shook my hormones into a cocktail of lust. I could enjoy his company, enjoy him physically, and say goodbye at the end of the week anyway. I had no illusions that someone as into himself as Duncan Flyte truly had any interest in me besides gaining viewers of his comic antics. He was probably always counting his subscribers. But if I went into this week with eyes wide open — knowing he didn't want anything real, knowing it would all be over in a few days — I could keep my emotions in check and have fun.

Or have . . . *sex?* It had been forever.

I had kind of lost the knack of having fun. Or sex. And, I thought, maybe I needed some of both.

Even if this courtship was just a stunt.

Despite my overdeveloped sense of caution, after an afternoon of talking myself into it, I had to admit that I was nervously excited by the prospect of having Duncan Flyte to myself.

So when he knocked, I answered the door with a smile.

A smile that lasted about three seconds.

"I thought you were coming over to my flat!" said Duncan, surrounded by three other guys and a couple of women. I recognized the men as having been part of his moving party. Now that I saw them up close, I also recognized them from a few of his videos. The women were my opposite — petite, thin, thoroughly bejeweled, and made up to a T.

At least they had pizza.

Duncan, wearing the same pants and shirt from earlier, led them past me as I gaped.

"Wow, this place looks great," he said. "Now I know what I have to aspire to."

"You have better furniture," the blonde told him, looking bored under her heavy eyeliner. Her hair was cut short, and her low-slung halter top and high-riding denim shorts left little to the imagination. She stood by the window, lit by the early-evening sun of summer, annoyingly hip.

"The couch is comfy, though," said the brunette, who plopped herself in the lap of one of the guys on my sofa. Maybe the guy was comfy. The couch was debatable.

Couch Guy pushed her long hair away from his face. "Put the pizza here, dude," he said, pointing to the coffee table.

Another guy grabbed my art books and magazines off the surface and dumped them next to the table. The dude with the pizza covered the table with four big, flat boxes.

"Everyone, I want you to meet Thea," Duncan announced as they dug in. "Do you have any beer, darlin'?"

"A — a little," I said, wondering how soon I could get these people out of my apartment. I wasn't angry so much as flabbergasted.

"Great!" Duncan said, heading toward my fridge. He emerged with a twelve-pack of assorted Bohemia Brewing Company beers that I'd just bought.

"I claim the wheat," Couch Guy said around a mouthful of pizza.

"Do you have any hard lemonade?" asked the brunette on his lap.

"Definitely not," I said.

Duncan laughed. "Good call."

My expression must have been as easy to read as a Times Square billboard: *Who the hell are these people?*

"Oh, I'm sorry, love. These are my friends." Duncan rattled off a bunch of names. The only one that stuck in my mind was Lolly, the bored blonde. He winked at her, and she smiled. The exchange spoke of something more than a casual acquaintance.

As they manhandled their slices, I went to the kitchen and brought back a roll of paper towels in hopes of preventing a pizza-related accident.

"So how did you meet Duncan?" Pizza Guy — Pete, I think — asked me.

"You should know that," Couch Guy said.

"What?" asked Pete as the others laughed.

"It was on his vlog," the brunette said.

"I can't watch that every damn day. I have things to do."

They all laughed again.

"I met her at the theater after a play," Duncan said.

"Woo-hoo, the theater. Fancy," said the dude who was sitting on the only soft chair. Lolly had perched next to him, making Duncan and I the only ones standing. I was the only one not eating.

"Smack him, will you?" Duncan said to Lolly. She slapped the back of Chair Dude's head. "Get yourself some culture, wanker," Duncan continued. "Would you like a slice, Thea?"

I scowled at him and grabbed a slice with pepperoni and mushrooms. Might as well eat. I stood there as they chattered, closed my eyes to shut them out and lost myself in the taste.

The pizza was delicious. My empty stomach offered a small purr as the scent of garlic invaded my nostrils. I wasn't sure when I'd gotten into the habit of eating so little, but it felt sort of nice to eat real food.

"Looks like a foodgasm to me." Duncan's voice interrupted my flavorful escape, and I opened my eyes to the others' chuckles.

"It was great to meet you all," I said, placing the remaining bit of my slice on a paper towel on an end table. "I think you'd better go."

"But we're not done!" Couch Guy said.

The brunette rolled her eyes. "You'll eat all night."

"There's not enough pizza for that," he countered.

"She's right. Time to go," Duncan said. "Take the boxes, Bruce." Also known as Chair Guy.

They took their beers and boxes and slices and left, still bantering, unfazed by my kicking them out. Almost as if it happened to them all the time.

I followed them to the door and watched Duncan unlocking his apartment for them. Dazed by the invasion, I closed my door and squeezed my head with both hands.

"What the hell was I thinking?"

"What was that, love?" My door was open again, and Duncan stood there. He stepped inside and closed it.

I dropped my arms. "What are you doing here?"

"Seven nights, remember?"

"Oh, no. You came. You went. I think that visit by you and your clown posse fulfilled my obligation. In fact, I think that'll do it for the week."

He laughed. "Clown posse. I'll have to tell them that one."

"Go, Duncan."

"Oh, no, my dear," he said, his voice softer. "Our deal has not been fulfilled. Unless, of course, you want me to do another video about you today."

"You promised!"

"Only if you spend your nights with me."

I rolled my eyes, walked back to the living area and dropped to the couch. I crossed my arms and closed my eyes, trying to visualize my quiet, private life in my cool, empty apartment.

"Do you have a headache, love?"

Damn it. I opened my eyes. He was still there, now standing in front of me. Beams from evening's golden hour poured through the windows and cast him in the kind of glow a Hollywood lighting director only dreams of.

"I'm fine," I ground out, trying to ignore his beauty. "What was that all about?"

"They came over with pizza, and I thought you might like some, since we had a date anyway."

"Not a date."

"Oh, Thea." He sat on the couch next to me, almost rocking the furniture. Somehow he seemed even bigger sitting down, his body large and warm next to mine. "Look, I can tell you're annoyed. They're my peeps. Like a third arm. I didn't think you'd mind. Please forgive me. Can we start over?"

"Start what over? The torture session?" I found one of the few remaining beers and opened it, dropping the cap on the coffee table. I took a sip and glanced up at him. To my surprise, he looked hurt. Genuinely hurt.

"I'm not that bad, am I?" he asked.

"Well, I — "

He leaned closer. "You're gorgeous tonight. Your hair, it's like a sunrise. And the rest of you . . . " His gaze unabashedly slid over my body and back to my eyes.

My mouth dropped open in stunned silence, whether at his brazenness or the compliments, I wasn't sure.

He closed it with his lips.

One moment I was staring at him as he leaned close to me, and the next, he'd captured my mouth with his.

And it was like fireworks going off. Lightning, thunder shaking me to my toes, a storm under my skin. And he was only tasting me, sipping my lips as one arm slid up and around my shoulder to cradle my neck. With his other hand, he smoothly took my beer bottle and set it on the table, never losing contact with me.

He tilted his head to take more of my mouth, and I melted like a puddle of butter. I should have pushed him away, but I moaned instead, and he answered me with an "Mmmm" tinged with amusement. He deepened his kiss. His tongue touched mine, teasing, and his mouth opened, hungry, devouring me. His free hand slid to my knee, squeezing, caressing. He drew his lips over my jawline, my neck, sucking and tonguing my electrified skin as I leaned against the back of the couch, feeling his big, hard body bending into mine.

Stop this! I told myself.

But I didn't want to. But I had to. *Oh, my God, Duncan Flyte is kissing the hell out of me.* It was a disaster in the making. But it was so delicious.

His hand moving up my thigh brought me to my senses. Too much, too fast.

I sat up, interrupting his kiss. Not that I wanted to. *Damn it.* "Duncan."

"Thea," he whispered, moving in to kiss me again.

I held up a hand in front of his face. He pressed his lips lightly against my fingers.

I couldn't help a tiny sound, somewhere between a whimper and a groan. He smiled.

"Let me," he whispered.

"Just wait. I need to think."

"Don't think." He grasped my wrist, freezing the hand I'd put up to stop him, and sucked on the tip of my index finger, slowly, his eyes closed, turning it into an erogenous zone I didn't know I had. Heat blossomed between my legs, in places that hadn't been touched by a man in two years, as his other hand slid around my waist, slipping up under my shirt, caressing the warm skin of my back. I arched into his touch, and his mouth moved to the next finger, and the next, each digit a gateway drug to the high I wanted most of all: Duncan Flyte.

Oh, fuck. I wanted him. I *wanted* him. Would it be so wrong to have him?

But he'd had as many women as there were grains of sand on Bohemia Beach. I knew it.

Then again, with that kind of experience, he probably knew what he was doing.

I'd already rationalized myself into this devil's bargain. Maybe just a little more of him wouldn't hurt.

As if he'd heard my thoughts, he shifted me, pushing me down against the cushions of the couch, grasping both my hands above my head with his. He was over me, strong and smiling, mischievous, reckless. I should have been scared. Instead, I felt strangely protected.

My heart was protected. I'd already decided that. I was shielded by time. One week. One and done.

But damn, it was easy to look into those luminous blue eyes and see forever.

Forever is only for fairy tales.

"Kiss me," I whispered.

His face grew more serious. Then he did.

His hands held me fast as he pressed against me, heavy, but I was no wilting violet. I wasn't a big-boned girl for nothing. I could take the pressure of his body, wanted it, ached for it. And his mouth. Oh, his mouth. Sweet and hot and hard all at once, his kisses took my breath away, deep and light, bright and dark. I could taste the passion in them, passion I'd always dreamed of. So what if it was all physical? My weak objections faded in the glorious feeling of his lips and tongue, of one knee pushing between my legs, of his chest pressing against my breasts.

Duncan released my hands, and his began to move, his fingers gliding slowly over my body as he kissed me. I clasped his back, tentatively at first. So broad, muscled and warm. I'd never been with a man who felt like him. Oh, who was I kidding — I'd only been with a couple of men anyway. But Duncan filled all my senses, promised to answer all my yearnings. And we were only kissing.

And touching. One of his hands slid up under my thin black shirt and over my belly, slowly, and I reveled in the feeling of it. His fingers caressed the curve of one breast through the lace of my bra. His thumb traced small circles over the peak until the nipple hardened under his touch.

I tensed. This was all too much. So much.

"It's OK, Thea," Duncan whispered into my neck, kissing me there. He reached down and, in a swift motion, pulled my shirt completely off.

I froze as he looked down at me. His face was flushed, his lips wet, his hair mussed. He had a dreamy look as he cupped both breasts and squeezed.

I gasped, still tense, rigid now under him.

"Thea," he whispered again, rubbing my nipples with his thumbs through the bra.

"No. I don't know," I said hoarsely. "I — we just met."

"Should I stop?" But he didn't. His hands felt so good.

"I — yes," I said, chickening out.

"How about I pause here. Just here. No more than this. Just let me touch you like this. Yes?"

"No more?" I whispered, relieved and regretful at the same time.

"Just this. Trust me."

The tension in my shoulders eased slightly as his caresses became deeper. He kneaded me, cupping me, rolling my breasts in his big hands as he watched my reaction with a lust that thrilled me. I knew I had curves, though most of the time, my clothes hid them. Duncan made me feel every sweet undulation of my flesh, my skin under the snug lace. He leaned over me and touched his tongue to the deep cleft between my breasts, and then he ran it up that sweet valley and over one mound above the bra. He licked that pale rise much as he had sucked on my fingers, teasing out sensation with his nimble tongue until I arched up to meet him. He moved his mouth over my nipple, through the black lace, licking it until it was wet and tingling and hard, while he teased the other nipple with his fingers.

I had no idea how much sensation I could experience through just my breasts. What had I been missing? Heat began to shimmer through my body, radiating outward from my taut peaks. I moaned and bucked under him.

"Shhh," he said as he nuzzled and stroked me, his body bearing down on mine until I was acutely aware of his hard length pressing against me through his clothes. He moved his mouth to the other nipple, teasing it with his tongue while flicking the first one. Then he pinched it.

I cried out in pleasure and pain, but he didn't stop. He rolled the nipple between his fingers while sucking on the other one through the fabric until I became enthralled to the sensation, surrendering to the tension coiling inside me, between my legs, in my most private places.

As he pinched the nipple he'd just been licking, the tension snapped, and chords of pleasure sang through me with my cry. I rubbed against him, against his erection through our clothes, and for the first time, he seemed to lose a thread of his control. He groaned and held me as I gasped and shook, as my orgasm blossomed and faded.

Breathing hard, I held him tightly. And then the reality came back to me. This man I barely knew had just brought me to release with only his mouth and fingers — on only my bra-clad breasts — and I was half-naked and nestled against what felt like an epic hard-on.

"Oh, Duncan — I — you ... "

"Think nothing of it, love," he said, easing off me, helping me sit up next to him.

"But you — " I couldn't help glancing down at his lap and up again. I was sure my cheeks had gone pink.

"Noticed that, did you?" He chuckled. "My pleasure." His voice lowered, suddenly more serious, and he held my gaze with his bright ice-blue one. "I'll consider it my punishment for wanting to fuck you on the first night."

His language snapped me back to something resembling reality, even as I felt his intensity. I tasted the phrase in my imagination. *Wanting to fuck you.* He wanted to fuck me. Coarse words, but I took strange pleasure in them, because he wanted *me*. And I could picture him doing it. Could almost feel him doing it, the way he'd been pressed against me, making me wet with desire.

Duncan cupped my cheek and looked into my eyes, my face, perhaps reading some of my ambivalence.

"It's not just that," he assured me. "It isn't. I want to spend time with you. I just — seeing you with your hair, and that shirt, and — I just couldn't keep my hands off you. Forgive me?" He released my cheek and held out his hand, palm up.

Forgive him? For giving me one of the best orgasms I'd ever had?

I couldn't let my emotions get the better of me. Feelings certainly didn't seem to have any kind of hold on him.

I placed my hand in his palm and tilted it, turning the touch into a handshake.

"Of course," I said softly. He seemed taken aback for a moment, but my small smile brought out a larger one on his face, the one with the dimples.

Oh, God. A week? How am I going to make it without losing my mind? Or worse?

"I'm still hungry," Duncan said a few minutes later after he'd spent some time in the bathroom — I didn't want to think about what he was doing in there — and I'd put myself back together. "Want to go out?"

"I have projects to work on. And we already ate."

"You call that eating? Don't you eat, Thea?"

I shrugged, uncomfortable. "Of course I eat. Just not as much, lately."

"Tell me you're not on a diet. I hate it when girls are on diets."

"I'm not."

He walked around my space, poking among my stuff, stressing me out. He shook my *Wizard of Oz* snow globe and grinned at Dorothy fleeing the tornado, scanned my small bookcase, which was heavy on children's books, then moved on to my work table, piled with paper cutouts, pop-up pieces and plans.

"OK, let's go." I stepped up to him and touched his arm. He looked up and smiled. Good. I didn't want him to see my art in progress. I wasn't sure I wanted anyone to see my art in progress.

"We've already done pizza," Duncan said. "Shall we continue the theme? Italian?"

"Well, you know what they say. You eat Italian and three weeks later, you're hungry again."

He chuckled. "Not me. And I'm buying."

"That's not necessary." I grabbed my bag, a soft fabric satchel that often held an iPad or a sketchbook.

"Oh, but it is. Call it a business expense. Besides, I want to go to Marco's, and it's expensive." He exited, and I locked the door behind us. From the hallway, I could hear rock music and laughter leaking from his apartment.

"You're just going to leave them in there?"

"Sure. What could go wrong? Maybe they'll actually unpack something."

The moment had a surreal quality. I'd just had an orgasm under this man, this stranger, and here we were, engaged in small talk on the way to the elevator.

"Is something wrong, Thea?"

"Does this not seem the least bit awkward to you?" I blurted as the elevator dinged. I was never good at hiding my thoughts.

We stepped inside, and the doors closed. Duncan moved his face close to mine, his eyes sparkling. "I think the awkwardness is what makes this interesting." He kissed my neck, the lightest brush of his lips, and stood straight, leaving me flushed and trembling as the elevator doors opened.

A couple stood there waiting, a handsome dark-skinned man and a lovely Asian woman, holding hands. The woman looked at me. The man looked at Duncan. Both smiled, and we all exchanged nods. *Geez.* It was one of those interactions I imagined couples had with each other all the time. Couple culture. I had no idea what it entailed and probably never would.

They entered the elevator; we left the building.

"That was weird, wasn't it?" Duncan asked. "Do you think couples always communicate telepathically like that?"

I laughed, and the tension broke. "Probably. They were pretty cute together, though."

"Not as cute as you. I'll drive."

There was no use arguing. I'd have to pick my battles. The sun was going down, shooting rays between towering clouds to the west, and the scorching heat of the day had eased to somewhere below the boiling point.

"Storms coming," Duncan observed as he started up his SUV and pulled out of the small parking lot, heading toward downtown.

"Summer in Florida."

"Yeah. And it'll give me something to film later, maybe."

"What? I thought you weren't doing videos with me."

He smiled. "That doesn't mean I'm not shooting videos. I have to feed the beast, love."

"Why do you have to post so many videos? Don't you have a job?"

"Where have you been? This is my job. Six hundred thousand subscribers and counting."

"So?"

"So, ad revenue," he said, turning onto the main street, with its busy bars and restaurants.

"Ad revenue? I mean, what does that buy you? A burger a day?"

He laughed. "Try this car. Rent. Travel and cameras. I'm doing all right."

"Huh." I wondered what "all right" meant. My interest in him did not originate in what he earned — especially since I'd assumed he was a poor video artist — but my curiosity would warrant some Googling later.

"This beats what I was doing a few years ago," he said.

"Which was what?"

"Working in a movie theater in Texas, dreaming about becoming a director or an actor or a comic, playing minor roles in community theater. I started watching videos online and thought it looked fun. It turned out I had a knack for it."

"You really do," I admitted.

He smiled broadly. "Thank you. It's nice to hear someone say it in the real world."

"I guess so. Most of the online commenters are assholes."

Duncan chuckled. "They're like hecklers. You just learn to humiliate them with humor or ignore them."

"I don't think I could deal with that kind of feedback all the time," I said as he parked on the busy street. "I don't like people judging me."

"But you're an artist, aren't you? Don't people judge your work?"

"My graphic art is work. Paid. It serves a purpose."

"But that's not your art, is it?"

We got out of the car and started our stroll toward the restaurant among the colorful, cute storefronts and watering holes of Bohemia.

"What was all that laid out on the table at your apartment?" he asked.

I was hoping he hadn't noticed. "Just something I dabble in."

He looked at me for a long moment, so long I got uncomfortable.

I shot him a glower. "What?"

"What are you scared of, Thea?"

I harrumphed. "I don't think you know me well enough to ask me that."

"That's why I'm asking."

"Maybe I'm scared of questions."

"Then you never would have let me interview you," he said.

Maybe not, if it had been anyone else. As much as I'd wanted to flee him at the theater, something had made me stay. Someone. Him.

We reached the restaurant, on the corner of the block, and he opened the door for me. Immediately, we were immersed in a space of warm colors, amber light and dark wood, contemporary with a touch of Tuscany. Arched niches behind the circular, marble-topped bar held shelves full of liquor and extensive wine racks. High-backed booths ringed the room, offering cozy dining, with a couple of long tables on one end for larger parties. Frank Sinatra sang "Nice Work If You Can Get It" in the background.

The hostess sat us at one of the booths with big food menus and a massive wine list in book form that must have weighed five pounds.

"Do you want this?" I asked Duncan.

"No, thank you. But feel free to order whatever you want."

"I'm not in a wine mood." I set the menu on the table.

"How do you feel about whiskey?" he asked.

"I like it, though that's a little heavy for a Monday night, isn't it?"

"Whiskey's never too heavy." When our server came back, he murmured to her behind his menu. When she left, he lowered it, sporting a smile.

"What did you do?" I asked.

"You'll see. Do you know what you're getting?"

"My friend Penelope raves about the gnocchi gorgonzola. I've never been here, so maybe it's time I try it."

"Hmm, steak and pasta for me."

I laughed. "It's almost like you didn't have pizza an hour ago."

"I almost didn't! I had, what, one slice? Or two? Barely an appetizer."

"I don't know how you stay so fit."

Duncan grinned. "You think I'm fit, do you?"

My face heated again, and I opted to change the subject. "So how did you end up coming here from Scotland, anyway? Or going to Texas?"

"Ah, you're about to find out, lass." He emphasized "lass" in an exaggerated Scottish accent that made me smile.

"Are you sure that accent is genuine?"

"It's real, of course, though the burr can become *verra extrrreme* for *drrramatic* effect," he said, excessively rolling all his "R's."

"Faker."

"I just know how to use my assets when I need to." He wiggled his eyebrows.

"To get laid?" I asked drily.

"What? Will that work?" he exclaimed with mock innocence. "You're *verra rrravishing* tonight, *prrrincess.*"

I couldn't help laughing. The server turned up with two rocks glasses filled with glittering brown liquid over ice, took our food orders and disappeared.

"Whiskey, I presume?" I asked.

"Whiskey, indeed. I spell it without the 'e,' of course. It's a single malt from Texas."

"Texas?" I picked up my glass. "I thought you'd ordered Scotch from Scotland."

He clinked his against mine. "It's from the distillery where my father works. *Slàinte!*" He took a deep sip with closed eyes and a look of pure pleasure that was extremely distracting.

I took a smaller taste. The drink had a smoky-sweet burn.

"And what do you think?" he asked.

"I'm not an expert on whiskey, but I like it. It reminds me of toffee. And grilled pears. And maybe cinnamon?"

"I think you know more about it than you're letting on. Very good."

"What does your father do at the distillery?"

Duncan took another sip and set the glass down on the red tablecloth. "Actually, he owns it with his cousin, who was born here and decided to start his own distillery about twenty years ago. He recruited my father, who was a master distiller in Scotland, to help him do it right. They're doing nicely."

"So it's a family business." I took another sip. The whiskey's sharp edges softened the more I drank.

"That's what my father seems to think. It's why I finally left Texas for Florida. He keeps pressuring me to join them."

"Sounds familiar," I said. "Do you have any siblings?"

"A younger sister who's pursuing international law in London."

"And your mom?"

He blinked. "Still in Texas."

"Not in the family business, then?" I asked.

"She just enjoys the fruits of my father's labors." His tone was dark and sarcastic and entirely unexpected given his ebullient personality. I raised my eyebrows. "She's perfectly lovely," he added.

I wasn't sure how to respond, so I didn't say anything for a couple of minutes. I just watched him over my glass, feeling my nervousness erode under the influence of the drink. He made himself busy looking at the specials on the flip-over cocktail menu on the table.

"Is she OK?" I finally asked.

Duncan looked back at me and shrugged. "Sure."

He held my gaze, but something about the icy blankness of it, its refusal to yield his secrets, made me swallow nervously.

"So, um, when did you get into video blogging?" I asked.

His face relaxed. "I kind of stumbled into it. I wanted to be a big-time movie director at first. Austin had a lot of filmmakers, a lot of outlets for creative minds. In high school, I started fooling around with acting and movies. Then I made a crazy little short film of me interviewing partiers during South by Southwest and put it online. It got a zillion hits. I started to think maybe there was something to it. I watched all the YouTube stars. They were my friends in high school when things were shitty at home. Ah, rescued by the steak!"

I also greeted the arrival of the food with relief. Duncan was clearly holding something back, and why not? He barely knew me. But the glimpse of something vulnerable in him, some tender part he wanted to protect, softened my heart. He obviously didn't want to talk about his mother. Maybe I was imagining things, but I knew what it was like to live with a mercurial parent, even if my memories of my dad's rages were old and mercifully fuzzy.

The server placed a bowl of pasta in front of me — gnocchi, bite-size potato dumplings smothered in a gorgonzola cream sauce, garnished with basil — before setting Duncan's full plate in front of him.

"This is enough to serve an army," I said. "I'm already full from the pizza."

"Half a slice of pizza? You are not." He was already cutting into his slab of meat, so rare it oozed red juice. It made me a little dizzy.

"I don't know if I can do this." I closed my eyes.

"Thea? Thea, are you all right?"

I took a deep breath and opened my eyes again to catch Duncan staring at me with concern.

"Why did you bring all those people into my apartment tonight?" I asked.

"What?" His forehead crinkled. "I told you, they brought over pizza — "

"That's not it. You got rid of them soon enough. You didn't have to bring them over."

He turned his whiskey glass slowly on the table, making a wet ring on the tablecloth, then took a sip. "Maybe I was nervous."

"Really?"

"Naw, that couldn't be it." He smiled broadly and stuffed another big bite of steak into his maw. "Go on, try your pasta," he said around the food.

I scowled. This was going to be a long week if he never

gave me a straight answer. But I wondered if his first response could be true. Could this boisterous extrovert actually have been nervous?

I used a spoon to scoop up a dumpling and a dollop of creamy sauce.

"Mmmmm," I moaned as the rich, gently salty flavor exploded in my mouth.

"Hey." Duncan's voice had gone an octave deeper, and he raised an eyebrow. "Now we're getting somewhere."

"This is so fucking good," I said after the first bite.

Without asking, Duncan reached over and speared one of the little dumplings with his fork. He tasted it and made an "Oh, yeah" expression. "I'll help you finish that, darlin'."

"OK, but let me have a few more first."

He laughed. "That's my girl. I'm going to treat you all week just so I can see you foodgasm again."

I raised an eyebrow. "That's all you're interested in? Foodgasms?"

"What do *you* think?" He smiled cheekily.

"*Awk*-ward," I said under my breath, and took another bite.

He laughed. We ate in near-silence for a couple of minutes, until I noticed Duncan eyeing my hand.

"What?" I asked. "Do I have sauce on me?"

"No," he said. "A triskele."

"A what?"

"Your ring. It's a kind of Celtic knot, a triskele."

"It is?" I put down my spoon and looked at my mother's ring. "I mean, I knew it was a Celtic knot, but not what kind."

"Where did you get it?" He held out his hand and grasped mine, skimming my fingers and the ring. I tingled from his touch. Every time I thought I was distancing myself, there he was, physically in my space. Heat and presence and power.

"My — my mother gave it to me. It was her mother's before."

"It looks old. It's unusual. It's quite chunky, isn't it?"

I pulled my hand from his and touched the ring. After a moment, I pulled it off and handed it to him.

He took it, turning it over.

I watched the light catch the deep grooves in the silver, outlining the three interlinked spirals. "My mom said it was the key to time travel."

"Did she now? A triskele can mean many things: different energies in motion; or mother, father and child; or past, present and future, among others."

I sat up straighter. "Past, present and future?"

"Interesting, isn't it? Maybe that's what she meant. It's a legacy she passed to you. Unless you believe in time travel."

He grinned and handed it back, touching me again. *Duncan, giving me a ring.* An exotic thought.

I smiled wryly and placed it back on my right ring finger. "I don't believe in time travel, but she used to tell me — oh, it's silly."

"What?" He took a sip of whiskey and smiled again. That smile was so reassuring. Was it genuine?

I shook my head. "When we moved to Wichita, I didn't get along with the other kids. She used to tell me that someday, when she gave me the ring, I'd be able to go back in time and see how silly they were. I imagined myself as a fairy-tale heroine who could travel in time. Though I told her I'd rather have a tornado take me to Oz instead."

Duncan chuckled. "Kansas brainwashing. I always wanted to see one in Texas, but I was never so lucky."

"That's a funny kind of luck to wish for."

"Maybe I wanted to go to Oz, too," he said. "So does the ring have a trick or something? A secret compartment?"

"I — I don't think so. I mean, I never noticed it engaging in any strange behavior."

"Flying around the room, perhaps?"

I chuckled. "No!"

"I know a jeweler in Bohemia Beach. She was in one of my videos."

"Oh, the one where you filmed the couple picking out the diamond? That was, well, funny but excruciating."

"You saw it?" He looked pleased.

"Yeah," I said. "He was cheap, and she wanted to buy a rock the size of the Hope Diamond."

Duncan nodded. "I'm afraid the engagement ended after they saw themselves in the video."

"Then maybe it wasn't meant to be."

"Maybe that was the only way they could see the truth about themselves," he said.

"That they were arguing about all the wrong things?"

"That, and water and oil don't mix." He polished off his drink. The steak was long gone. "Anyway, we can have my friend look at it. Maybe there's something in your mom's story. So you grew up in Wichita?"

"After my parents divorced. I was born here, but once my parents split, my mom wanted to go to where my grandma lived. Unfortunately, she didn't last long. My grandma, I mean."

"Sounds tough."

"At first. Mom was an art teacher. She struggled some, but she did OK. She brought art books and projects home for me when I was little. That's where my interest in art and design started. After I graduated, I got into art school in Kansas City. Only I had to drop out a semester shy of graduating after she got sick. So then it was tough again, even though I worked in an ad agency and did some waitressing that last year to help pay the bills."

"Cancer?" Duncan asked softly.

I nodded. "There was an ice storm, the night she gave me the ring. I still remember the cracking sounds and the branches glittering at night under the streetlights outside. And Pookie resting his head on my leg as we were all sitting on the couch, knowing it was near the end."

"Pookie?"

"Our dog. A beagle mix. He was old and sweet. My mom going broke his heart, I think. He died not long after."

"Holy Christ, you're killing me!" Duncan exclaimed. "Not the dog, too! Grandma and then your ma and then the bloody dog! Your dog died?" Other diners were looking our way as Duncan's face reddened. "Next you're going to tell me you have ten days to live. That's bloody *awful!*"

His outburst shouldn't have been funny. He was recounting most of the tragedies of my life. But his high sense of outrage and theater were just a little bit hilarious. I felt the giggle bubbling up, and it burst into a full-bore laugh that went on and on. It was like some cork had popped, and all my angst blew out into the atmosphere and evaporated. He looked at me in astonishment.

"Sorry," I managed to gasp. "I didn't mean — I'll just shut up now." I dashed back the rest of my whiskey, getting myself under control.

"No, no, I don't want — please, talk to me." He brusquely waved away the attention of the other diners, and they turned back to their meals. "It's just so damn sad. Are you still sad?"

"I'm not that sad now," I said. "Not all the time. I mean, I miss Mom. The dog, too. But I'm OK. Pathetic, maybe, but not sad."

"Whew. OK, then," he said in his facetious manner. "Pathetic. Thank God. I can deal with that."

A smile stole over my face, and Duncan answered it, at least partly in relief, I thought.

"Do you want to get out of here?" he asked. He caught the server's eye and made an air-writing motion with one hand so she'd bring the check. "Maybe we can catch some lightning."

"Great idea," I said. At least outside, no one would stare at us.

"WE'RE TOO LATE," Duncan said as he drove us over the causeway.

The bridge soared high above the wide lagoon — the river, as so many called it — that separated Bohemia from the barrier island and Bohemia Beach. The inky sky was mostly clear and salted with stars, though the fat sliver of moon setting behind us cast a glimmer on a few clouds to the east. The night was beautiful and calm, and I had a little warm sun inside me from the whiskey and the laughter at dinner.

As we swooped over the highest point of the bridge, a flash briefly illuminated a storm just offshore.

"There's still lightning," I said.

"Not enough. It's dying. Typical. I don't think the storms ever really got going today."

"Isn't it hard to film lightning?" I strained to see the cloud light up again in the darkness. We were coming into Bohemia

Beach. Duncan drove through the business corridor of restaurants, bars and beach emporiums on the main east-west road, then turned north onto A1A.

"I usually don't film it, exactly. I set up the camera to take a series of stills and make a time-lapse movie."

"But how do you film your standup thing in front of the camera?"

"Oh, I always film myself before or after. I'm always on camera. You should know that, as my one true fan," he joked.

"I guess I do, which is why I asked." His barb sort of annoyed me. It's not like I was a groupie or something. "Do you put everything on camera?"

He glanced over at me, a mischievous look in his eyes. "What do you mean by everything, darlin'?"

"Not *that,* whatever you're thinking. I mean, why do you feel compelled to be on camera all the time?"

"Everything's better on camera," he said, pulling into the empty parking lot of a beachside park.

"No, it's not!"

"Well, then, I make it better."

"You make reality suck less?"

He chuckled. "That's a perfect way to put it. But I don't think reality sucks, exactly. It's all in how you choose to look at it." He turned off the car, glanced at his radar app and popped his phone in the glove compartment. I stowed my purse under the seat, and he locked the SUV. "Should we walk on the beach?"

"Not worried about getting struck by lightning?"

"Hardly," he said. We walked toward the steps of the wooden crossover. "I mean, it's possible, but that thing hasn't flashed in an age."

It was true. The last dying storm might actually be dead.

But the stars were pretty, and the furnace of summer had lowered a few degrees to a comforting warmth. A light breeze whispered, echoing the waves, softening as the night deepened.

We walked over the platform at the top of the dunes, the wooden planks echoing hollowly under our footsteps. Then we took the stairs down to the sand. I took off my sandals, and Duncan kicked off his sneakers and yanked off his socks.

And then he took off his pants.

"What the hell are you doing?" I gaped at his loose boxers, which were covered with Darth Vader heads.

"Getting comfortable. I don't want my pants to get wet, do I? Besides, I'll wrap our shoes in them and stuff them under the stairs, and no one will bother them."

I had my doubts about this logic, but I handed over my sandals while trying not to stare at his legs. He rolled the bundle and hid it in the shadows.

"We could take a few more things off. Go swimming," he suggested with his usual cheek as we walked toward the water.

"Sharks."

"What?"

"Sharks. Everybody knows you don't go swimming at night." By now the warm, foamy waves were washing up around our ankles, and I looked at the water suspiciously. "They say that's when the sharks are out."

"Do 'they' say that? The last poor bastard who was nipped at Bohemia Beach was surfing in broad daylight."

"Oh," I said. "Well, I haven't lived here that long."

"So the answer is no?"

"Go ahead and swim. I'll go back to the car and dial nine-one."

"Don't you mean nine-one-one?"

I shook my head. "Nine-one, so I'm ready to hit the last 'one' when your screams start."

His grin was visible even in the darkness. My eyes were adjusting, too. So many more stars twinkled overhead.

At that moment, a fork of lightning shot through the distant, dwindling storm and pierced the ocean below.

"Awesome," Duncan breathed. He put a hand on my arm, and we stopped walking. "Wait for it," he whispered.

A moment later, it came: the thunder, a low and lonely rumble, rambling through the night like a train that had lost its tracks.

"Nice," I said. "Do we have to go back and get your camera?"

"No. It's still dying. But that was a *verra prrrretty* last gasp."

"Uh-oh," I said as we resumed our stroll. "You're rolling your 'R's' again."

"Is it working?" He looped his arm in mine, and I smiled. It kind of was. Something was — the stars, the waves, the fading storm. His good humor and warm body.

"So as part of this deal, are we going to stay up all night, every night?" I asked, feeling a touch of nerves again. His touch meant a touch of nerves.

"Depends on if we can think of something to do," he answered puckishly.

"I see." I could imagine a few things, as much as I tried not to. "I have a day job, you know."

"Are you tired?"

"Sort of, but that's not the point. Anyway, I don't want to rush home."

"Good." He stopped and turned me toward him. He was a shadow in the scant moonlight, blocking out the stars. The breeze ruffled his hair. His pale blue eyes reflected a hint of moonlight just before he gently clasped my arms and lowered his lips to mine.

Damn it. Why did he have to keep doing that? I resisted, thought I resisted, but like a stolen car, I was gone in sixty seconds, lost in him all over again. I allowed him to pull me against him, his broad chest, as he opened his mouth to taste more of me. His tongue tangled with mine, and his arms moved to my back as his lips brushed the sensitive skin under my ear. I sucked in a breath as his hands slid down, grasping my ass, pressing me closer. Oh, God, he was hard again, and I could feel a lot of him through the thin boxers.

Those boxers. Those Darth Vader boxers. A laugh bubbled up from my belly, and I stumbled back from him, giggling.

"You know how to wound a guy," said Duncan as I doubled over, clutching my middle, trying to stop, laughing even more. But he didn't sound particularly miffed.

"I'm so sorry. I — that was nice, really. But Darth Vader. I mean, Darth Vader." I broke into another peal of laughter.

"I take it you don't want to rule the universe with me?"

"At least not as father and son."

"Ew, you *are* twisted!" He laughed, too. "I could take them off. Would that help?"

"NO! No, don't do that. Maybe we should head back home."

"You're not much for a romantic evening, are you, darlin'?"

"Not with Darth Vader."

"Don't underestimate the power of the dark side."

I burst into a new gust of laughter.

"It's good to hear you laugh. I don't mind. Our week has

only just begun." Duncan's voice was filled with devilish promise. He took my hand, and we turned and walked back the way we'd come.

I had a feeling I was going to regret making fun of him.

Or was I?

"WE LIVE across the hall from each other. Why don't you go home? Doesn't this count as a night?" I asked when we got back into my apartment. "Because otherwise, I don't foresee getting much sleep."

"That's my plan," Duncan said.

I crossed my arms, hovering, standing in the middle of the room. "Look, I don't know what you expect — "

"What do *you* want?" He sat on the couch and quaffed one of my last two beers, utterly relaxed. At least he was wearing pants again.

"What do I — what are you talking about? I want my life back."

"Was this evening so unpleasant for you?" Duncan's tone was humorous but gentle, too. Almost as if he wasn't punking me. "Was nothing about tonight pleasurable?"

I felt my face heat again, and my skin was so damn transparent, it probably looked like it was on fire. "That's not the point."

"That's the entire point. Why not live for pleasure, Thea?"

"There's more to life than pleasure." I sat at my work table, with its piles of paper in a kaleidoscope of colors, and busied myself rearranging my knife and stylus and ruler.

"Like what? What else is in your life?"

"Don't be rude."

"I really want to know." He set down his beer, crossed the room and hovered behind my shoulder.

I grabbed my cutting mat and slid it over my works in progress.

"You deserve pleasure," he whispered.

I tensed as his hands rested on my shoulders. Then I relaxed, involuntarily, as he dug his thumbs and fingers into my rigid muscles, pressing, kneading. A long sigh escaped me. "There's no such thing as pleasure without a price."

"Now that's cynical, darlin'. Maybe you haven't had the right kind of pleasure."

Oh, and he could give it. My head drooped as his thumbs moved to the back of my neck, rubbing in little circles, and his fingers dug in.

My words came out in little sighs between his strokes. "I find I can't — have pleasure — without some kind of — emotional toll." I didn't want to say *emotional investment,* though that's what I was thinking. I wanted my life back, but I didn't necessarily want to scare him off. Yet. His hands felt so good. And deep inside me, petals were unfurling, the nectar begging for the bee. A longing I'd forgotten, made myself forget. Because it hurt so much when the flower withered and died.

That hurt was in my mind when I shrugged him off and stood. "I can't handle this, whatever this is."

"It's whatever you want it to be."

I turned to face him. He radiated calm and confidence, but around the edges of his placid demeanor was a crackling energy, like the lightning from that storm, that bespoke a need to connect. Cloud to sea. Him to me. The want in his eyes was palpable, and I wanted to fall into that pool of blue desire and lose myself.

But I wouldn't. I couldn't. I'd lost too much already.

"We have an agreement," I managed to say. "You can stay. The couch is yours if you want it."

Duncan reached out and touched my jaw, caressed it, sliding his finger to my chin. His hand fell. "All right, darlin'. Better than sleeping among the boxes."

"And your clown posse."

He smiled. "And there's always tomorrow."

He turned and went to the couch, took a final long sip of his beer, settled against the pillows and closed his eyes.

A handsome prince from a fairy tale, waiting for a kiss.

Ha.

And my bed was just across the room, because this *was* a studio, however big. At least there was a built-in closet next to the bathroom. I grabbed my sleep shorts and T-shirt, went into the closet and changed. I moved around the apartment and turned off all the lights, acutely aware of him, his breathing. Was he asleep?

I didn't know. I slipped under the covers and didn't sleep for a long, long time.

You know when you're dreaming, and somehow you know it's a dream because you're not that far from being awake, but you try to hang on to it anyway, guide it toward that lovely thing you want so badly but can't have in real life? That's where I was, on a warm beach, running, Duncan laughing behind me. I tumbled onto a huge, soft beach towel, blue like the sky, and he dropped next to me. Shifted over me, smiling, his eyes sparkling, his chest bare and broad. And without hesitation, he touched me, and my swimsuit vanished. It was a dream, after all. Around us, the dune grass grew and swayed, hiding us from the world, and the sounds of waves rushed in my ears as he caressed my breasts and eased one hand down the curve of my belly to my patch of red curls, my folds. It felt so easy, so natural, as if we'd done this so many times already. His eyes told me so. His finger slid inside me, penetrating me, curling to touch that place that made me writhe in ecstasy against his hand as he thrust it against me, awakening my clit, making me wet with desire.

"Please," I whispered.

That's when the wave washed over me and I awoke.

I froze in my bed, my wretched reality returning as morning light filled the apartment. Above me, my flock of origami birds turned slowly in imperceptible breezes. Guided by the dream, my hand had slipped inside my sleep shorts and was curled around my mound. I withdrew it, embarrassed that he might have seen something. Heard something.

But the apartment was quiet. I eased out of bed and tread softly across the wooden floor to peek over the top of the couch. He was gone, like my dream. Was last night a dream, after all? The way he'd touched me, the dinner, the walk on the beach, the laughter? And the moment I'd turned him down?

I suppressed a little swell of disappointment, started the coffee and got ready for the day. I was going back to my dad's office today. And tonight — tonight, I would see Duncan again. That was our bargain. What would I do about it?

I didn't hear from him during the day, but before I headed home from work, I checked his vlog to see if he'd posted anything. I was mortified to see he had. Had he kept his promise to stop his theatrical courtship?

I felt a little guilty about my lack of trust when I saw he'd kept his word. The video consisted of him unpacking a moving box while one of his drunken friends — Pete, I think — snored on the couch behind him. In droll fashion, Duncan presented each odd object that came out of the box — a baseball autographed by a star I'd never heard of, a medal from a 5K, a drinking horn, a lightning calendar, a talking Yoda and more stuff, running it all by his unconscious friend. The snoring lump in question didn't stir until the bagpipe emerged and Duncan stood and blasted out a passable version of "Scotland the Brave." A moment later, my dad poked his head out of his office and looked at me funny. Guess he'd never heard me laugh like that before.

When Duncan's friend had fled, Duncan turned back to the camera and said, "Now, about that little bet I have running — all I can say is, it's still on. And if you have no idea what I'm talking about, see yesterday's video." He winked, and a link to the video of him bargaining with me popped up. I had to hand it to him — he was always pushing those clicks. And I was just another one. The thought dried up my humor pretty quickly.

The knock on my apartment door came at 7 p.m. on the dot. Tonight, I hadn't gone to any special trouble over my clothes — just shorts, a V-neck T-shirt and sneakers. I'd twisted my hair up in a clip, though strands kept escaping. I had no idea what was in store, but I wasn't about to get all dressed up for another invasion by his friends.

So when I opened the door, my breath stopped for a moment when I saw what he was wearing: black tux. Crisp white shirt. A bright red bow tie shot through with silver threads that sparkled almost as much as his pale blue eyes. Despite the silly tie, he was *devastating*. Roguishly debonair.

Insanely fuckable.

Stop it, Thea.

"You're going to sweat to death in that," I said, trying not to reveal how blown away I was.

"So you think I'm hot, darlin'?" Duncan winked.

I swallowed and tried to find my voice. "I think I'm under-dressed."

"Not at all. This is for the game show."

"The what?"

"I've got a collab tonight. A collaboration," he said to my confused stare. "We're doing a video downtown."

"We?"

"Don't worry," he said. "Not you."

"You mean you and someone else? So I could just stay here, right?"

"Our night has begun. So, no, you can't. Besides, I'm going to buy you dinner when we're done. Unless, of course, you want the video to be about you instead."

"No! No," I said hastily. "Let me just get my purse."

I made a stop in the bathroom and added lipstick. The rest — well, it was too late to swan-ify this ugly duckling.

Tuesday night in downtown Bohemia in the off-season wasn't exactly bustling, but one could always count on a certain number of cocktail-swizzling hipsters and beer-swilling partiers to keep the bars busy. Carrying his tripod and backpack, Duncan led me into one of the bigger ones, a cavernous place called Decadence with a busy patio outside. Indoors, a long bar stretched along one wall, and a dozen patrons played on a few pool tables in the middle. The "Decade" part of "Decadence" shone in red on the logo, outlined in cursive neon above the bar, with the rest in white. Befitting the theme, each night featured music from a different decade. Tonight it was '80s, and Frankie Goes to

Hollywood pounded through the speakers as we walked up to the bar.

"Relax," I said to myself, as much identifying the song as telling myself not to be nervous.

"What, darlin'?" Duncan asked over the thumping beat, seeming not to notice the stares he drew as he toted his gear.

"Are you going to do your video in here?"

"Too loud. We're going outside, but I had to check with Hank and make sure it's cool if we film on the patio. And we're meeting Lolly here."

Lolly. The bored blonde from last night. Great. Just what was she to Duncan?

I didn't want to compete with the bass beat, so I didn't ask. Duncan introduced me to Hank the bartender and ordered beers. I had no sooner taken a sip of my IPA when Lolly walked through the open door, in a hot little black slip dress that clung to her braless breasts and barely covered her butt. Her eyeliner was thicker and darker, if anything, than it had been yesterday. Her lips were a deep, dark, angry red, and her short hair stuck up a little on top, giving her a punk diva look.

"Lolly! Hello, gorgeous!" Duncan exclaimed. He leaned in to kiss her cheek. I swallowed an unwelcome surge of jealousy as she nodded coolly at me. After all, what claim did I have on Duncan, besides a week's worth of nights?

"Babe," she asked him, "did you get mine?"

Duncan waved down Hank and murmured something in his ear. The bartender grabbed a bottle of tequila off the top shelf and filled a shot glass to the brim. In a ritual that seemed familiar to all of them, Hank plunked it down in front of Lolly, who knocked it back in one go.

Duncan dropped money on the bar and led the way to the patio, where he set up his camera, bristling with a bracket weighed down by a complex-looking box and a light. The music wasn't quite as loud out here, but Duncan hooked himself up with a wireless microphone instead of his usual stick mike. It took him a couple of minutes to figure out where to put the battery pack for Lolly's, given her minimal clothing, but finally, he hooked it to the back of her dress. When he started to tuck the wire under the fabric, she smacked his hand away and did it herself.

"Always trying to cop a feel," she said to me as she smoothed her dress and Duncan laughed. "OK, dude, how are we doing this?"

"We work off the list," he said, a piece of paper in his hand. "We flip a coin to determine who picks first. Say you win and pick the firefighter. I might pick somebody with a guitar. Whoever finds their person and gets back first in each round gets a point, and we interview them on camera to confirm their existence. You have, say, ten minutes to find someone, or you forfeit that round. After five rounds, you know who won."

"Five? Forget it. This'll take all night," Lolly said. "Make it three. No one can watch a video for that long, even with editing."

"She has a point," I said.

"Even with me in it?" Duncan teased.

"Especially with you in it," Lolly said. "And don't forget to plug my vlog. I'll do the same for you next time."

"Of course," Duncan said. "I'm not a click whore for nothing."

His words sent my mind into the gutter, thinking of my first impression of him as a man-whore. Just who was the whore here, given how easily I'd entered into our little deal?

"Carry this." Duncan handed Lolly a GoPro. "Get video of

you running around talking to people. I'll carry one, too. I'll edit it in later. Thea, can you stop the camera after we go?"

"I think so." And what was I supposed to do while they were scavenging for random people?

"Cool," Lolly said. "Let's do it for the camera."

Duncan switched on the light, and he and Lolly, bathed in its harsh white glow, explained their game to the lens, quipping and elbowing each other as if they'd known each other forever. Maybe they had.

"And my lovely and unwilling assistant, who is stuck spending a week of nights with me, will time us to make sure we don't go over our ten minutes," Duncan said, winking at me behind the camera. "Are you ready?" he asked Lolly.

"Let's do this," Lolly affirmed.

Duncan flipped a quarter, and Lolly called heads and won. She looked over the list.

"I'll find someone with a guitar," she said quickly, then handed the list to Duncan.

"OK," Duncan said, perusing the list, "then I'll find someone with a cup of coffee." He reached beyond the camera, where I was hiding in the shadows, and handed the list to me.

"Three — two — one — go!" Lolly said.

They ran through the patio gate and down the street, leaving me alone with the camera. Curious bar patrons watched them, then looked at me. I shrugged at them, figured out the basics of the camera and stopped the recording. Then I sat, pulled out my phone so I could keep track of the time, and worked on my beer.

Lolly was back in eight minutes with the down-at-heel busker who always claimed the corner outside the pizza shop. "Turn the camera on!" she snapped.

I scowled, stood and got it rolling. After Lolly spent a minute interviewing the guy about his nonexistent music career, Duncan appeared towing a frazzled-looking woman with a stroller sporting a fussy baby and a cupholder with, yes, a coffee.

"Don't say I lost!" Duncan cried.

"Two more rounds, buddy," Lolly said, dismissing the bemused guitar player, who shambled back down the street to his usual post. "You're going down in one."

"Thank you, ma'am," Duncan told the mom, "and I hope you enjoy the coffee."

"Thanks," the woman said drily, looking askance at the camera before heading down the street.

"You didn't buy her that coffee, did you?" Lolly asked.

"There was nothing in the rules about buying things," Duncan said innocently.

"*Your* rules."

"For all I know, you bought Al his guitar."

"You know Al plays that shitty guitar every night at Mango and Main, so shut up," Lolly said. "Give me a quarter."

She flipped. He called tails. She won again.

"Damn it," he said.

"I'll find the firefighter," she said.

"I'll find — um — a scientist," Duncan said.

Lolly laughed. "Good luck with that."

Duncan just smiled, like the cat who'd been in the cream, and they were off and running. I shut off the camera and waited.

Duncan was back in six minutes with a sinewy guy in khakis and a white golf shirt (rather muscular for my precon-ceived notions of a scientist, I thought admiringly) who was a few inches shorter than he was — not surprising, since Duncan was nothing if not physically imposing.

"Is this going to take long?" the man said, running a hand through his wavy dark hair. "I have to get back to my presentation."

Duncan double-checked the camera and gave me a thumbs-up before introducing him, an astronomer who worked at the technical university down the road.

"And what can we be looking for in the sky anytime soon?" Duncan asked.

"We have the significant Perseid meteor shower coming to us starting in mid-July and peaking in mid-August," the astronomer said, warming to his topic and seeming to forget the presentation he'd been worried about a moment before. His eyes lit up with enthusiasm. "And there's the Alpha Capricornids starting in July. Not as many meteors, but you're likely to see a few fireballs. Of course, nothing beats —"

"Hold it!" Lolly had run up, dragging a hunk of man wearing a Bohemia Fire Department T-shirt and a huge grin.

"You're too late," I said.

"Bitch, please," Lolly said. I held up my phone with the clock on display. "Shit," she added when she saw I was right.

"Is that the time?" the astronomer exclaimed when he saw it. "I have to get back to the Rotary Club. They'll never invite me again." He shook Duncan's hand and ran off down the street to the meeting he'd come from.

"And so we're even. Hello," Duncan said, shaking the hand of the firefighter.

"Guess I'm not needed, then?" the man said, his voice deep and amused.

"I'll let you know," Lolly replied with a sultry look. He grinned again and wandered off.

"One more round," Duncan told the camera. "Before we get to it, don't forget to check out Lolly's vlog. You should be seeing the link above my head."

"Your giant, swelled head," Lolly said. "But thanks. Are you ready to get your ass kicked?"

"We shall see," Duncan said, flipping his quarter. Lolly called heads and won again, prompting his *"Och!"*

"I'll take the chef," she said. An easy bet, since downtown Bohemia was full of restaurants.

"Then I'll take . . . " Duncan's brow creased under his unruly reddish hair. I leaned over a bit so I could see the list, but not enough so I was on camera. He glanced up at me and I mimed taking a photo. "The photographer," Duncan declared.

"All right," Lolly said and counted them down again. "Go!"

I paused the video.

"Have something in mind, or were you just taking a mental picture?" Duncan asked after she ran off.

"I think Cali is working late tonight. Calista Goode. You know her gallery?"

"Oh, yes! I was there a while back, actually, for the opening party." Duncan suddenly looked at me funny.

Oh, hell. That's right. I'd seen him across the room at that party, interviewing some of the pinups Cali had featured in that show. He'd come late, and I was mostly avoiding people in the back room, before that whole thing exploded with the band. There was no way he'd noticed there was a photo of me — was there?

"You want to come along?" Duncan asked, his face still wreathed in puzzlement.

"I have to watch your camera. Go!" I said.

He ran off. Five minutes later, he was back, towing Calista Goode.

"Cali!" I grinned as I got the camera rolling. My friend's blond hair was up in a ponytail, and she was wearing a tank top and denim shorts. Clearly in work mode.

"I noticed Ms. Calista Goode was keeping late hours at her gallery when I was out on my last fool's errand," Duncan explained to the camera, "and here she is. Why are you working late?"

"Getting ready for Friday's show opening, 'Waveriders.' Awesome photos of surfers. You should come!" Cali said, shooting a conspiratorial glance at me. I rolled my eyes.

"Excellent," Duncan said, just as Lolly jogged up, tugging along a rough-looking young man in a stained black T-shirt and apron.

"You did *not* beat me," she said.

"Ta-da," answered Duncan. "And who's this?"

"Meet Rudy, chef at —"

"I'm not the chef," the surly guy said. "I told you, I'm a line cook."

"That's enough!" Lolly said, as Duncan shouted, "Ha! Not only did I beat you, but you cheated?" I noticed he didn't mention getting outside help himself, even if a hint wasn't strictly against the rules. I had to smile.

Lolly pouted. "Apparently chefs don't want to leave their kitchens during dinner rush."

"And there we have it! I've triumphed again!" Duncan said.

"What do you mean again? I'm going to crush you next time."

"Thanks for watching, and thanks to my lovely assistant.

Goodnight from *Flyte Night!*" Duncan said. He grinned and nodded at me, and I turned off the camera.

Lolly looked from Duncan to me and back as the cook shuffled off to his workplace. "Hey, is something going on here?" she asked suspiciously.

"I hope so," Duncan said.

I laughed. "Nicely played."

"Duncan knows all my moves." She sniffed, looked me up and down, then turned to him as if finding me unworthy. "Want to get dinner?"

"We have plans," I said without thinking. *Fuck.* I was claiming my territory, and Duncan, eyes twinkling, hadn't missed it. She actually made me *jealous.*

"Quite right," Duncan said, quickly packing up the gear. "But I'll see you for the next one."

"OK, losers." Lolly tossed her head and strode into the bar, no doubt for more tequila shots.

"You're quite the secret weapon," Duncan said, slinging his pack over his shoulder.

I grabbed the tripod. "I'm a danger to myself and others."

"Dangerous, indeed," he murmured, leaning over to kiss my neck. A shiver ran through me. "Now I'm taking you to dinner."

"Um, you know, maybe I should change. I'm kind of underdressed."

"There's no such thing as underdressed in Florida."

"Says the guy in a tux."

"Then we'll go somewhere I can guarantee you won't feel underdressed," he said. "Besides, the less dressed you are, the happier I am."

I smacked his arm lightly. But I smiled back.

Oh, hell, he was handsome. And the more dangerous one by far.

ONLY DUNCAN COULD CARRY off a tux at a beachside burrito shack. I'd heard about this place from Cali, but I'd never been here — just four tables, a counter with barstools where a couple of customers were eating, weathered wood and corrugated metal decor, and a big TV playing surf videos.

"We'll have two Big Blaster Burritos and a couple of Bohemia Brewing ales," Duncan told the guy behind the counter.

"Can we expect the rest of the wedding party?" the clerk deadpanned.

"I hope not. I'm a runaway groom. That's the home-wrecker right there." Duncan pointed his thumb over his shoulder at me, sitting at one of the tables. I shook my head, and the counter guy grinned, popped the caps on two bottles and turned to pass our order through the window to the tiny kitchen.

Duncan joined me with the bottles of beer. "Thanks for helping me tonight."

"My pleasure." Actually, it had been my pleasure to see Lolly lose their little game, but I didn't want to sound as petty as I felt. And then I felt bad for feeling petty. And jealous. And inadequate.

Duncan nodded. "Sounds like we need to go to Calista Goode's gallery party Friday night."

"I was planning to go anyway, I mean, before you roped me into this deal." I sipped my beer.

"If I were *roping* you into the deal, I would have tied you up and had my way with you long before now," he teased, and my heart did a little flip. "We'll definitely go, then. Are you having fun yet?"

I could have said no, but something was happening with each minute I spent with him. A little green shoot had sprouted in my heart, and I watched its tender unfurling with a mixture of excitement and alarm. I couldn't get attached to him. I just couldn't. This was a seven-day wonder, and then I had to get rid of him and get my life back.

"Yes," I said anyway, dazzled by his dimples, by the light in those pale blue eyes. Ice and indigo.

"Good," he said, his voice husky. He held my gaze for an extra few seconds as the server put two baskets in front of us, and a shiver ran up my spine. A good shiver.

I want him I want him I want him! a little voice insisted from inside me. My id, no doubt, jumping up and down, making my heart beat faster. Demanding little tart.

We ate, and I quizzed Duncan about life as a video blogger, about how often he did his "collabs" (a couple of times a month), whether he posted daily (only when he felt like it, which was almost daily), and whether he'd consider any other career ("I wouldn't mind being Steven Spielberg"). I carefully avoided asking about Lolly, though I was burning with curiosity about how they knew each other. I figured he didn't need to know how much I cared.

And then we were flying back over the causeway to Bohemia under the stars in Duncan's car, racing toward the half-moon as it lowered in the western sky. Duncan blasted Celtic folk music from the car stereo.

"Laying it on a little thick, aren't you?" I teased.

"Are you kidding?" he shouted over the loudly skirling

tune. "I love this stuff. Besides, I need to test your reaction to bagpipes."

"Why?" I couldn't keep the suspicion out of my voice.

He laughed. "Oh, no reason."

That got my mind running. But I had to admit the music was kind of catchy. I felt a compulsion to do a jig and tapped my feet against the floorboards.

As Duncan pulled into the parking lot of our building and parked under its lone oak tree, his phone rang. He shut off the car, cutting off the rowdy tunes so only the ringtone, the looped opening strums of the Proclaimers' "I'm Gonna Be (500 Miles)," cut through the night. He pulled the phone out of his bag, frowning at the screen.

"Go on up, darlin'. I'll join you in a minute."

"Isn't my obligation to you discharged?" I asked, feeling nervous again.

"Absolutely not!"

I suppressed my smile and told my happy id to shut up. As I walked toward the building, I heard Duncan.

"Dad. What's up? . . . You know that's not possible. I'm not . . . She can't expect, not after . . . You can't know what you're asking of me."

And then I was out of earshot, wondering what was up with Duncan and his dad. And whoever "she" was. His mother? His sister? A girlfriend? I knew so little about him. But there was something I recognized in him, I thought as I rode up in the elevator. A weird kinship. He was nothing like me, but something in him spoke to me. Or maybe it was just that he literally spoke to me. So few interesting men did.

I shook my head as I unlocked my door and went inside, flipping a switch that turned on the stained-glass floor lamp in the living area. It cast a subtle, warm glow in the room.

Mood lighting? Oh, hell. He was coming up here. Should I change? I was still casual. He was still in a tux. I could put on a dress or something.

But that was ridiculous. This was the point in an old movie where the slinky woman with the bullet bra would go "put on something more comfortable." Usually involving satin, of which I had very little.

One thing I *could* do: Put on music and get us something to drink. They did that in old movies, too, and not much had changed, right? I found my favorite hip lounge mix on my phone and got my wireless speaker going, and then I rummaged in the kitchen for alcohol.

"Thea?" Duncan called from the door.

"Come in!"

He entered the tiny kitchen just as I pulled a bottle of port out of a cabinet.

"Port? Do you have cigars, too?"

"Very funny. Somebody gave this to my dad to thank him for a job, and he gave it to me since he doesn't drink anymore."

"Huh." His response was muted. Kind of strange, actually. But he took the bottle and looked it over.

"Is it OK?"

"What?" He looked up at me and then back at the label as if he hadn't really been looking at the bottle at all. Then at me again, his gaze clearing. "Oh, yeah, it's fine. I'll open it, shall I?"

"Great," I said, handing him my corkscrew, admiring how he filled out the tuxedo. "Where'd you get that ridiculous tie?"

"Secondhand store. The tux, too."

"No way. It fits you perfectly."

He popped the cork out of the bottle. "Ah, you noticed?" He shot me that smile that turned my insides to hot cocoa. Spiked hot cocoa. I was tongue-tied. "Have a decanter?"

"Uh, no."

"That's all right. Normally we'd have to pass the bottle clockwise, but since it's just the two of us, I think I can pour."

"Why clockwise?" I asked, pulling two wine glasses out of the cabinet. I didn't have anything fancier.

"The devil's always lurking over your left shoulder. Or over mine. It wouldn't do to rile him." His face darkened for a moment, and then he was filling our glasses and handing me one with a smile that, I thought, wasn't altogether real.

Then again, was any of this real?

"Thank you," I said, heading for the living room and the couch.

He was right behind me, carrying the bottle and his glass, which he placed on the coffee table. He shed his jacket and tie on a chair before dropping down next to me. The furniture quaked. He kicked off his shoes and draped an arm over my shoulders as if it was the most natural thing in the world.

"That's very nice," he said after a sip of the port. "I mean, *verrra* nice."

"No fair, rolling the 'R's,' " I said, following his lead and toeing off my sneakers.

"If I don't bring out the 'R's' now, when would I?"

He had a point, but I wasn't sure he needed the sexy Scottish accent to get my attention. My body temperature was soaring through the stratosphere like a lit rocket. I sipped the port, hoping it would cool me down, but all it did was add to the warm feeling I got nestled against him. Because I *was* nestled, as he somehow got closer to me without seeming to have moved at all. Or maybe I'd shifted closer to him.

We drank the port, and Duncan refilled our glasses. The chocolaty sweetness of the wine should have made me more relaxed, but a tension grew in my body as we listened to the music and I inhaled his nice smell of soap and spice and felt him shift against me, a solid block of heat.

"What's this?" Duncan asked, nodding at the speaker.

"Huh?" *Stop daydreaming, Thea.* "Oh, the music? This band is Tape Five. I like this kind of retro-modern stuff."

"Like spy movie music."

"Kind of, yeah. You're dressed for it. We really should be drinking martinis."

"But this is just right." Was it my imagination, or did his arm pull me a little closer? I felt hot. I shivered. A little kernel of panic popped in my head. This was crazy. He'd asked to spend seven nights with me on a video blog, and I said *yes?*

"What the hell are we doing?" I blurted.

Duncan seemed completely unfazed. He looked directly into my eyes, his handsome face a revelation in the low, warm light. "Anything you want, Thea."

Anything I want? Anything I want . . . the idea was, well, *radical.* When was the last thing I did something I really wanted? Had let myself want something and believed I could get it and *taken* it? Last night I'd tasted his passion, but I'd hesitated, and later, I'd turned him down. Why? Why deny myself this thing — no, this man I wanted, based on fear? No one knew what the future held.

Maybe all *he* wanted was a quick physical connection, but he wanted me. *Me.* The very idea went straight to my head. And the feeling was mutual.

He held my eyes with his, blue on blue, giving me permission. Permission I should have been able to give myself. Only,

I realized, Duncan wasn't judging me, not the way I judged myself. He was — he was *inviting* me.

Anything I want.

I wanted him.

I took a gulp of port and shakily set the empty glass on the table. It had done something to me, softened my edges, but then again, so had he. Duncan. Staring at me with just the hint of a smile around his mouth.

I took his glass, too, and put it on the table. His eyebrow twitched, a hint of surprise. And then I cupped his face in my hands and slowly, so slowly, moved toward him.

He sat very still, as if he were the lion and I was the unsuspecting gazelle who just wanted to give him a sniff, not knowing I was about to be devoured.

But I knew. I was counting on it.

He made a small sound, a shaky intake of breath as I paused a hair's-breadth from him, searching those eyes. The ice blue there seemed fathomless.

I pressed my lips against his and closed my eyes.

Duncan's kiss was soft heat, sweet wine, rough where his stubble brushed my cheek. I tasted him, sucking on his bottom lip, licking it until his mouth opened wider. I flicked my tongue against his as heat focused in my breasts, between my legs, an ache that demanded an answer. But I wasn't there yet. I wanted to kiss him, to revel in his kisses.

Something in him snapped. His arms wrapped around me, yanking me hard against him; he sucked in my tongue, hungry. It was that passion again, the fire I'd only tasted last night. I whimpered into his mouth as his hands moved farther down, encircling my waist. He pulled me onto his lap, sideways. One of his hands slid down my waist and hip, running along the skin of my thigh below the shorts. I pressed against him and caressed his hard back, warm through the thin shirt.

"Mmmm," he murmured, cupping my bottom with one hand as the other pulled the clip from my hair. The tendrils swished around my face, against my shoulders, and he rubbed his face in my curls, inhaling.

"Oh, I'm — I'm sweaty," I said, embarrassed. I'd had a shower before the evening's activities, but the hot night meant I didn't feel quite as daisy-fresh now.

"Not yet," Duncan quipped, running his fingers through my hair, pushing it back and kissing my neck.

"Oh, God," I murmured, tilting my head to make room for his kisses.

"Mm-hmm," Duncan said, his lips trailing little blossoms of heat toward my collarbone. He stretched the neckline of my shirt as his kisses moved south. Then, in a swift move, he pulled it over my head and tossed it aside.

I gasped as he cupped one breast and squeezed — and as he squeezed my ass through my shorts. His hands were big. I wanted to curl up inside them, give myself up to them. Would this be a repeat of last night?

No. It would be more. Duncan slipped his fingers under one cup of the cotton bra and lifted my breast, releasing it, exposing me, shooting electricity through my body. Then he released the other one. There was no fabric shield tonight, just my naked flesh, my curves. He cupped one breast, massaging it.

As he cradled my behind, he latched on to a rosy nipple with his mouth, suckling, tonguing. The sensation sent fingers of fire over my skin, through my blood. I arched into him, wanting more. He chuckled and licked and blew on the peak. It hardened in response, and the heat between my legs grew.

"You're so sensitive," he whispered, now using both hands to deftly unlatch my bra and drop it on the floor. All my doubts took a vacation as he cupped and stroked both breasts, licking and suckling on one and then the other until the ache between my legs became almost unbearable.

I reached up to unbutton his shirt and a tiny, reflective bit of hardware popped out, clattering on the floor. "Oh, shit. What did I do?"

"It's the studs, darlin'. I don't care if you lose them. Here." And he shifted me and yanked his shirt open with a pop and a clatter of the little pearl fasteners.

A giggle escaped me, muted almost immediately by admiration. No undershirt stood between me and his torso. I still thought his dimples were his sexiest feature, but his chest? He was magnificent. His pectoral muscles were large and defined, lightly accented by those wisps of reddish-gold hair I'd glimpsed the night I went across the hall to yell at him. His tummy didn't have that exaggerated six-pack that gym rats got, but it was solid. Rippling. Irresistible. I lay my hands against his firm warmth, and he grunted. I looked up at his face in surprise. That look in his eyes — it bordered on pain. And then I realized that I was still sitting on his lap, and the shape of his lap had become a lot less flat.

"Oh," I said softly, my eyes widening.

"You're the best kind of torture," he said, slipping his shirt off, revealing the hard, thick muscles of his arms. He leaned in and kissed my mouth with soft, sensual attention. "Somehow I don't mind."

"Duncan," I whispered, shifting so I straddled him. He let out a breath and sucked it in again as I placed one hand on his bulge. My God, he was hard. And not small, either. I wondered just how not-small and felt my face heat.

"If you could see your face now," he said softly. "Your freckles are lit up like a constellation."

I said nothing, but I started to move my hand, rubbing, squeezing him lightly through his pants. I sat up and began to unfasten them. He closed his eyes, his mouth open, his breaths coming short, and I smiled. For just a moment, he was at my mercy. It was my turn.

I got the pants open, stood and, with his help, pulled them off. His erection tented his boxers, and I tried not to stare. OK, I didn't try very hard.

"No Darth Vader tonight?" His black shorts were printed with tiny bottles of Guinness, though.

He chuckled through his agony as I straddled him again, perching on his knees. I grasped him through the thin fabric. *Wow*, was all I could think for a minute.

"Fuck," he hissed. "What you do to me ... "

A heady feeling of power rushed through me. I stroked him and squeezed him, and after a minute, I reached to his waistband and pulled down his shorts, letting his erection spring free.

It was my turn to suck in a breath. I knelt on the floor before him and got an eyeful. His cock was thick and impressive, befitting his physique. I looked up, and he was looking down at me with pure lust. I don't know what he expected of me, but I followed my instincts and touched him again.

"Christ, Thea," he said as I began to run my hand up and down his shaft, circling it with my fingers, teasing the moistening tip. I gently cupped his balls, then slid my hand up and down the length of his cock again, marveling at how hot he was, how hard and silky at the same time. It had been a long time since my last lame sexual experience, and — well, I hadn't had anything like this to play with.

I adjusted my touch as he responded. He lifted his hips so his shaft slid against my hand. I brushed my palm against the slickness emerging at his tip and slowly increased the pace of my strokes. It was thrilling, watching him come undone. Watching his brash façade come apart as he twisted, as he groaned, as he watched me with hooded eyes. I caressed him faster and faster until he bucked against my grip and erupted. His come coated my hand. Drops spattered my naked breasts. It was primitive and messy and, somehow, incredibly arousing. I was breathing almost as hard as he was as I let go and he grasped his shaft and pumped a few more times, completing what I'd started.

The air seemed to go out of him, and his head dropped back against the couch.

"Fuck," he said. "I can't remember the last time I came like that."

I smiled. "Good."

He lifted his head and looked down at me in surprise. And then he laughed, a short, sweet laugh. "Wicked lass." He leaned over me, slipped a hand behind my neck and pulled me in for a hot, hard kiss.

When he released me, I had to catch my breath. "I'll be back in a second." I stood and went to the bathroom to wipe myself off and retrieve a towel for him. He took it and cleaned himself up, and then I curled up next to him on the couch.

"Well, this is a change," he said. "I'm completely skuddy and you still have your shorts on."

"Skuddy? Oh, naked." I giggled into his neck and kissed him there, slipping my arms around his waist, melting into his size and heat. "I like it."

"Do you now? I'll have to be naked more often."

"We'll see," I said, but who was I kidding? I yearned to be naked with him. Or at least my body did. I was wet and wanting between my legs. My skin tingled. I snuggled against the comforting warmth of his body as the air-conditioning blew over us, as he dozed, and I drifted in the pleasant buzz of the port and the afterglow of making him come. I wasn't much of a siren, but in that moment, I felt like one.

I could have stripped and spread wide for him right then, but something held me back, that cautious girl inside me who'd suffered the emotional consequences of physical attachment. No sense in going all-in now and frying my overloaded circuits when I had five more nights to go.

WHEN I AWOKE, sort of, the barest hints of dawn glowed through the windows, and a large, warm body shifted and moved me so I lay by myself on the couch against the pillows. A blanket settled over me, and a soft kiss touched my cheek, and I closed my eyes and settled back into the dream.

Dream?

The sound of the door closing popped my eyes open again, and then I remembered. I still had my shorts on, but my breasts were naked under the soft throw. He'd touched me. Kissed me. I'd touched him. I'd — oh, boy. How weird was it going to be to see him tonight?

And why was I so eager to throw myself off that cliff and into his arms?

I closed my eyes and tried not to worry, tried to rationalize all my fears. I sank into an unsettled sleep for another hour until the noise of the beeping garbage trucks outside cut through the fog, and I got up.

I rubbed my eyes until they came into focus and saw a note on the coffee table, written with a favorite purple pen.

Let's start our night early. Knock on my door at 4. We have an important mission.

   — D.

WELL, that was intriguing, and a bunch of things jumped out at me. *Our night . . . my door . . . mission.*

Another night. I couldn't put my little genie of desire back in the bottle, could I? Especially when that genie had grown way too big to fit.

His door. His apartment? I wasn't ready to think about what that meant.

Four o'clock would be no problem. I was working from home today on a dreary website project, with maybe some stolen time for my paper art, since the last two days hadn't given me a chance to work on it. I had ideas for a story I could tell with the pop-up sculptures, but I needed to work out some concepts.

It was all I could do to ignore the tantalizing pieces of paper and settle down at the computer after a shower. But the hours slipped by quickly enough, and after a mid-afternoon peanut butter and jelly sandwich, I gave myself time to play. Geometry had always come easily to me, and visualizing paper constructs worked both sides of my brain. A class in origamic architecture had reinforced my love for paper and pop-ups, and ever since, I'd been trying to create more intricate and beautiful designs. More than that, I wanted them to tell a story, have an impact. But there was something missing.

For now, I designed a drawbridge and then a bigger bridge that would span an enchanted river, imagining the princess's escape into the wild, wide world.

If my phone hadn't buzzed a reminder at 3:30, I might have forgotten my appointment. I hastily organized my project's pieces, fluffed my hair and dove into my closet in search of something to wear. I began to regret my lack of interest in clothes. I mean, casual was still my religion, but with Duncan showing up in wrinkled shorts one night and a tux the next, I had no idea what was appropriate.

With fifteen minutes to spare, I opted for simple — a breezy, light skirt in tiered shades of blue and a thin, dark gray T-shirt. V-neck. Again. I was one of those lazy (or practical) shoppers who, when finding a garment she liked, bought it in five colors. The blue bra was pretty nice, though. I slipped on my sandals, grabbed my bag and headed across the hall.

I stopped outside Duncan's door for a moment and sucked in a few deep breaths, trying to quell my nerves.

I raised my hand to tap on the door, and it magically opened.

"I thought you'd never bloody knock," said Duncan, who was back in his adorably-rumpled mode in a light blue T-shirt and khaki shorts. "Are you ready to go?"

"I — I — OK," I stammered. "Go where?"

"On our mission." He closed the door behind him, smiled and leaned in to kiss my cheek.

Oh, my. I swallowed, touching the newly warm spot on my cheek, and found myself half-jogging to catch up with him as he strode down the hallway.

"Where are we going?"

"You'll see." He grabbed my hand after we got on the elevator, rubbed his thumb over my ring, then lifted my hand and kissed my fingers. "I like your skirt."

"You do?" *Nice response, McKay.* Why was I so dumb all of a sudden?

"I do." His hand strayed to my bottom and caressed it just as the elevator doors opened, revealing the same handsome couple we'd seen two nights before.

"Oh!" I exclaimed as he let go. I followed him out, mortified. The woman quirked her mouth at me. And out of the corner of my eye, I saw her guy grab her ass, too. She was giggling as we left the building.

All men really were the same.

"Try not to do that in public," I said.

"Oh, good, then I can do it in private?" Duncan grinned, opening the passenger door of his car for me.

I rolled my eyes and sat. "Turn on the A/C, will ya? It's hot as the hinges of hell out here."

In a moment, he drove us out of the lot and through downtown Bohemia — this time to a more conventional rock soundtrack — with the vents mercifully blasting cold air.

"What did you do today?" he asked.

"Web work and stuff."

"Tell me about the stuff."

"Just, you know, stuff," I said.

"Those pieces of paper that were on your desk?"

"Oh, it's boring."

"Nothing you do is boring," Duncan said. "Tell me."

"It's just some pop-up art I'm working on."

"Pop-ups? Like cards?"

"Cards, books, art."

"What do you do with it?" He went through the green light that led us onto the causeway. We were heading toward Bohemia Beach, soaring toward the bright blue sky.

"I'm still trying to figure out what I'm doing with it."

"That's a peculiar thing to do. I mean, interesting, but ... "

"There's actually a lot more to it than you might think." I heard my defensive tone and declined to tone it down.

"I didn't mean —"

"Origamic architecture can be incredibly sophisticated. Some of it takes real engineering. Some of it's even being used for scientific purposes, like robots and heart stents and solar arrays."

"Ah," Duncan said, sounding a bit abashed. "I'm sorry. You're not working for the space center, are you?"

I laughed, relaxing a little. "No. I just didn't want you insulting my art."

"That's a good thing, then," Duncan said with a smile. "You *should* be proud of your art. I want to see it later."

"Oh, I don't know." I wasn't ready to show my art to anyone.

"I insist," he said. "As much as I like cheese, I may need an origami heart stent soon."

I laughed again. He always seemed to know how to make me laugh. "So are you going to tell me where we're going?"

"I don't have to," Duncan said, turning off Bohemia Beach's main drag and taking a side street lined with more shops and restaurants. "We're almost there."

He took another turn up an alley that led to a small lot behind a row of shops and stopped the car. The sign said "Parking for Beachside Jewelers."

"Oh, now I get it," I said, rubbing my mom's ring with my thumb. "You're going to solve my mystery."

"Well, I can't promise that much." We exited the car and headed through the alley toward the front of the building. "But maybe we'll learn something."

The jewelry store wasn't large, but it was elegant, decorated in black, cream and gold with pale marble floors and wall accents. A large, round chandelier dripped with crystals that glittered like diamonds, complemented by tiny, bright recessed lights that lent extra sparkle to the jewels in the glass cases.

A silver-haired man in a jacket and tie was showing a young couple the diamond rings. He looked up, saw Duncan and scowled.

"Apparently he remembers your video," I murmured.

"Holly!" the man called. "Your *appointment* is here." He made "appointment" sound like something nasty he'd scraped off a movie-theater floor.

"Duncan!" came a lilting voice from a doorway behind the main counter, followed by the appearance of a diminutive blonde in her 40s with sculpted hair, an adorable nose, gleaming pink lips, striking green eyes that surely did not occur in nature, and a waterfall of pearl necklaces over her sleeveless black dress. In short, she was everything I was not: chic, coiffed, elegant and expensive.

"Hello, darlin,' " Duncan said, leaning down to kiss both her cheeks as she came out to greet him. A cloud of jasmine scent followed her.

"You're not here to pick out a ring, are you?" she asked in a richly deep voice, shooting me a coy glance.

Duncan stuttered for a moment. "Ah, no. I have a little mystery for you." He reached out and grabbed my hand. "This is Thea."

"Are you a mystery, Thea?" Holly asked.

"Transparent as glass," I said. "But I have a ring that's kind of interesting."

"Oh, you already *have* a ring. That means all hope isn't lost for me," she said, winking at Duncan.

I couldn't tell if she was kidding or not.

"Hand it over, my dear," she said.

I pulled the ring off and dropped it into Holly's well-manicured hand.

She led us to the counter, leaving us in front while she slipped behind it to pick up a loupe. She pressed the small black cylinder to one emerald eye (those *had* to be contacts!) and held up the ring so that a light from above gleamed off its silver surfaces.

"Hmmm. Poison ring?" she asked.

"What?" I gasped, letting out a tensely held breath.

"Is it a poison ring? A pillbox ring. You know. With a secret compartment?"

"That's what we'd like to know," Duncan said. "It's Irish, isn't it, Thea?"

"Yes. It came here with my grandmother. My mother gave it to me."

"Hmmm," Holly said, turning it over carefully. "Needs cleaning."

"Probably. Sorry," I said.

"No problem. I can do that for you, sweetie," she said, still turning the ring slowly. "I don't see anything that looks like a hinge or latch or even a fine line that might give away a compartment." She put down the loupe and loudly rapped the ring three times against the glass countertop, making me jump. "I think it's just a thick old ring. It's not delicate, but it's well-made. This engraving is very precise; stamped and engraved, I would think. Nice quality silver. A pretty curiosity. Shall I clean it for you?"

I sighed. I had put more hope into her examination than I'd realized, and now I felt deflated. "Thanks," I said, and Holly nodded and disappeared through the doorway, ring in hand.

"At least she didn't spontaneously teleport back in time," Duncan said.

"Maybe if she rubs it hard enough. So," I said, "do you have any other rhyming friends I should know about?"

"What do you mean?"

"Lolly. Holly. Maybe an Ollie somewhere? Dolly?"

"Oh, I think that's all," Duncan said, a twinkle in his eye. "Though I knew a Wally back in Texas."

Holly emerged and handed me the ring. It shone more brightly, now, and the grooves looked less dark. But it was still the same solid, timeworn ring, and a tear came to my eye as I put it back on. *Sorry, Mom.*

Duncan's brow furrowed, and he put an arm around me.

"Thanks, Holly," he said. "I owe you one."

"Bring back another couple to do a video," Holly said. "That was so fun."

"Will do!" Duncan called, guiding me to the door.

As we walked out, I heard Holly's colleague say in a stage whisper, "Are you *crazy?*"

I chuckled and tried to be subtle about wiping my eye as I blinked in the bright afternoon sunlight. "You must be bad for business."

"Oh, he owns the place, and he's an old stick in the mud," Duncan said, adding softly: "Are you all right?"

"I'm fine. It just made me think of my mom and — and everything."

"Then I hope I made the right choice about dinner." Duncan still looked concerned.

I narrowed my eyes at him, forgetting my sorrows. "What did you do?"

"Oh, nothing. Nothing at all. We have to make a stop, and then — dinner."

Duncan said "dinner" as if it would spontaneously appear wherever we were. I shot him a dubious look. He shrugged and smiled, and we headed back to the car, then back over the causeway bridge. He had me sit in the car while he went into a chain steakhouse; a couple of minutes later, he was back with two big white bags bulging with food boxes.

"Home, then?" I asked.

"Sort of?" he answered with a wan smile.

He hit the road without another word while I tried to figure him out. Ten minutes later, meandering through one of the older neighborhoods in Bohemia as he consulted the map app on his phone, I had a bad feeling.

"You are not going where I think you're going."

"It's all arranged," Duncan said, a rueful note in his voice. "I said I'd bring dinner, and he agreed."

"Why would you want to have dinner at my dad's house, for God's sake?"

"He seems nice. Why don't *you* want to have dinner at your dad's house?"

"It's not that he — I mean — Duncan! I told you to leave my dad alone."

"He cares about you," Duncan said. "He wants to know more about the man who's courting his daughter."

I guffawed. "Really? Courting? You're killing me."

"It'll be fun," Duncan said, reacquiring his boisterousness. "Or I can put you *and* him on camera again and call off our deal."

"No way!"

Duncan said something under his breath as we pulled into my dad's driveway.

It might have been, "Good."

THE ANNOYING OLD mantel clock was bonging the Big Ben chimes and then 6 p.m. in the foyer when my dad let us in. That clock was one of the few things I remembered from when I was a little girl living here, marking out our lives in quarter-hour *BONG-bong-BONG-bongs*, unless someone forgot to wind it. Only its environment had changed. The skinny hall table that held it had filled up with grubby knick-knacks, a bowl of keys and a stack of outdated magazines.

The antique Irish timepiece looked dingy now, its intricate wooden carvings, once pristine, dulled by dust. Hearing the chimes always made me tense, remembering how they'd played in the background as my parents screamed at each other, as I heard my name dropped between the low notes that marked their dwindling time together.

The rest of the house had the same feeling the foyer had acquired — a tad outdated, a bit dusty, but basically livable. Dad had been a bachelor for years and, as far as I knew, had never entered into a committed relationship after my mother divorced him. I hadn't seen him much over the years, either, except for a few random holidays, and those were short visits packed with trips to the zoo and the movies and the beach that didn't allow much time for personal conversation. He'd been on his best behavior then. When I came back to

Bohemia this year, he'd seemed like a totally different person from the raging, charismatic character of my childhood, steady and restrained almost to the point of suffocation, his rages dissolved by time or maybe sobriety. We were cordial, but somehow, I still heard the echoes of my childhood, felt the guilt for driving my parents apart. Living with him for a few months was enough bonding for a lifetime.

"You can put that in the kitchen," my dad told Duncan. "Through there."

"Hi, Dad." I hugged him. "Are you sure you want us here?"

"Of course I want you here. Not so sure about him." He smiled, his eyes crinkling.

"You and me both," I said. But Duncan's cheerful whistling in the kitchen as he set out the food alighted in my heart like a bird of happiness.

"So he's your boyfriend?"

"Um, no. A friend. We're just hanging out this week. It's complicated."

"It's always complicated with you young people," my dad said, leading the way. "Maybe you just need a normal boyfriend."

"Let me know when you find me one. No, scratch that," I said. "I don't think a normal boyfriend is my destiny."

The kitchen was still stuck in the 1980s, with white laminate cabinets, blond wood trim and a cobalt-blue tiled kitchen island. That's where Duncan was opening the boxes. Dad had already put out plates, glasses with ice and a pitcher of iced tea.

"Hope you like steak, Dad," Duncan said, grabbing a fork, spearing a slab of meat and adding it to his plate.

"Please call me Milt."

"Aw." Duncan shot him a pathetic look.

"Please," my dad said, popping a couple of pills from the bottles he kept on the counter as Duncan watched curiously. "One child is enough."

"Thanks a lot, Dad," I said, putting down my purse and picking up my own plate. Duncan was trying to smother a laugh.

We loaded up the plates and sat at the round wooden table.

"So you don't sound like you're from around here," my dad ventured to Duncan.

"I'm from Texas."

"Texas accents must have changed a lot."

"Well, via Scotland."

"Really?" Dad, who was clearly enjoying his meal, looked impressed. "I have Scottish ancestors. Did you live in a bog?"

Leave it to my dad to ask the weirdest questions.

"No," Duncan said, swallowing a bite of roll, "but I could get to one if I had to."

"Did you have to much?"

"Mostly we brought the bog in."

Dad's brow creased. "You brought it in?"

"Peat. For the distillery."

"Ah. You made whiskey?"

"My father did. Still does," Duncan said. "Only now he does it in Texas."

"I used to like whiskey." My dad chewed another bite of steak, looking morose.

"So if you didn't live in a bog," I asked Duncan, "where did you live?"

"Muir of Ord. A village in the Black Isle, in the Highlands."

"You lived on an island?" my dad asked.

"It's a peninsula, actually."

"Sounds quaint," I said.

Duncan shrugged, polishing off a mouthful of string beans. "We had a train station and a football team. It was all right."

"Ah, football," my dad said knowingly. "You look like the kind of guy who'd play football. What position?"

"Well, it's what you'd call soccer," Duncan said. "They tried to get me to try out for the American football team at my Texas high school, but I was hopeless. I think you have to be raised on it to do it properly."

"Huh." Dad chewed some more.

I had given up on my steak and was nibbling on the mashed potatoes, which had about a pound of butter in them. Not that that was a bad thing.

"Have you slept with my daughter?" Dad asked.

I choked on my potatoes and sputtered a few blobs onto my plate as Duncan leaped up and slapped me on the back. He was stifling another laugh. "No, sir."

Not unless you counted two sessions of heavy petting and his night on the couch.

"Maybe we should go," I creaked after getting down some iced tea.

"No need for that," Dad said. "Just thought I'd ask. What's for dessert?"

Topped off with apple pie, we finally said our goodbyes.

On the way back to the old ice-plant-turned-apartments, I struggled to come up with something to say.

"You know," Duncan said, "your father really should be a video blogger. He's a hell of an interviewer."

"Oh, lord, please do not put him on video ever again. I have no idea what he'll say next."

Duncan laughed. "That's what makes him so delightful. What if I'd said 'yes'?"

"Yes?"

"You know, to his question about whether I'd slept with you? I'd have loved to see his response."

"Oh, no. No, no, no. You can't ever tell him 'yes.' "

"But what about after I sleep with you?"

"Even then." And then I realized what I'd said. I looked over at Duncan, who sported a broad grin. "I mean, if — I mean, that's not an issue. This is never going to come up again."

"Isn't it?" Duncan asked innocently, pulling into our lot and parking. "Because I want a reason to tell him yes, Thea. And I think maybe you do, too."

Maybe I did, but I suddenly felt hot and overwhelmed and wanted to get back to my place. I got out, slammed the door and walked double-time toward the building.

"Wait!" Duncan called. I heard the beep of him locking his car, his steps as he ran to catch up with me. He cupped my elbow. "Slow down. There's nowhere to run. And no need."

"I'm not running."

"You're speed-walking, then. I've always thought speed-walking was absurd. I mean, why not just run?"

"I don't know. Knees?"

"Why does everything you say make me want you more?" Duncan asked as we entered the coolness of the lobby.

"Knees? What — oh." I instantly imagined myself on my knees in front of him, looking up into those blue eyes, taking his big cock in my mouth. And a hot little ember of need flared in my belly as I pictured it.

I couldn't look him in the eye as he pressed the elevator button, but I felt him at my back. He put his big hands on my shoulders and squeezed, digging in his thumbs as he'd done the other night, coaxing the tension out of my muscles.

It was hard to argue with him when his touch was the one thing I really wanted. I thought I'd already convinced myself that taking a chance on him — or, rather, on the pleasure he could afford — was worth it. But there was still a part of me that recoiled in fear at the idea of becoming so intimate with a man again.

I shrugged him off, those strong hands, and stood there paralyzed in thought.

It was dumb, really. I'd always been too romantic in my sensibilities. So what if guys had always been mean to me? So what if the one dickhead I finally fell for had screwed me over? It didn't mean it would happen again. It couldn't happen again if I went into these last few nights with my eyes open, knowing this was a fling.

Yeah. Just a fling.

Only it felt like so much more, with his body so close I could feel his heat, with his presence, his energy wrapping around me.

It was terrifying.

The bell dinged, and I stepped forward into the elevator. When I turned, he was still standing there. In his eyes was a kind of resignation.

"Go on, love. I'll take the stairs."

The elevator doors closed as I opened my mouth to say — say what? Object. Bring him back. I wanted him. Needed him.

I'd lost him, and I'd never even had him.

PART 2

What was I doing? Why was I always the cautious one, Rapunzel trapped in a tower of my own making? The look in Duncan's eyes told me he didn't want to push me anymore. Maybe he didn't want me anymore, either — want me in that way that made me melt. Made me burn.

Fuck it. There was one way to find out. My heart beat faster as my mind made lightning-fast choices in the time it took to rise two floors. I was not going to let Night Three be my last chance at joy for the foreseeable future.

The elevator dinged again at the third floor, and I pressed my hands against the doors. "Open, open, open . . . "

I almost fell out as they did. I twirled and headed for the entrance to the stairs, yanking the door open. I dimly registered the red brick walls, black iron railings and windows on the landings as I practically flew down the steps. Even the stairs were hip in this building.

I ran smack into Duncan as he reached the landing for

the second floor. Reeling, I grabbed his arms so I wouldn't topple. With a gasp, I looked up into his face.

"Miss me, darlin'?" he asked, his voice soft and teasing, his eyes warm.

I let my purse fall to the floor and threw my arms around my neck and kissed him.

He almost staggered with the force of my assault, and then he wrapped me up with his muscular arms, pushed me against the wall and opened his mouth over mine, taking what I'd given. I whimpered at the force of him, his strength. He still wanted me, all right, even if it was only in this minute, this second. And God, I wanted him. My body seemed to boil over with red-hot lust. It shot through my veins and out my ears and twisted through every curl of my red hair, which he fisted, tilting my head back so he could suck on my neck, licking and tonguing and scraping my skin with his teeth. I made a low sound in my throat, and he released me, panting, looking wildly into my eyes.

"Shit," he said.

I looked up at him with a question. And perhaps a glimmer of panic.

He bent over, picked up my purse and thrust it in my arms. And then, to my astonishment, he scooped me up in his arms and stomped up the stairs.

"I — Duncan?"

"Sex on the stairs can come later," he said, his voice gruff. "I'm taking you to my bed."

"OK," I replied, breathless. I let my head fall back against his shoulder, reveling in the fact that this big hunk of guy was carrying my gangly self. Somehow he got the door open at the top of the stairs and strode down the hallway with me, but he let me slide to my feet so he could fish out his keys and open his door.

He grabbed my hand and pulled me inside. A twilight sky cast a dim orange glow through the windows, but I could tell his pad was very much the mirror of my apartment. He really did have nicer furniture than I did. Only there were still boxes everywhere, and an ungodly sound came from the vicinity of the couch.

"Pete! Up! Out!" Duncan bellowed.

A lumpy, prone form resolved itself into that of his skinny friend, who stumbled to his feet. "OK, man. Where's the fire?"

"OUT!"

"Going! Jesus!" Pete picked up a piece of pizza from a plate on top of a pile of boxes and shuffled to the door. It slammed shut behind him. I dropped my purse on a chair.

Duncan turned to me. The dwindling light caught the blue in his eyes, flecking it with gold. Time stood still. He cupped my cheek, leaned in and kissed me again.

Only this time, the kiss started softly and increased in intensity as he reached around my waist and pulled me closer. He sucked on my lower lip, then kissed my chin, my neck again — God, he could do that all day if he wanted to.

"Thea," he whispered between kisses, one hand moving up to cup a breast through my clothes. "You want me, then?"

"Yes, Duncan," I whispered back.

This time when he scooped me up (twice in ten minutes!) the walk was a lot shorter. He practically threw me on his bed. It was a lot bigger than mine, king-size, I thought, with a black box base and a black quilted leather headboard. That was my visual brain taking snapshots again — not that these details were at the forefront of my mind, because Duncan was stripping with astounding speed. I sat up enough to watch. I didn't know how engrossed I was until I licked my lips and he groaned as he caught me doing it.

And he was naked, gloriously naked — and crawling toward me on the bed, pushing me back against the soft bedding (I would laugh later about it being splashed with *Star Wars* graphics) and hovering over me on his elbows, slipping his hands into my thick curls, pressing his mouth against mine.

I slid my hands around his back, reveling in his hard muscle, his hot skin, enjoying the weight of him against me. He pushed a knee between my legs and drew my shirt over my head, and then my bra was gone, almost as fast as in that dream I'd had. I had never moved this fast in my life.

He pushed my skirt up around my waist and reached between my legs to touch me through my underwear. Then he slipped a finger under the fabric and stroked me.

"You're so wet," he whispered in satisfaction and wonder.

God, yes, I was wet. I closed my eyes and lay back with a moan, letting him touch and tease my clit with his clever fingers. He made little circles over the sensitive bud, lightly, then pressed harder, making me arch in want, before he resumed the delicate dance that slowly pushed me to the edge. I wanted more, *fuck,* all of him.

And then one of those fingers pushed inside me, deep, curling against my hot spot. I involuntarily bucked against the invasion. "Yes, Thea, that's *verrra* good. You want this, don't you, Thea? You want me inside you?"

"Yes," I almost sobbed, looking up at him. "Please, yes."

"Thank God," he said. "Because you're about to make me explode."

He yanked off my panties and tossed them aside — the

sandals had vanished already — and reached into a night-stand drawer. In a moment, he was rolling on a condom.

"I'm OK, but it never hurts to be cautious," he said. "Are you ready?"

"I'm protected, too. But yes. I'm ready. Now, Duncan."

My skirt was still bunched around my waist. It didn't matter. He hooked his arms under my knees and hitched me closer to him, sliding his cock against my wet cleft. I felt so empty. I wanted him inside me so badly. I opened my legs wider, and his mouth opened in a kind of half-smile that spoke of his arousal, that said he was barely on the edge of control. His eyes were hooded, dreamy, intense.

And then he was sliding into me, thick inch by hard inch. So big. I moaned as he stretched me. It had been a long time. I wasn't used to this kind of invasion. But I needed it, wanted it, and my slick arousal eased his passage until he'd sunk all the way to the hilt. There was a hint of pain, but more than that, a fiery need.

"More," I whispered, and he eased out partway and pushed again. I didn't think he could go deeper, but he did, and I made a little mewling sound.

He ran a finger around one nipple and sucked in a breath. "You're so fucking tight, Thea. Jesus." He pulled back and thrust again, this time harder.

"Yes, God, *yes.*"

And then he pounded me. Deep. Deeper. So hard. I wanted it hard, fast, and I wrapped my legs around his back, clutched the bedspread beneath me. His fucking was almost a punishment, a glorious punishment for making myself wait so long, and a reward, too. He was magnificent above me, a beautiful beast, his usual humor displaced by raw desire.

He shifted, making me groan anew, and leaned over to

suck on one breast, squeezing the other with one hand, still thrusting, his flint striking a spark that quickly caught and flared and burned. The flames of pleasure threatened to break through my brick walls, and then my walls were straw, tinder, paper, engulfed in fire.

I cried out as the blast of ecstasy ripped through me, and Duncan grasped my hips, yanking me tighter against him. The intensity of my orgasm tripled, and I moaned even as I heard Duncan's primitive cry, felt him pulse inside me, holding himself there as he pressed even harder against me. The slide of his body against my clit had me crying out again, and I wrapped my arms around him, pulling him down, holding him tightly as he quaked and then, slowly, calmed.

His stuttering breaths eased. Still holding me — still inside me, so intimate, *oh,* so good — he rolled us so we were sideways on the bed. For once, he didn't say a thing, except with his hands. He caressed me: my shoulders, my breasts, my still-hard nipples. My cheeks. My lips. He kissed me again, this one slow and simmering, and I lost myself in the play of his tongue on mine, drowsy, spent.

Finally, he slipped out of me, went briefly into the bathroom and returned without the condom. He bundled me under the covers, slipping off my wrinkled skirt, wrapping me up in his arms, warm and strong. And then he fell asleep.

I held my breath for a while, not wanting to wake him, to break this sweet cocoon. Was I really in the arms of Duncan Flyte? And was this what it was like to have someone? Really have someone?

Tears came to my eyes, and I wiped them away, not wanting him to feel them, to know. Stupid tears. Foolish tears.

Duncan might play the field, I told myself, but tonight, he was playing with me.

I HAD TO ADMIT, I felt a little slutty to be the one leaving before dawn, but it was kind of fun for once. Plus, I wasn't ready to face whatever reality the morning brought.

Duncan snored lightly as I eased out of the big bed. I slipped on my skirt and shirt and, clutching my undergarments, purse and sandals, slipped out his door and across the hall to mine. I took a long, hot shower and thought about what last night meant, and then I told myself to stop thinking. It didn't mean anything. This was what it was: glorious sex. All the kids were doing it.

Only I wasn't, usually. Fucking emotional baggage. Why did it have to follow me, even when I left it somewhere in Kansas? Did a tornado bring it back east to Florida and drop it at my doorstep?

I got myself together and headed downtown, grabbing a doughnut and coffee at Sugar Shack. Ez was heading in as I was heading out, and she stopped just outside the door to look me over.

"Bitch, you got laid," she said.

"Ez!" I shrieked, then looked around. Passersby had an appalling lack of curiosity.

"Just saying. Good for you." She made a rude gesture with her fist, shot me a lopsided grin and disappeared into the store.

I hoped my dad wouldn't have the same reaction. Fortunately, he was still waking up and didn't say much other than "Thanks for the steak." I spent the morning working on a sign design. This one would be made the new-fashioned way — digitally. The art of sign painting was fading, no doubt, but I was weirdly proud that my dad and I both still knew how to do it. Anybody could do what I did with a computer. It looked good, but it lacked a certain tactile authenticity.

Dad went out to paint the sign for a new gallery — Cali's sign seemed to have started a trend — and I got to work. Around noon, just when I'd retrieved my PB&J from the refrigerator, a delivery came to the front desk. My jaw dropped when Connie brought in the huge vase of roses, the petals fiery orange edged with red, and plunked it on my desk.

"Two dozen, I think," she said with feigned indifference. "There's a card."

"Thanks. Yeah. Wow."

She smiled. "Oh, yeah. Big wow. He's a keeper."

I'm sure all the girls thought that about Duncan when he turned on the charm.

These were only the second roses I'd ever received, and by far the most exquisite. I hated that these beautiful blooms dredged up that bitter old memory, and I closed my eyes and imagined Duncan's mouth on mine and brought myself back to the present.

When I opened my eyes, Connie was there hovering, waiting for me to open the card. I didn't bite. I knew who they were from.

I raised an eyebrow at her. As soon as she went back out front, I grabbed the card and opened it.

Verrra beautiful redheads, just like you. See you at 7.
— D.

Could roses turn a girl on? Because, imagining his words, his delicious rolled "R's," my lady parts tingled and my face grew hot.

I ate my sandwich and drank my water slowly, staring at the flowers as if they were a really good movie on TV. Lines and color. Symmetry. Circles within circles, deep in the heart of each bloom. I pushed my nose into one, inhaled its sweetness and let its velvet touch tickle my skin.

That's about when my dad walked through the door. I sat back abruptly, almost spilling what was left in my water bottle.

He looked at me shrewdly and didn't say a word before heading into his office.

Oh, shit. What was I supposed to say? Was it that obvious? *Yes, Dad, I slept with him, and it fucking rocked.*

Instead, I emailed my father a proof of the design I'd been working on with a line that said I was leaving early. I left the roses on my desk, but I took the note. That was for my eyes only. And then, as much as I dreaded it, I walked downtown to shop for clothes.

By 7, I looked as close as I ever looked to good. I didn't want to scare Duncan by dressing up too much, but I wanted to emphasize what few assets I had. Given that I rarely dressed up, achieving the balance between *looking* dressed up while also appearing to be casual was way too much for my unfashionable mind to comprehend. Fortunately, a bored clerk at one of the boutiques downtown took me in hand and found me a hand-dyed blue-green sundress in a light fabric with a halter neck.

"You can't wear a bra with this," she'd insisted.

"I have to wear a bra."

"You can't. It will ruin the line. Here, see how the bodice sort of cups and pushes up your breasts?" She patted me under my bosom in a far too familiar way, but I had to admit, the girls looked pretty good, enhanced by the deep V-neck.

"But it's too short," I said.

"Oh, it's just because you're tall. The more leg, the better. Trust me."

So here I was in my apartment, fluffing my hair like a dope, considering what shoes to wear, hoping he wasn't taking me horseback riding or something tonight. I was just wondering if I was supposed to knock on his door when the knock came on mine. Barefoot, I ran to open it.

It was Duncan, slightly sunburned, toting a couple of fabric grocery bags and wearing familiar loose khaki shorts and a black T-shirt that said, "I'm Scottish and We Don't Keep Calm."

His eyes widened as he scanned me. "Uh-oh."

"What? What is it?" Had I gotten lipstick on myself? Was one of my boobs hanging out? I looked down at myself in worry and up at his face.

"I really should be taking you out on the town in that getup, darlin'. Not cooking for you at home." Duncan leaned in and brushed my mouth with a feather-light kiss that nearly took my breath away.

"Oh, this old thing," I said, not very convincingly, as he carried the bags to the kitchen. *Yes! He liked it!* "You're going to cook for me? After sending me those beautiful roses?"

"You liked them, then?" He started unpacking the bags. Something green wrapped in plastic. Something wrapped in paper . . . "Good. I hadn't heard from you, and I hoped you weren't annoyed with me."

"Oh, no! They're gorgeous! I left them at the office to cheer me up there. I'm sorry. I don't really know the, uh, etiquette of receiving roses."

He stopped what he was doing and moved closer, slipping

his arms around my waist, letting his hands stray south to cup my bottom.

"This dress is all the thanks I need," he murmured, leaning over me to kiss me again with more heat, more intensity. He slid his tongue over mine, constantly moving, tasting, as he pressed me against him. I hung on to his neck and kissed him back, my awkwardness forgotten in my need. One of his hands bunched up the skirt of my dress. I sucked on his tongue and he pushed me away with a gasp.

"But I was going to cook," he said, his voice rough.

"I'm not hungry yet," I whispered.

"I am," he said, grabbing me with urgency, kissing me, steering me toward my bed. He pushed me back against the mattress, and I bounced. And giggled. He grinned, and his shirt was off in a second. The golden light of early evening streamed through my windows and lit him up like a god, every ridge and valley of his muscles, every copper curl of hair.

He leaned over me, smiling, and kissed my neck, licking that spot under my ear that made my toes curl. I made a soft sound.

"That's right," he said, kissing his way down into the V of my dress, onto the soft curves. "Don't hold back. I want you, Thea. All of you. All of you."

He traced the outline of my hardening nipples through the fabric of the dress, and little arcs of electricity seemed to spark wherever he touched me. With his big hands, he swiftly scooped both my breasts out of their slings. I bit my lip at being so exposed.

"Oh, I like this dress very much," he said softly, delicately tracing my pink areolas.

"Duncan." I arched, needing more, needing it fast.

"Patience. I want to admire you." He licked one stiff peak, and I moaned. And then he was licking, suckling, drawing out the nipples gently with his teeth. I writhed under him, and he chuckled. He unfastened his shorts; from a pocket, he pulled a small square packet and threw it on the bedspread. And then he yanked off the rest of his clothes as if they were on fire and reached up under my dress.

"Ah, what's this?" he asked.

"I — I got some new underwear today."

"The same place you got the dress? Let's just see, shall we?" He pushed the dress up around my waist — it didn't have far to go, given how short it was — and I tried to own my inner siren.

"Oh, darlin'," he said. "I like you in a thong."

I gasped as Duncan rolled me over with no effort at all and cupped my ass cheeks. "Your skin is so pale," he said, running a finger down the crevice, under the string of the thong. And then he hooked his finger around the wisp of fabric and pulled the whole thing off.

"Spread your legs," he said, a note of command in his voice.

"Oh, God," I moaned into the bedspread, but I complied, liking the feeling of him caressing my bottom. He moved one hand between my legs, stroking my folds, finding my nub and teasing it with excruciatingly delicious skill.

He pushed a finger inside me. "Jesus, you're wet." He added a second finger, thrusting with his hand, teasing my clit with his thumb. "Oh, yes, darlin'. You're so pretty like this, your pussy wet and hot for me. Sweet little red curls. Do you like this, Thea?"

I breathed out a "yes," and he clutched my ass with his free hand, squeezing, rubbing. He kissed one cheek and ran a finger down the center again, stroking my nether hole with the lightest touch, ramping up my sense of forbidden pleasure before his fingers probed deeper into my slick cleft. When he abruptly stopped, I made a whimpering sound, and then I felt the mattress shift. I looked up, and he was moving onto his back up against the pillows, reaching for me.

"Come," he said. Though he didn't mean it *that* way. God knows I'd been close. "Take that dress off and straddle my head, sweetheart. I want to taste you."

"I — are you sure?" Because I wasn't a small girl, and . . .

"Get up here."

I pulled the dress off as he watched. The pure lust in his eyes set me on fire as I crawled to him. I settled gingerly on my knees, hovering over his face. He grasped my behind and shifted me, and then his tongue flicked my clit and I gasped. I grabbed the headboard, leaning over as he pulled me against his mouth, licking, teasing. He sucked hard on my nub and then swirled it lightly with his tongue. He grazed it with his teeth and licked some more, his nimble tongue never resting in one place.

An aching, wrenching pleasure began to radiate from my clit. It throbbed, an overwrought nexus of sensation, building and expanding like a cosmic explosion in slow motion, until I was gasping and crying out and moaning in complete abandon. I didn't know myself, this ravenous sex goddess whose inhibitions had burned away in one flash of fire.

"God, yes — yes — Duncan. Oh, my God!" And it didn't stop. Waves of pleasure, wave after wave, until it was almost painful, almost too much. I tried to disengage, but he held me fast for another minute of luscious torture until I cried out again and fell back.

This time, he let me go, and I could hear him panting, feel

him shifting. He moved over me and kissed my mouth, salty and wet and hot. "Do you taste yourself?" he whispered, kissing me again. "God, I love licking your pussy." Another kiss. "So juicy for me." His mouth descended on mine in a deep, open kiss, and I wrapped myself around him, giving him back what he gave, hungry and grateful. He broke away for a moment. I was vaguely aware of him grabbing and opening the condom, rolling it on, and then he pushed my aching legs wide.

The touch of his cock against my still-pulsing clit was like a brand, and I cried out. He slid the tip over my apex, dragged it through my cleft and thrust into me, hard. Again. Again. *Again.* And I wanted more. Harder. Deeper. Every molecule of his big body ravishing mine.

The late-day light wreathed his head in fire. The blue in his eyes seemed to darken to sapphires with flames at their hearts. The muscles in his arms flexed as he supported himself over me; every movement of his body as he thrust into me was rough, sensual poetry.

The lingering ache from my previous orgasms evolved into renewed pleasure, deeper and even more satisfying, and then I was clutching him, wrapping my legs around his back, groaning as he convulsed in my depths.

"Fuck," he said. "Fuck, oh God, yes." He held himself hard inside me, shaking as my sheath clenched around him in yet another dizzying orgasm. "Thea," he moaned.

"Yes, Duncan. Oh, yes. Stay inside me."

And he did, for another couple of minutes, as we slowly came down. When he finally eased out of me, I was exhausted. He lay next to me and cradled me in his arms. The sun was lower now, the light more mellow. God, it wasn't even night yet. Would we do that again? I couldn't imagine it.

"What are you thinking?" he asked, kissing my hair.

"Just wondering how many times a person can do that in a night."

He laughed, a low rumble against my ear. "You want to go for the record?"

"Ah, no, I mean . . . " I had to chuckle too. "I mean, how much can a body take? Because that was a lot."

"Did I hurt you?" He sounded worried.

"Oh, God, no. That was unbelievably — I don't even have words for it. How good it was, I mean."

"Now that's a compliment a guy can take to the bank," he said, and I remembered that I was far from the first and wouldn't be the last girl from whom he'd collect his kudos.

He kissed my hair again and added, "And I have to agree with you on how good it was, lovely lass. You set my kilt on fire."

And my heart melted anew. I lifted my face to his and kissed him. We kissed for a while like that, trading touches of tongues and lips and hands, until he paused and pushed my hair back away from my face.

"Now I'm really hungry. Stay here in bed, darlin', and I'll cook that dinner, OK?"

"Do you need help?"

"Not at all. In fact, it'll do me good knowing I can glance out here and see you naked and gorgeous and waiting for me."

If I didn't blush before, I was pretty sure I did then. I smiled as he rolled out of bed and pulled on his shorts (leaving his briefs on the floor and my mind in the gutter) and headed toward the kitchen. I curled up against the pillows and dozed off.

When I awoke, it was past dusk, and delicious smells arose from the kitchen, along with a loud grinding sound.

I sat straight up. "Duncan? What is that?"

"Food processor!" he shouted from the kitchen. "I had to bring it over from my place. Did you know you have absolutely nothing useful in your kitchen?"

I knew. I wasn't much for cooking, though I occasionally baked cookies as therapy.

It seemed kind of silly to put the dress back on, so I found the thong (also kind of silly, but I smiled when I thought of Duncan's reaction to it) and slipped it on, along with an over-sized Bohemia Beach T-shirt. I stopped by the bathroom, then padded to the kitchen in my bare feet.

"Wow," I said.

The limited surfaces were besieged by controlled chaos — a cutting board with half a bulb of garlic and miscellaneous green bits, a cast-iron pan sizzling with small cuts of delicious-smelling meat next to a boiling pot on the stove, and Duncan stuffing basil leaves into an already-loaded food processor before making it roar again. As it ground up the basil with the other items, he poured in extra virgin olive oil. He noticed me, quickly glancing at my legs and then back at my face, and smiled.

"Pesto," he shouted over the machine.

"Awesome." And I was in awe.

"And lamb chops," he said as he turned off the processor, ducked over to the stove and used tongs to flip the chops in the frying pan. He opened the lid of the tall steaming pot and stirred the contents with a wooden spoon. "Pasta's done." He turned off the stove.

"You're amazing," I said.

"Wait until you taste me. I mean them." He grinned, and I felt a rush of mortification — and desire.

I smiled back shyly, imagining the pleasures afforded by both the food and Duncan.

I put plates and utensils on the small retro table in my living area. He wrapped up his culinary masterpieces and slipped on his T-shirt as I opened a bottle of cabernet sauvignon.

When Duncan dished up the lamb chops, redolent of garlic and rosemary, and spooned pesto-smothered farfalle noodles onto my plate, my stomach growled audibly.

"That's what I want to hear," Duncan said.

"I should put music on to cover up my stomach's gymnastics," I said, a trifle embarrassed. Which was ridiculous, given I'd done much more embarrassing things already tonight. I got my wireless speaker going and poured the wine. I sat and toasted Duncan. "To the chef."

"To a woman with excellent taste," he joked, and we both drank. "Damn, that's delicious," he added.

"You'll have to see Alex's wine room. It's ridiculous."

"Alex?" There was something in his tone. Was he jealous? *Of course not.* I just wanted him to be.

"My friend Sloane's boyfriend. He's on the art museum board. He gave me the bottle when I did some free graphics for the museum's marketing campaign."

He nodded, smiling now. "It's always good to know someone who knows wine. I'll bring you whiskey next time. Now dig in, before it gets cold."

After a couple of minutes of food heaven, I came up for air. "This is *soooo* good, Duncan. Where'd you learn to cook like this?"

"Oh, you learn to cook when you have to," he said, not really answering the question.

"I used to have this friend in Kansas who cooked for me a couple of times."

"Ah! A romantic interest?" Duncan asked.

"No. I mean, he was definitely romantically interesting, cute as hell, but he was way out of my league. So we cooked meals together and stayed squarely in the friend zone."

Duncan's brow creased for a moment. "Well, his loss is my gain. At least this week," he added, reminding me of our temporary arrangement. I was starting to hate the stupid deadline, especially since I'd already plunged into the deep end. "So was this the handsome prince who screwed you over?"

"What?" I paused with my fork halfway to my mouth.

"The guy you mentioned the first night I met you, at the theater. You said you preferred handsome princes who didn't screw you over."

"Oh, that." I chewed on the bite of pesto pasta, hoping somehow the question would dissolve into thin air, but he was still looking at me when I was done. "It was just a guy I knew back in Kansas City at art school."

"And?" Duncan started on his second lamb chop. He wasn't pressing me. He just seemed curious, and for some reason, I wanted to tell him. Maybe to see how he'd react.

"We were really good friends. I mean, I didn't have many friends, so maybe I didn't know any better. But we spent a lot of time together, especially around the time my mom was first diagnosed, before we knew how bad it was going to be. I wanted to come home right away, but she didn't want me to drop out. I agreed to finish the semester, but I was anxious about what would happen. What had already happened. I poured out my heart to this guy. We were friends, and then we were more than friends." That had been a huge night for me. And he'd sent me roses the next day. Those fucking roses that I thought meant everything. "I *thought* we were more than friends, anyway. But it turned out I wasn't a good judge of what it all meant."

"What it all meant?"

"The talking, I guess. And what we were doing. You know, the physical part."

Duncan nodded sympathetically, probably not seeing the parallels I couldn't help but draw, so I continued.

"I put a lot of trust in him, which was a big deal for me, because the guys in junior high and high school were so mean."

Duncan's brows came together. "How?"

"Oh, I don't want to get into it."

"You've already started."

I frowned. "It's not like I want to relive it. It started in junior high. I was one of the first girls to, uh, develop, and so I got a lot of juvenile comments, along with overtures from some of the more confident guys. Not the nice ones. I was a real wallflower, you know? I wasn't ready to deal with what they were throwing at me, and I pushed them away. They started calling me stuck-up, and then worse. Said some really cruel things. Vandalized my locker. Stupid crap like that. I don't want to go into it."

But shit, junior high was horrible. The least of it was the endless teasing about my red hair, and not just the hair on my head, not that any of those creeps ever got a look. By the time I'd hit high school and everyone had grown up a little, I was generally viewed as a freak. I stayed on the fringe with the rest of the outcasts and skipped all the social events that other people fondly remembered. I had a couple of bad years when my grades spiraled and I thought about death a lot, wished for it. My mom tried to get me into counseling, but I wouldn't go. It got a little better by senior year, maybe because I knew I was about to get out.

"I'm sorry," Duncan was saying. "Junior-high boys can be ory little knobs."

I chuckled in spite of my painful memories. "What's that?"

"Dicks, basically." He had that right. "But what about this prince in art school?"

"Oh, I thought we were exclusive for weeks. One night he invites me over to his apartment, and I walk in and he's on the couch, making out with another girl. He introduced me as 'Thea, this girl I know from art class.' "

"Ouch," Duncan said.

"And then he asked me if I'd like to join them."

"Did you?" Duncan's gaze lit with more than curiosity.

I rolled my eyes. "Leave it to a guy to ask that. No, I didn't. He'd just proven himself a first-class asshole."

"Point taken, point taken." Duncan refilled our glasses. "I'm just imagining you in a threesome, and it's kind of hot."

"You're talking to the girl who still hasn't figured out how to deal with one man, let alone two, but thanks."

He laughed, but the sound had an edge. "You were vulnerable. The bastard was using you."

"I guess he was. I'd like to think there was something there, something at least in our friendship, but I know better now." I paused. The putative prince was the reason I swore I'd never let my guard down again, yet here I was, spilling my guts to a new candidate for the throne. "I hate to admit it, but that guy was probably one of the reasons I didn't go back to finish art school after Mom died. I thought maybe I'd pick up some classes here at the Bohemia School of Art and Design, but I just haven't found the time."

"Handsome prince," Duncan scoffed. "If you ever introduce me to him, I'll thrash him."

Hearing laid-back Duncan speak so casually of enacting violent revenge on my ex-fuck-buddy kind of, well, turned me on.

"I'd like that," I said, sipping my wine, looking him in the eye.

"You're quite medieval, aren't you, lass?"

"You have no idea."

He laughed again, more lightly this time. "Come here."

Oh, the twinkle in those eyes. I keep drowning in those pools. Just remember, he's not your prince. Only the prince of pleasure. And that's all you really want.

And I was going to take advantage of these few days, even if it killed me.

"Take off your shirt first," I said in a soft voice.

His gaze darkened, and he pulled the shirt off and tossed it aside.

"Now the shorts. But get whatever you need out of the pockets."

He stood, pulled a condom packet out of his pocket and dropped his shorts. He pushed his chair back and sat again, beckoning to me.

I stood and slowly, teasingly removed my thong. I sauntered over to him and, at the same pace, pulled my T-shirt over my head, dropping it on the floor.

He swallowed, his Adam's apple bobbing, his face serious now, his mouth slightly open as he took in my nakedness. His was devastating; his hardening cock towered from his lap.

I took the condom packet out of his hand, ripped it open, grasped his shaft and rolled it on.

He hauled me into his lap without hesitation, positioning me so his tip breached my cleft. With a groan I slid down onto him, gripping his shoulders. And then, looking into those crystalline eyes, I started to move, up and down, hanging on to his muscled neck, shifting so I took him even deeper.

"Fuck," Duncan growled. "I like you like this."

I said nothing, but I pressed my lips to his, opening to his ravening tongue as he thrust upward into me. I moaned against his mouth and increased my pace, urgent now, meeting his thrusts with a wild need I didn't know I possessed. He struck me in a place so profound, so primitive, so gloriously raw, I couldn't imagine ever getting enough.

He grabbed my waist with a groan, holding himself deep within me as he bucked. He threw his head back as his deto- nation rocked through me, precipitating mine. I convulsed around him, bending forward, pressing my breasts against his hard chest, wanting to meld with him in every way possible, holding him tight until we both stopped shaking.

At last, Duncan eased me off his lap and scooped me up, carrying me to the bed, laying me against the pillows. He went into the bathroom to dispose of his condom, turned out the lights and came back, curling around me, hot and protec- tive against my back.

"I rather like eating garlic and kissing you," he said. "You're even more delicious."

A laugh rumbled up from my full belly, as sated as the rest of me. "You're a hell of a cook, Duncan Flyte," I whispered.

CALI'S GALLERY WAS PACKED, and Duncan was roving it with his camera, interviewing people for the vlog. I'd taken a moment to check his channel this morning and found he'd interviewed people on the beach yesterday, including a hilariously taciturn fisherman who continued to give one- or two-word answers no matter how long Duncan persisted. And Duncan knew how to persist.

So that's why he'd looked a little sunburned. I should have asked him about his day, but things had moved so fast last night. He hadn't seemed to mind.

It was weird to be in a crowd with him after our intimate night. Though "with him" was an exaggeration. Truth was, while he was roving, I hung out with Sloane and Ez by the snack table in the interior studio, eating cheese and crackers and drinking champagne. We watched Cali and Wyatt, flushed and happy, moving through the crowd and talking about the big, beautiful images of their trip to Tahiti and the surfers there and in Bohemia Beach.

The photos hung in the lobby — astounding waves, graceful surfers, black-and-white beaches. In the studio, a big screen displayed their short, stunning time-lapses and surf videos, some with Wyatt himself riding the board.

"Do you wish the Emeralds were playing tonight?" I said to Ez over the surf music rocking the sound system.

"Naw." In a black tank, jeans and dangling silver jewelry, she eyed the crowd from behind her swoop of dark bangs and sipped her third glass of champagne. "After the disaster last time, it's kind of nice to sit back and let somebody else do the work."

"But that disaster led to Gary," observed Sloane, cute in

one of her short dresses and an airy scarf. Her long hair was up, given the brutal summer heat outside.

"Poor Gary," I said. Duncan had cornered Ez's curly-haired artist boyfriend with his camera, and Gary gestured wildly as he talked.

Ez's mouth quirked into a smile. "Gary can hold his own."

"I think Alex went out for a breath of air. He's not big on crowds. I'm going to go see how he's doing," Sloane said, moving off.

"So how's it going with video boy?" Ez asked slyly, and then: "Wow, I didn't know anyone could still turn that red. I guess that answers my question. Good for you."

I sighed, fingering the fabric of my dress — the same one I'd worn last night. Duncan had asked me to wear it again, and its soft touch on my skin reminded me of him.

"I can't believe I let things go so far when I only have a week with him," I said.

"Who's to say it's only a week?"

"He did. We did. That's the deal. I give him a week, and then I can tell him to go away so I don't have to undergo the torture of being broadcast to his legions of fans."

"I'm sure you could work something out," Ez said.

"I don't see how. He lives his whole life on camera. Anyway, you've seen how he flirts with every girl he sees. I'm just a moment's distraction until he finds the next one."

"Just because he's got the goods doesn't necessarily mean he's into every vagina he meets." Ez eyed him appreciatively. "Though I doubt many women turn him down."

"It's none of my business anyway," I said. "I'm not setting myself up for disappointment."

Ez leaned closer so she wouldn't have to shout. "I'd say

you've already set yourself up for something. And that's OK. Sometimes you just have to take a leap."

The very idea started a bubbling in my belly, fizzy nerves that popped in little bursts of anxiety.

"Maybe," was all I could manage.

Ez squeezed my arm and smiled. "I guess I'll go rescue my guy. Maybe I can get some airtime and plug the band."

"Good idea." I was left standing awkwardly by the snacks, marveling at how all of my friends had found love in the past year. Penelope and Jace, the only close friends who were missing, were busy with their play tonight.

And me? I sort of wished I were home working on my pop-ups.

I refilled my glass and wandered away from the snacks, as if movement would prevent anyone from finding me. And then I almost bumped into Lolly.

Duncan's blond friend was wearing platform heels, a teeny-tiny purse and a silver strapless mini-dress so miniature, her ass cheeks hung ever so slightly out of it. What was she, some kind of astronaut envoy from Planet Sex?

"Oh, it's you," Lolly said.

"Hi, Lolly."

"I'm sorry. What's your name again?"

"Thea." I tried not to be insulted. I was used to being both invisible and forgettable.

"So you're not the Key Grip tonight?" she asked drily.

"The what?"

"Camera carrier. Whatever. Duncan's in fine form."

"He's a one-man band, as far as I can tell," I said. "He doesn't need me."

"Ha, that's the truth. He doesn't need any of us."

"Us?" I sipped my champagne and tried to pretend I wasn't curious.

"Women. Don't get me wrong. He's a fine fuck. But his only queen is the click. If he's not getting clicks, he's not interested."

The bubbles of anxiety fizzed in my stomach again. I knew Duncan lived for his audience, but hearing her state it so baldly — and worse, picturing her with him — made me feel ill.

"You've known him a long time?" I creaked. And drank more champagne.

"Since he came to Bohemia a few years ago. I got to know him at a meetup. That was fun, if you know what I mean." Lolly grinned.

"Meetup?"

"Where video bloggers get together."

"Oh, yeah."

"Well, have fun." Clearly bored, Lolly wiggled away, dragging with her the eyeballs of several guys in the vicinity.

I sucked in some deep breaths, drank the rest of my champagne and went back to the table for more. Then I wandered out to the lobby, a smaller space still thronged with people, and sat on the mod couch in front of a huge photo of Wyatt surfing a glassy wave. The colors were astounding — green and blue and yellow and hints of red as the sun, kissing the horizon, gleamed behind him. He was a pro surfer, and he looked it, every inch of his body working with his board, with the wave, like a dancer's. Motion frozen in time.

I'd been frozen in time until this week. Until Duncan came along and wound my clock again. I wished I could be cool like Lolly, look on him as a "fine fuck" and nothing else. That was the bargain I'd made with myself. But her words made me realize I was falling into the emotional trap of connecting feelings with sex, an extremely dangerous thing to do with someone like Duncan. Why wouldn't a guy who was so obviously adroit with women enjoy the fruits of his charms? He wasn't looking for anything more, and damn it, neither was I.

The couch cushion bounced next to me. I looked over, my eyes focusing again.

I should have known.

"Ugly, isn't he?" Duncan remarked, looking up at Cali's photo of Wyatt.

A small laugh escaped me. "I know. All those muscles. That cool white streak in his dark hair. And the tattoo."

"What woman could possibly like that?"

"Right. Hideous."

Duncan leaned over and spoke softly in my ear. "I love you in that dress."

I turned to look at him and found my face barely an inch from his.

He sucked in a breath, then leaned back and smiled. "And out of it," he added.

A corner of my mouth lifted, but I held something back. "You done filming?"

"Yeah." He gestured to the camera bag sitting next to him. "I got more than enough."

"I ran into Lolly."

"Oh, I thought I saw her in her silver space-slut outfit," Duncan said, picking up one of the photo books Cali had placed on a clear acrylic end table. "I thought she only wore that to conventions."

Great. Now I would not only picture them together, I'd picture him with her wearing *that dress*.

Duncan thumbed through Cali's photos of pinup girls, subjects she had been cultivating for months, starting with a photo shoot with her friends. Including me.

Oh, crap.

There I was, filling a page, teetering atop a ladder, holding a paint brush, exclaiming in a red-lipped "Oh!" as a can of paint toppled in front of me, throwing out a frozen wave of blue color. My denim overalls were falling off my naked shoulder, showing a hint of a white lace bra and cleavage. The image was modest, but for me, it had been a huge step to let Cali bring out my sexy side. I mean, my would-be sexy side.

"Holy Christ, I knew I'd seen you before! You were in that exhibit!" Duncan exclaimed, attracting a few curious glances. He held the book closer. "God, you're delectable. And somehow softer in this photo. I like it. You. Your look. My God, your breasts."

I punched his arm and glanced around to see more leering lookie-loos. "Shut up!"

"How can I? Do you think I can buy this?"

"It's a demo to attract customers."

"It's attracting me."

I couldn't help but laugh. "You don't have to flatter me, Duncan."

He turned to me. "Flatter you?" He lowered his voice. "Darlin', if you think this is flattery, you should feel my hard-on right now."

I swallowed, holding his gaze. He leaned closer as if he were going to kiss me, then seemed to recover himself and pull back. "Don't get me started, or I'll lay you down right here on this couch," he muttered, putting down the book. "Want to get out of here?"

"Thea!" Cali and Wyatt appeared before us, making the rounds like the bridal couple at a wedding.

I stood and swayed a bit. Too much champagne. Not enough Duncan.

"Whoa." Duncan grabbed my arm as he stood, too.

"Wonderful show," I said.

"Thanks," Cali and Wyatt said in tandem, then laughed at their synchronicity.

"I'm more interested in a show you had several months ago," Duncan said, to my growing mortification. "Can I buy a print of that photo of Thea?"

Cali grinned, flicked her gaze at me and returned her attention to Duncan. "I actually have the original print still framed in the back. It's pretty large, though. Do you want to see it?"

"Absolutely. I'll be right back," Duncan said to me, and then he went off with Cali into the studio.

Wyatt and I stood there awkwardly for a moment.

I nodded at the surf picture. "How would you feel if that photo of you were on someone else's wall?"

He shrugged. "I've been photographed for most of my professional life. I've been in magazines and on TV. You get used to it. Though when a collector bought that photo I took of Cali, I had a bad day picturing other people looking at her."

Oh, yeah. I remembered that photo. "It was very tasteful and artistic."

"That's what she said." Wyatt smiled. "So is the photo of you. And at least you have clothes on."

"True." I returned his smile at his easy response and gave myself up to my champagne buzz. No use creating stress out of nothing. "I have to remember it's all about the art."

Just then, Cali's brother Damien strolled up, absorbing all light around him as usual in a pure black suit, relieved only by a white tie punctuated by flying black crows. His longish black hair mostly stuck straight up, and his eyeliner completed the upscale-Goth look.

"Did someone say art?" Damien asked. "Go on, ask me about my latest commission."

"How's it going?" I asked.

"Fucking awesome," Damien said with a grin. "So what gives, Thea? Cali says you're working on something but won't talk about it."

"Oh, I don't mean to be mysterious. It's pop-up art, with paper. I have the skills to build what I envision, I think, but I'm trying to develop a killer concept."

"When I can't figure out why something I'm doing isn't working, I just add multimedia," Damien said. "Makes it better every time."

"I'm no programmer," I said. Damien did stuff with monitors and computers that was not my speed at all.

"Whatever you do," Wyatt said, "there's a new gallery opening down the street, and their first exhibit is going to be called 'Three-Dimensional.' They have a call to artists online. I'll have Cali send you the link so you can check it out. I think the deadline is the end of July."

"Really?" I couldn't deny a dose of excitement. Maybe, just maybe, I could put together something worth exhibiting. "That would be great. Thanks."

"No problem."

A commotion at one end of the room distracted us: Duncan coming through the doors with a huge, paper-wrapped rectangle under his arm, followed by an amused Cali.

"Made a sale," she said, raising an eyebrow and looking at me as if she were dying to pull me aside and pump me for details.

"Great," I said drily.

Duncan appeared to be delighted. "This will look fantastic in my apartment. I have big walls."

"So you're saying I'm big?" I asked.

"No, darlin', but this photo sure is."

Wyatt and Cali chuckled. We said our goodbyes. I grabbed Duncan's camera bag since he was hauling the picture, and we headed out of the gallery. Partiers and art lovers crowded the sidewalks; Bohemia was having one of its occasional street parties tonight. Duncan managed not to whack anyone with the photo.

"Shall we check out the scene?" he asked after he stuffed the art into his car and took the camera bag from me.

"Only if you explain to me what possessed you to buy that picture."

"It's a great photo," he said as we strolled toward the heart of downtown.

I wasn't sure how to answer that. "Cali's an excellent photographer."

"Yes, she is, but it helped that you came up with the concept for the photo. She told me about it."

"Not the spilling paint. That was her."

"Still. You're an adorable pinup, and I love pinup art."

"Are you a collector?" I asked.

"You could say that." He had a funny little smile on his face. Great. I was one more pin in the wall, one more pinup, pinned by Duncan.

But I did so *enjoy* being pinned by Duncan.

Go with the buzz, Thea.

I took his arm, noting his look of surprise and pleasure.

"I think I love champagne," I said. "I've always put beer first, and then cocktails, but champagne has this wonderful bubbly lift, you know?"

Duncan glanced over at me with a sly expression. "Are you drunk?"

"Not quite."

"I rarely encourage drunkenness — "

I rolled my eyes. "Oh, come on."

He chuckled but stood by his statement. "I *rarely* encourage drunkenness, but I'd like to see you drunk, darlin'."

"Maybe if you play your cards right." *Shit, that third glass of champagne may have already done the job.*

"Oh, I think I have just the place."

It was a warm night, and I shouldn't be clinging to Duncan's arm — which threw off heat like the rest of him — but it was fun and kind of nice to have this big tree trunk of a man to lean against, especially when I was tipsy. And not just nice, because my thoughts strayed frequently into naughty when flashes of the last two nights popped into my mind. I remembered what he looked like under the loose button-up white shirt and long, navy-blue shorts. As an artist, I appreciated that he didn't clash with my dress, and a little giggle escaped me.

"What?" he asked.

I just looked at him and shook my head and smiled, and he answered me with a broad grin. And a quick kiss.

We'd entered the part of town where the street party was barricaded to cars, right in the heart of the bars and restaurants, augmented by food trucks. Revelers carrying cups —

and carrying on — were all around us. A rock band played on a small stage at the end of the street.

"Damn, that smells good," Duncan said as we passed a food truck selling barbecue. A black cylindrical cooker behind the truck billowed with smoke that caught the street lights as the vendors slung juicy shredded pork onto soft rolls.

"We can stop," I said, inhaling a lungful of the divine aroma.

"Oh, no. I want to take you to a nice little bar. They have food."

"OK," I said, strangely happy and much more compliant than usual. Was that a good thing? *Sure,* the champagne said. I liked it when the champagne did my thinking for me.

A few minutes later, we arrived at the bar called Nola. Carved wood and gilded trim, dark damask wallpaper and elaborate Mardi Gras masks gave it a New Orleans atmosphere. It was dark in here, and the bar was busy, though not as packed as the crowds outside might suggest.

"Hey, doll," Duncan called to a striking bartender with short, dark hair, deep red lips and a black zip-up vest over a scrap of a white T-shirt that brought out her eye-popping cleavage.

Her eyes warmed instantly. "Duncan, sweetie, where have you been?" She stuck out her cheek for his kiss.

"Oh, you know. Here and there."

"Yeah, I know," she said archly. "What can I get you?"

He leaned in closer, and I leaned in, too, to hear him murmur: "Is one of the private rooms available?"

She looked me over and asked, "How big is your party?"

Duncan grinned at her, and she shrugged. "Sure, the Bienville Room is open. Can I bring y'all something?"

"The cheese plate, two French 75s and a bottle of my good stuff."

"You mean your dad's good stuff. Go on back. It's on its way."

"Who's that?" I whispered as Duncan tugged me down a dark hallway.

"A good friend. She was kind to me when I came to town. Thanks to her, this was one of the first bars in Bohemia to carry my dad's whiskey."

"Your charm at work, no doubt."

"Actually, my dad's. He went bar to bar when he visited me to talk up the brand." Duncan paused in front of a dark wooden door labeled BIENVILLE, elaborately lettered in gold. He turned the brass knob, and the door opened into a magical space, a cushy cocoon of decadence.

"Oh, wow." I dropped my purse next to Duncan's bag and turned slowly. The room was barely eight feet square, with built-in seating around three sides — wide benches, though that word was too harsh. These were more like lounging sofas, with deep, plush upholstery in jewel tones and layers of pillows in velour, satin and brocade. A square table held candles and an elegant, antique-style French phone in black, and above us, a bronze-finished chandelier dripping with gold crystals glowed softly with flickering candle bulbs. Burgundy wallpaper flocked with an elaborate, traditional pattern in black made the room even more intimate. Soft jazz played from hidden speakers.

"You like it?" Duncan asked.

"It's gorgeous. This is a room made for sin." I clapped my hand to my mouth after I said it.

He laughed and sat in the corner, leaning back and

spreading out his arms on the pillows. "I hadn't ruled it out. Come here."

I looked at him in the warm, golden light and got lost in those eyes. Just one dimple showed as he teased me with a half-smile, and I almost couldn't breathe. *Stay calm, Thea. This is all part of the fantasy. The handsome prince for rent. One week, and you're out.*

I scooched around the table and sank into the softness next to him, nervous. He slipped one hand into my loose hair, leaned forward and touched his lips to mine.

His kiss started lightly, but it didn't stop. He clutched the back of my neck and tilted his head, taking more of my mouth with his, slipping his tongue between my lips. I moaned and leaned back against the cushions, and he followed, a growl in his throat as his kiss grew deeper, hungrier.

"Ahem."

Duncan broke the kiss, and dizzy, I looked up to see the bartender with a loaded tray.

"Let me help you," Duncan said briskly, as if he hadn't been about to eat me alive. He hopped up and removed the two cocktails, then the whiskey bottle, as his friend set down the cheese plate, a small ice bucket and two more highball glasses.

"You two enjoy yourselves. Call me if you need anything." She nodded at the phone on the table.

"Thanks!" Duncan said brightly.

The bartender shot him a wry smile. And turned the lock on the inside of the door before closing it on the way out.

"Well, wasn't that nice of her," Duncan quipped.

"Does she think —?"

"Oh, I *hope* so." He picked up the cocktails and joined me on the bench. "French 75."

I quelled a flutter and took the flute from him, holding it up to the light. Bubbles danced in the amber glimmer. "Champagne?"

"Yes, and gin and lemon. Try it."

I did, sipping around the twist of lemon peel. "Oh, *yeah,* that's good."

Duncan took a big sip of his, too, and sighed. "A New Orleans classic. I should take you there."

"Take me? Ha. You'll never see me again after this week is over."

His eyes narrowed. "And why is that?"

"Because you're going to give me my life back," I said, though less emphatically.

He didn't say anything for a minute. Then he took another sip and grabbed a piece of cheese. "Well, I can always find someone to go to New Orleans with me," he said, "but I think you would enjoy it."

"I probably would," I said in a small voice. Damn him for teasing me.

"Yes, you would. Definitely. The restaurants are incredible. And the bars — forget most of Bourbon Street. The best bars are in other parts of the Quarter, of the city. The French 75 bar, for instance."

"There's a bar named for the drink?"

"They share a name, and it's a fine old NOLA place in Arnaud's, just off Bourbon Street, actually."

He held the cheese plate out to me, and I took a piece, along with an olive. Both were divine.

We drank and ate for a few minutes until our cocktails were gone, as Duncan told a tale of a cemetery tour he'd once taken in the city that ended with a voodoo priestess liberating most of the crowd of its money as she told outrageous fortunes. He had a way with a story, and I forgot the earlier tension and settled back against the bench, giggling, nodding, feeling as if I were drifting on a cloud. In my hand I held the next course, a glass of the whiskey.

"You like it, don't you?" Duncan asked, leaning an elbow on the cushions, facing me. In his other hand, he swirled the whiskey around a big cube of ice.

"It grows on me," I said, taking another sip. "Is this the same one we had at the Italian place? It tastes different. More — I don't know, chocolaty."

His eyes crinkled with his smile. "That's right. This is different. This one is aged in French oak casks. There's a touch of fruit."

"Yes!" I sipped it again. What a delicious, slow burn. "I taste it." I licked my lips and looked up at him.

Duncan's eyes were smoky, blue flecked with gold. "Go ahead," he murmured. "I'm not sure if you're drunk yet. Wasn't that why we came?"

"Was it?" My voice was soft, too. I took a long sip, closing my eyes, feeling the room tip a little. "I'm pretty sure I'm drunk." I looked over at him and licked my lips again, more slowly. "Do you want to take advantage of me?"

"Only with permission," he said gruffly. He took a deep drink from his glass, his eyes never leaving mine.

I became conscious of an ache between my legs, of heat flowing through my body from the whiskey. From him. He was perfectly still, but I could feel the tension coiled in him, the desire waiting to be sprung.

I wanted to set it free. Set myself free. The drinks had taken me halfway.

I took another deep sip and set down my glass, and then I leaned into him and tasted his mouth, barely touching his lips with mine, running my tongue along his bottom lip, feeling his hot, short breaths against my mouth as he let me sip and taste. Was this what it felt like to be wanted? The feeling went to my head even more than the alcohol as I took more of his mouth, felt him start to respond.

I took his glass and set it down on the table, then slipped off my sandals and knelt before him, looking up at him much as I had the other night. Only this time I was fully clothed. I reached for his shorts, unfastened them, and his mouth opened. His breathing quickened. He didn't talk, didn't touch me. It was as if he didn't want to break the spell.

For I was under a spell, entranced by his rough, sweet magic. I was someone else with him, more confident, prettier, more sensual. Right now, I had power that I'd never had before as I pulled his shorts down and off with his sneakers. He wore black boxer briefs tonight, sexier than his usual fare. His erection was beautifully sculpted against the black fabric, and I caressed it once, twice, before I slipped the briefs off, letting his hard cock spring free.

Oh, yes. He wanted me. A high-proof thrill of lust and power shot through my veins as I grasped the base of his shaft and slowly, so slowly worked my hand up to the tip. He let out a ragged breath and sank back into the cushions. I leaned forward and languorously licked the dark, engorged head and the glistening drop of moisture there.

"God, Thea," he groaned.

It was all the encouragement I needed. I took him into my mouth.

I was floating thanks to the champagne and whiskey, overwhelmed with sensation — the silky heat of his skin under my tongue, the musky, spicy scent of him, the music in the background, and the primal drumbeat of need that struck up in my core. Guiding him with one hand, I took him deeper, sucking harder, letting his tip touch the back of my throat. His shaft filled me, hot and alive, the physical essence of the man against my tongue, molding to my mouth as I sucked. I savored his taste and his low groans, the way he lifted his hips to meet me, wanting more. I made a sound of satisfaction as I tasted the salty hint of what was to come. I looked up as I drew him in deeper to see Duncan's eyes burning into mine, his mouth open as he panted. Gone was the jokester. Here was the man, and right now, he was mine.

Abruptly he touched my head, making me pause, and I let his slick cock slip out of my mouth as I caught my breath.

"I don't want to come yet," he said. "I want to fuck you."

God, hearing his blunt words almost made me come right there.

"I want you to," I whispered.

"I told you I was safe. Do you trust me?"

I nodded, giddy at where this was going.

"And you?"

"Yes. And I have an IUD from back when I thought things would last with the ex-prince."

His voice lowered, dark and lascivious. "Are you ready for this?"

In answer, I swirled my tongue around the tip of his shaft one more time.

"God," he said, hoisting me, twirling me up onto the couch, pushing a hand up under my dress as he pushed me back against the cushions. "You make me crazy."

"Good," I said with a giggle that he smothered with a searing kiss.

His hot hand slid up my thigh. Overwhelming my hungry mouth with his, he stroked me through my very damp underwear. I moaned against his mouth in response, giddiness replaced by pure want. He yanked my underwear off and pushed two fingers inside me, pumping. I made more noises of pleasure and need, spreading my legs.

"That's right," he said. "You're not so ready to get rid of me now, are you?"

"No," I said breathlessly. "Please, Duncan."

"Do you want me inside you? Say it."

"I want you inside me." *His fingers, holy fuck!* I bucked against him, trying to take in more of him as pleasure radiated from where he stroked me.

"Is that all?"

I let the whiskey talk, this time. It had no inhibitions. "I want you to fuck me hard, Duncan. Take me. Take all of me."

"Fuck, yes." His control seemed to snap, even as he exerted more of it. He pulled me roughly to the edge of the seat, flipped me. "On your knees," he whispered in my ear.

"Oh, God." I knelt on the edge of the wide seat and supported myself against the cushions as he pushed up my dress.

"I'm going to fuck you now, Thea, and fuck you properly."

"Oh, please do it improperly," I said, and he laughed. And then I felt his hard heat pressing against my folds, slick and naked. I moaned again as he dipped his tip into my juices and let his cock glide through the furrow of my slit, teasing.

I became conscious of noise through the wall, laughing and chattering, the boisterous conversation of loud drunks entering the adjoining private room.

Duncan pushed his cock inside me, and I gasped with the fullness of it.

"They're having a party right there through that pretty wallpaper," he said in his delicious accent. "And they have no idea that you're getting fucked right now."

He pulled out partway and thrust more deeply, holding himself there. He felt so good, filling me, sweet and easy without the condom, hard and hot and nasty, too. He eased back and then slammed into me, and I groaned.

"What if they hear you?" Duncan said. "My sweet, fiery lass." He kissed my neck, pulled back and slammed into me again.

"God, yes," I moaned. I didn't give a fuck who heard me.

"That's right." He thrust again. "Say my name." Again, again, again ...

"Duncan. Oh, God, yes, Duncan ... "

He grasped my waist, the dress pushed up almost to my breasts, and pumped into me, increasing his pace, finding that sweet spot that spawned little sparks of ecstasy that morphed into whirlwinds of fire. I slammed back against him, picking up his rhythm, and he groaned. He reached up and pinched one nipple through my dress, and I cried out and came like an erupting volcano.

Only it was Duncan who truly erupted. I felt his explosion deep inside me as he spurted his seed into me, spearing me with his cock, lighting me up with his hot jets of come, and I responded, clenching him, making him groan anew as he shook against me, squeezing me hard.

I was almost crying from the pure release of it as he eased out of me. I had never had sex like that, ever, *ever*. I hadn't had all that much experience, but I had never given myself, all of me, over to anyone the way I had to Duncan.

Somehow I knew it was the greatest gift I could have given myself.

I turned and collapsed onto my back against the softness and watched his face in the light. He looked serious, spent. He cupped my cheek and kissed me softly. The crowd next door was singing "Happy Birthday," and I had to smile at the completely surreal moment.

"I would have at least expected 'For He's a Jolly Good Fellow,' " Duncan said with a tiny grin, and I giggled. He grabbed his whiskey and nestled next to me, curling a muscular arm around my shoulders and entwining one leg with mine.

"Which nobody can deny," I said, looking up at him.

"Well, you're my one true fan. I'd be wounded to the quick if you denied me." Despite his light tone, his eyes were still hooded, dreamy. He leaned over me and kissed me again, tasting of whiskey and desire.

"You could take me home and try to impress me again," I whispered.

"That is a very, very good idea." After several minutes of kissing, and Duncan almost spilling his whiskey, we put ourselves together. He paid the bill that hid under the cheese plate and left what looked like a crazy-huge tip, then tucked the half-empty whiskey bottle in his camera bag. After a stop by his car to get the photo ("I don't want anyone stealing it!"), we took a cab back to our building.

We stumbled into my apartment. Duncan used the bathroom, and I went in afterward to wash up properly. When I came out, he was face-down on the pillows on my unmade bed, unconscious. I couldn't help but smile. I was barely conscious myself; only anticipation and adrenaline had kept my head above water — or whiskey — on the ride home. I got his shoes off, and then I stripped. Somehow I got the blankets over both of us and curled up next to him, my hot skin against his rumpled clothes.

As I tried to get comfortable, drunken swirling thoughts raced around my brain. A devilish feeling of satisfaction warred with my analytical angel, who said nights like this would make it harder to tell Duncan to go to hell, and if I wanted my privacy back, I had no choice but to tell him so at the end of our week. But the little she-devil on my other shoulder whispered that any pleasure I had now could be converted into seductive wiles I could use on men who weren't adorable Scottish playboys who snored, and wouldn't that be nice? Because Duncan was education and ecstasy all in one.

But the analytical angel suggested that maybe Duncan had more substance than he let on, and that I shouldn't condemn him outright, as the she-devil laughed and laughed and laughed and I drifted into uneasy sleep.

I AWOKE SUDDENLY, shaken by a nightmare in which my ex-prince from Kansas City was in bed next to me, laughing. I rolled over in horror and saw — no one. Not even Duncan. Somehow, that was worse.

I sat up and groaned and became aware that I was still naked. *Holy shit.* I'd liked the way the alcohol had turned me into a sex kitten last night, but today I felt like an alley cat who'd been trapped in a storm drain. My teeth were covered in shag carpeting, the morning sun shot lasers into my eyeballs, and my head was somehow too small for my brain.

And Duncan — where had he gone?

Across the hall, I supposed, and the photo along with

him. Across the hall, where he'd still be after this week was over. How fucking awkward was that going to be?

Not awkward at all, I told myself as I showered, threw on a robe, brewed coffee, and sucked down the caffeine and an ibuprofen. This was the twenty-first century, damn it, and I was a modern woman. I didn't need to be bothered by the idea of running into an ex-paramour on the elevator, maybe as he came back sweaty and hot from the weight room. An ex-paramour who smelled like spices and soap and maybe, I dunno, Scotland and thistles and whiskey and laughter.

"Oh, fuck." I sank into my computer chair and stared at the screen. I had more than an alcohol hangover. I had a Duncan hangover. He was fucking addictive. Compulsively, I clicked to his video channel to see his latest. He hadn't posted the gallery video yet, so I scrolled through his channel to one of my favorites from about a year ago. In it, he was lying on a towel on the tawny sands of Bohemia Beach, leaning on his elbow, shirtless (I refused to admit this was one of the reasons it was a favorite), but close to the camera. Actually, it was probably just a phone video, but it was bright and clear in the sun, and his eyes seemed to glitter like the blue ocean behind him as he spoke.

"I'm here at the beach on a beautiful day, and it puts me in mind of a favorite Robert Burns poem. As I'm sure you know if you've watched me at all, I'm legally bound to love Robert Burns because I'm Scottish. Allow me to indulge."

And with that, he began to recite: "O my luve is like a red, red rose, That's newly sprung in June . . . " It was only after those cheesy, immortal lines that I sank into Duncan's voice, his accent thick and devastating with lines that squeezed my heart, speaking of how fair his *luve* is and how deeply he loves her, continuing:

And I will luve thee still, my dear,
Till a' the seas gang dry.

Till a' the seas gang dry, my dear,
And the rocks melt wi' the sun;
And I will luve thee still my dear,
While the sands o' life shall run.

At last, the poet says farewell but promises to come again, "Tho' it were ten thousand mile."

"And on a day like this," Duncan wrapped up after a suitable pause, "I believe the rocks might just melt with the sun." And then he winked, and his smiling face dissolved to his *Flyte Night* logo, and it was over.

And I was clutching my chest and fighting back a sniffle, because it got me every damn time. And it wasn't even for me. It was for everybody, that wink, that sweet sincerity that made everybody his friend, his intimate, his true *luve.*

Lolly. Holly. The bartender from last night. God knows who else. I was his latest distraction. No, worse. His latest clickbait.

But oh, to hear him say those words and know they were for me would be like drinking from a fountain of champagne, pre-hangover. And now I was back in fantasy territory, the way I'd been before I met him, when I'd watch his vlog and imagine him. I didn't know him then. Didn't know how funny he'd be, how protective, how, well, *hot.*

Didn't know how he would feel inside me.

"Fuck," I said again, finishing my coffee. And I went back to bed.

∼

THE THIRD TIME I woke up on Saturday (the second was for a peanut butter and jelly sandwich and two hours on the couch watching *Outlander* on my laptop) was to a pounding on my door, the kind of pounding cops do in TV shows. It felt as if I'd been sleeping for weeks, and I almost had, making up for months of sleep deprivation. I rolled out of bed, cinched the belt on my short robe and shuffled in that direction.

"Thea!" came the familiar voice through the door. Curse me for not hesitating to open it.

Duncan seemed completely unaffected by the imbibing of the night before, clean and energetic in a Yoda T-shirt and khaki shorts. But his eyes widened as he took in my mussed hair and my long, bare legs.

"Damn it, Thea," he said.

"Damn it, what?"

"Where have you been?"

"In bed," I said.

"With who?"

"Are you kidding me?" I stood aside and let him enter, closing the door behind him.

"There's no way you can still look that just-fucked at 6 p.m.," he said, dropping his bag and enfolding me in his arms. His hands slid under the robe and cupped my ass. He groaned as he found naked flesh.

I melted into him, not wanting to wake up from the dream.

"My God," he said. "I can't let you tempt me again."

"Let *me* tempt *you?*" I dropped my arms and stepped out of his grasp, gazing up at him.

"You look so delicious right now." He stepped toward me again and tugged at the belt of my robe, loosening the knot. It fell open, and he reached up and cupped my breasts, thumbing my nipples, shooting exquisite darts of sensation through me. "Oh, Thea."

And then he was kissing me, and Robert Burns be damned, he was roses and sand and sea and heat, lifting me and carrying me to the bed.

I was a rag doll in his arms as he lay me down and kissed my neck while one hand slipped down between my legs.

"But why are you here? Aren't you early?" I mumbled.

"Damn it!" Duncan said as if shocked. He stood up straight. "You almost made me forget. Get dressed."

I sat up and raised an eyebrow at him, thoroughly awake now and spoiling for a fight. "So you don't want me?"

He groaned again. "Yes, but — damn it. Damn it, we don't have time!"

I slipped the robe completely off and lay back, spreading my arms wide, tilting my head to the side to look at him. "You sure?"

He sighed in exasperation. "Oh, fuck me." And started tearing his clothes off.

He was on me so fast, I almost laughed, but then he was ramming inside me, taking my breath away, and in no time at all I'd wrapped my legs around him and was crying out his name as he pounded me into the bed.

"God!" Duncan shouted as he came inside me. Fuck, it felt so good to have him like this, bare and slick and hard, triggering an explosive orgasm that left me limp and sated and entirely forgetful of all of my morning angst.

"That wasn't so bad, was it?" I murmured in his ear.

"Christ, I can't resist you," he said, slipping out of me and heading for the bathroom. "Now get dressed, darlin'. We have to go."

I frowned and lay there, not ready to move.

"You're not dressed!" he said as he came out of the bath-room and started yanking his clothes back on.

"Because it's been, like, sixty seconds," I said. "Why the hurry?"

He took a deep breath and smiled, and then I felt the full sun of his charm, the kind that demanded SPF30-level defenses. "You'll see. Casual is fine. Hurry."

His eyes followed me appreciatively as I slid out of bed, grabbed a couple of things out of my dresser and went into the bathroom. Ten minutes later, after a super-fast shower and hastened ablutions, I emerged in denim shorts and a clingy blue V-neck T-shirt (another of my V-neck family) that brought out my eyes. I tied my hair up in a scarf and put on sneakers as he ogled my desktop computer.

"Fan of Robert Burns, are you?" he asked with a twinkle.

Oh, shit. Of course, his video was still up on my screen.

"I prefer Yeats," I said with feigned indifference.

"*Och,* Irish," he said, but he was grinning. "If you have a camera, bring it."

"I don't." But I picked up my small sketchbook and a pack of colored pencils and dropped them into my bag. "Ready."

A half-hour later, we were west of Bohemia and headed down a winding semi-rural highway toward the center of the state. We'd traveled in companionable silence (except for the rock music blaring from his stereo) up till now; I, for one, felt dreamy and sated after my dissolute day and that thorough rogering by Duncan.

"Are you going to tell me where we're going?" I asked.

Duncan looked up and out of the windshield, then turned south onto a narrow gravel road that ran along a cow pasture. "About here should do it."

"Where's here?" Because there was basically nothing that I could see.

"The sea breeze," he said, parking in a turn-off next to a gate in the pasture fence. Thirty yards away, a half-dozen brown and black cows stared at us curiously from under the scant shade of a cluster of palm trees.

I followed Duncan's lead and got out of the car, wincing against the blast of summer heat. "I'm not sure there's a breeze, and there's definitely no sea."

"The sea-breeze boundary. Right there!" He pointed to the sky.

I looked up. Just to our west, filtering the slowly descending sun, white clouds towered in the blue sky, all in a line.

"Oh, the clouds!"

He laughed as he set up a tripod next to the fence. "Yeah, the clouds. Tonight we're going to get our lightning. I can feel it."

I shaded my eyes and took a closer look at the piles of white cotton candy lofting into the blue sky.

"You're a man of many interests," I observed.

"That I am."

"Got any sunscreen?"

"Of course. I'm Scottish." Duncan stopped toying with the camera long enough to find a bottle of the stuff. He tossed it, and I put some on. He finished setting up his shot and turned to me. "I wanted to get a time-lapse before the storms were well under way. That's why I was in a hurry. Sorry about that."

"It was an interesting way to wake up."

He walked over to where I was leaning against the hood of the car, bent over and pressed his mouth against mine, slipping his tongue between my lips, coaxing me to open and lose myself in his hunger and heat. He lightly grasped my waist with both hands as he pushed his tongue in further, and I sucked on it, lost in the taste of him.

"Hmmm," he murmured, breaking the kiss. "I shouldn't have done that. Now I want to pick up where we left off."

"Too bad we can't," I whispered.

"Why can't we?" he whispered back, licking my earlobe.

Despite my un-Thea-like behavior of the past couple of days, I was still capable of being shocked. "Because we're outside in public in daylight?"

"Nobody's around except the cows." He kissed my neck.

A tingle ran up my spine. "But your camera — it will record us."

"Not even the sound. It's a time-lapse, and it's pointed the other way." His hands were under my shirt now, caressing my back, and he tongued my neck, rough and hot, even hotter than the ninety-three-degree day.

"But I — I —" *What in the hell am I doing?* Pressing against his body. Letting him lick me, caress me.

He unclasped my bra, and I let out a little gasp. He grabbed my hand and tugged me toward the back of the SUV. He opened the back and lowered the tailgate, lifted me, sat me on it and pulled my shirt over my head. His lips crashed into mine, and I moaned. At least the tailgate faced away from the road.

"But Duncan ... if someone comes ... "

"You're the only one who's going to come," he said, his voice commanding now, and I melted like an ice cream left out in the sun.

"Those stupid cows," I said, still nervous as he pulled off

the bra completely and cupped my breasts. The animals were looking at us.

He chuckled, and then his hands were in my hair. He pulled out the scarf, and my curls came tumbling down around my face. "If you can't see them, they can't see you." He slipped the scarf over my eyes and tied it in back.

"Oh, my God . . . "

Now I could only feel. And fear, yes, a little. But Duncan's big, strong body seemed to envelop me, protecting me, and his mouth was everywhere, sucking on my nipples, moving down my belly to where he was unbuttoning my shorts and pulling them off with my underwear. An ache pulsed between my legs as his tongue touched my clit, dancing over the sweet bundle of nerves. I threaded my fingers into his thick, wavy hair, hearing, smelling, feeling everything. I groaned as he licked me, sweeping his tongue through my ridiculously wet cleft.

"I think you like being naked where anyone can see you," Duncan murmured, sucking on my clit.

"No — it's not — oh, God," I groaned as he grazed my nub with his teeth and licked it with even more vigor. "I don't care. I'll do anything, as long as you keep doing that, oh, yes, *yes.*"

"You're gorgeous," he said as he took a breath. I felt a rustle against me — his shorts coming down — and he pushed my thighs apart roughly. "Anyone who saw you now would fall at your feet."

His words went to my head. And then he was pulling me to the edge of the tailgate, holding me steady, and his cock slid against my entrance. I moaned.

"Tell me what you want," he said into my ear, holding himself there, rubbing against me, teasing.

"I want you inside me."

"Even here? Even with everyone watching?"

I saw nothing through the scarf, heard nothing, not even the cows. My breaths came short as I imagined him fucking me with an audience. I trembled with the strange, dark thrill the idea gave me. And then a low rumble of thunder resonated through the thick, hot air.

"Yes, Duncan. Please. God, yes. Fuck me. I don't care."

"That's my girl." He teased me, just at the brink, before he pushed inside, thick and hard and somehow gloriously inevitable. I needed him there, had to have him. He fit even as he stretched me, snug and slick, stoking the fire that was already threatening to consume me.

He let out a long, ragged breath. "How you can feel so tight and so ready for me at the same time — fuck, so hot — so perfect," he whispered, thrusting again with deliberate, maddening control.

He slowly picked up his pace, going deeper, faster. And I was gone on the Duncan roller coaster again, clinging to his muscled arms as he pounded into me, taking me higher, hotter, until I was crying out his name, until the orgasm rocked me and I clenched around him and he grunted and spilled himself inside me, holding me tight.

I clung to him and kissed his neck, wrecked. *Wrecked for anyone else,* I thought.

"Sweet Thea," he whispered into my ear. And he kissed me, and tears leaked from my eyes, though he couldn't see them behind the scarf, through the sweat. I was drenched.

He eased out of me, and I sensed him getting dressed. He pulled my shirt on over my head, slipped my underwear back on, then my shorts, over my sneakers. I fastened the shorts, almost laughing to think what a sight I would have made, spreading wide for him, still wearing my shoes.

He pulled the scarf off last.

I looked into Duncan's eyes. For once, they weren't full of laughter. He looked serious and at least as hot as I felt. Hot in more ways than one. My breath caught.

He swallowed and took a step back. "You OK?"

I looked around. We were still alone, and even the cows had lost interest. I nodded, wondering what was going on in his head.

Thunder rumbled again.

"We'd better get in the car," he said. "I got enough of the clouds. Let's get east and get ahead of the storms."

He held out a hand and helped me off the tailgate. I stumbled and he caught me with one strong arm around my waist. He looked down into my eyes, and I was drowning in his again, in the pale blue, the endless sky of his gaze. He granted me a small smile, handed me my scarf and let me go.

Shaky, I walked back around the car and got into the passenger side.

After a couple of minutes, which he used to pack up his camera, he got into his side and tossed something over at me. My bra.

"In case you want that," he said. "Though I like you without it." And then he grinned one of those Duncan grins, complete with dimples, and everything was all casual and fun and light again.

Only it wasn't. Not for me. I was still high on him, and those chemicals everybody warns you about were going crazy in my brain, crushing on him, binding me to him. I shook my head as if I could make them go away, stuffed the bra in my bag and looked out the window as we headed back to Bohemia.

I had to get a grip. We had tonight and tomorrow, and that

was it. The affair would be over. I had no illusions that he would want to stick around, and besides, I couldn't live life on camera the way he did. I didn't want my life to belong to six hundred thousand Internet trolls.

The next couple of hours gave me a chance to regain my equilibrium. We didn't so much chase the storms as have them chase us. Typical of Florida, they popped up and faded, kicking off more cells to the south, then to the north. Duncan cheerfully drove in circles, getting video here and there. He filmed a standup shot of himself talking in front of a dramatic shelf cloud as it moved toward the beach just after sunset, and I did my best to sketch the scene in my notebook. Coming in behind it was the lightning he wanted. We took shelter in the car, let the storm go out to sea and re-emerged to film a time-lapse from the beach.

"This isn't the safest thing in the world because of the lightning, so if you want to get back in the car, I don't mind," Duncan said as the camera clicked repeatedly, getting long exposures of the flashing, retreating storm in the darkness. The rain had cooled the air, and now a soft breeze accompanied the lightning show.

"It's really beautiful," I said. "I don't think I've ever just stood on the beach and watched the lightning like this."

"Then you're smarter than I am. But you're right, it is beautiful. That's why I do this once in a while, to capture lightning in a bottle. In the camera."

"And for the clicks," I said.

"*Always* for the clicks."

His answer depressed me a little, but I watched the strobing within the storm and found a sense of peace in it. Peace and electricity. In the blue of post-twilight, against the soundtrack of the crashing waves, the cloud lit up from within — an electric brain, sparking with light and imagination. Duncan, his hair ruffled by the breeze, put a hand on my shoulder and rubbed my back. We both gasped as a bolt arced out of the top of the cloud and zapped the sea beneath it. He pulled me closer, and I shivered despite the warm evening as thunder rumbled through the night.

This week was a storm blowing through my life, powerful and wonderful. Though it would leave a whirlwind's worth of debris behind, I had to admit that maybe I'd needed the rain.

Duncan eased behind me and slipped his arms around my waist, pulling me to him. As always, I felt a flutter of desire, but I reckoned this was what I'd miss the most. His warmth. The way he touched me. I put my hands over his, and we looked out over the waves into the descending darkness, toward the diminishing flashes. Above the storm, stars had come out in a magical display of nature's wonders, and a fat half-moon hung overhead, illuminating lingering wisps of cloud.

Duncan was a force of nature, too. I couldn't beat myself up for giving in to him.

When the weakening storm was only a glimmer on the horizon, he turned to me. I could barely see his smile in the darkness. God, that smile. What secrets did it hold?

"Want to grab something to eat?" he asked, oblivious to my angst. "It's pretty late."

"I really need a shower more than I need food." I was sticky and gritty after the heat and the sand and our bucolic tryst.

"Nonsense. But I'll compromise. We can pick up a pizza on the way home and then you can shower before we eat, OK? There's a great place in Bohemia Beach."

"Sounds good," I said, already anticipating being cool and clean again and marveling at how domestic we sounded.

Duncan called in the order when we got back to the car, and we picked up the giant box on the way back to Bohemia. When we got into my apartment, I walked right into the bathroom, used the toilet and stripped. In a moment, I was under the shower, closing my eyes as I reveled in our awesome water pressure.

And jumped as I felt a body slide behind mine.

"I needed a shower, too," Duncan said in my ear, "and I hate to waste water."

"You're insatiable," I said, turning to face him. My mouth opened a little as I scanned his body. I'd never seen him like this, with water running over his gloriously naked skin, his gleaming muscles.

"You have a dirty mind, Ms. McKay. I'm only here to get clean." He grabbed a sponge from my shower caddy and loaded it with body wash, and then he soaped me up, every hot, slippery inch of me. I closed my eyes and surrendered to it, to him, his big hands, his deliciously thorough scrubbing. "Time to rinse," he said, turning me under the water, and a laugh bubbled up from my belly.

"Give me that," I said, taking the sponge from him and returning the favor until it was clear his mind was just as dirty as mine was. I dropped the sponge and clasped his thickening shaft between my hands, rubbing slowly up and down as he braced himself against the walls of the shower and held my gaze with those ice-blue eyes.

I didn't need him inside me again just then. But I needed to feel my power over him. I dropped to my knees, flicked his tip with my tongue and took him in my mouth.

He dropped his head back with an incoherent sound as I

sucked hard on his tip, then took his thick length in deeper, caressing him with my lips, laving as the water streamed down my face, over my lips, cascading over my body.

Duncan rested his one hand on my head, and he eased his hips toward me, shifting, pushing a little, testing my reaction. Wanting to fuck my mouth.

I made a low humming noise and opened wider.

"Yes," he hissed, easing into a slow rhythm, touching the back of my throat, and then I took him deep, feeling everything, loving his possession of me, pulling back and taking him deep again, sharing control. When he came, my mouth filled with his hot, salty seed, and I swallowed it all, reveling in my ability to make him shatter, more than satisfied. I'd never done that before, swallowed a man's essence like that, and it was impossible to shake the sense that Duncan had imprinted himself on me even more strongly. But as with every other step I took with him, I didn't care. I only wanted more.

He pulled me up and kissed me for a long time under the hot running water, and the heady feeling of abandon stayed with me. Finally, he turned it off, and we dried each other with a couple of fluffy towels, playful and brisk. I slipped on my robe, and he pulled on a T-shirt and soft shorts he'd grabbed from his place. We ate the pizza and chatted about movies until he declared himself tired and asked if I wanted to go to bed.

～

SUNDAY MORNING. Church bells rang in Bohemia, evoking services I'd attended with my mother before everything changed.

Light filled my windows, pure white light unfiltered by colored glass, an artist's boon.

A mockingbird sang in the oak tree outside.

And Duncan was gone, again.

He really was like a prince in a fairy tale — one of those dark fairy tales that made him cursed to be mine only in the night. By day, he was a frog or a grasshopper or something. Only at night did he become a man, the man who held me under his spell. Otherwise, he wasn't real at all.

None of this was real, damn it. And tonight was our last night.

I had to start thinking beyond this week. This day. I dressed in shorts and a T-shirt, made coffee and wandered over to my pop-up projects. I really wanted to try to get into that exhibit Wyatt had told me about, but what would be special enough? What would make a statement? I didn't want to make just one pop-up sculpture. I wanted to tell a story about a princess who lives in an enchanted castle and escapes it because she wants to see the world. Only the world is dark and dreary and difficult, filled with monsters. Yes — fantasy creatures, contrasted with urban landscapes. A red and green dragon stalking a drab city street. A purple ogre under the arch of a white bridge. Cruelty and danger. I could imagine the scenes, was already calculating the architecture in my head. I couldn't wait to start the sculptures, but the story lacked an ending. Where would the princess end up?

I began with the castle, working through much of the day to create the moat and bridge that would let my theoretical princess escape. I wasn't worried yet about the princess herself. I might add her later or re-create the piece with her popping out of a window or taking a leap; inevitably, I made a sculpture two or three times before it was final. For now, I needed the parts to work together, the folds and slots and cutouts, so when the paper opened, the castle delicately exploded from two dimensions into three.

Mid-afternoon, I took a break and watched Duncan's videos from the gallery opening and the lightning storm. The latter took my breath away. After his intro, he'd stepped back and let the time-lapses speak for themselves, set to music. They were hypnotic. They were art. There was nothing wrong with being a video blogger, but I had a feeling Duncan was capable of so much more. He worked hard, but I wondered if he was coasting instead of really stretching his talent.

Oh, hell. I'm one to talk. I looked over my pile of half-constructed pop-up pieces and rubbed my ring. My mom's ring.

I was changing, wasn't I? I was going for it, would submit to the gallery show. And that's all I would have time to think about after Duncan was gone.

I showered and put on my short denim skirt and a soft, flowing, scoop-neck blouse in a blue tie-dye pattern over a tank top. The ritual of getting ready gave my inner voices time to argue. Of course, said the illusory angel who rode around on one shoulder, if I were really changing, I'd work on making this thing with Duncan last longer than a week.

The little she-devil inside me laughed as I put on lipstick, red with a hint of orange. Because there was no way I was misreading this situation. I was a brief stop on the Duncan Express, and after tonight, if I wanted male company, I had to find another train.

He knocked on my door at 7. I had to give him points for promptness.

And deliciousness.

"Hello, darlin'," Duncan said. He seemed to have gotten

the "dressed-up casual" memo. He wore long blue shorts in a minuscule checked pattern and a cream-colored Henley, half-unbuttoned, sleeves pushed up to the elbows, that was just thin enough to show off every muscle in his chest and arms.

"H — hi," I stuttered. All of my resolutions melted in the face of his smile as he watched me watching him.

He leaned in and kissed me, then wandered into my space, looking around. "Ready to go?"

"Go where?"

"I thought we'd start at Plumeria Bar, and then the sky's the limit. Oh, hey, is this yours? Good God, this is amazing!" He picked up a piece of the castle I'd been assembling.

"Oh, it's just a work in progress," I said, but I was secretly pleased that he was impressed. "Here, this is a better mock-up." I handed him a folded piece of cardstock.

Gingerly, he opened it. His eyes widened along with his smile as the first draft of my castle unfolded, parapets and turrets and towers and crenellated walls, with a moat and drawbridge. "This is incredible, Thea."

"Oh, it's not, really. But I hope it will be when I put it together with all of the other pieces in the story."

"A storybook?"

I shrugged. "Maybe someday. I'm still ironing out the concept for that gallery show Wyatt told me about."

"That's really good." Duncan set the piece down, and I wondered if he meant *it* was really good, or if it was really good that I was going for the show. "Art makes me hungry. Let's go."

"Everything makes you hungry."

He laughed. "Especially you." He kissed my neck, and it was all I could do not to throw him on the floor and have my way with him. We had all night. I was going to savor it.

He glanced at his phone as we got out of the elevator. "She's almost here."

"Who?"

"Rideeo driver. Just in case."

"Rideeo?"

"Like Uber, but it's cheaper, because there's no special vehicle requirements."

"That sounds safe," I quipped. "Anyway, I could drive. There's no way I'm drinking as much as I did the other night."

He grinned. "Might as well keep our options open." His phone buzzed, and he looked at it again.

"The driver?" I asked.

"No. My dad calling for the fifth time today. That's why it's on silent."

"You can talk to him if you need to."

"I do not." Duncan's syllables were clipped and brooked no argument.

A powder-blue vintage Mercedes pulled into the parking lot, and the woman driving it waved. She had short, white hair, big glasses and bigger jewelry. In age, I figured she was somewhere between eighty and Methuselah.

"You must be Duncan," she said as he opened the back door and we scooted in.

"And you must be Louise," he said, glancing at his phone to confirm her name. He looked around appreciatively as she whipped out of the lot. "Beautiful ride."

"I've had it since '72, but I barely drove it until I got into this taxi business. There are Cokes and waters in the cooler, and let me know if you need one of these coozies so your hands don't get cold."

I exchanged a smile with Duncan as Louise pointed to the

basket between the front seats filled with colorful crocheted drink holders.

"Did you make those?" I asked. "They're really pretty."

"I can lend you one for the ride, but they're a steal at five dollars if you want to take one home!"

I tried not to laugh as Duncan reached into his pocket and pulled out his wallet. "I definitely want one," he said.

"Plumeria Bar, right?" Louise confirmed as she got into downtown.

"Yes, ma'am," I said.

"Don't you go ma'am-ing me, young lady." She worked her way toward the harbor through light traffic. "We're almost there. Take one of my cards so you can request me next time. I do cash, too. Riders after 8 get homemade cookies."

"Yes, m— " I caught myself. "Yes, Louise, thank you." I grabbed one of the business cards in the crocheted holder hanging from the back of her seat.

The sunlight looked especially golden this evening, slanting over the sailboats and docks as the road curved toward Plumeria Bar. It caught the gold threads in Duncan's reddish-brown hair as we got out of the car and he paid for his coozie.

"What are you going to do with that?" I asked after Louise peeled away from the curb.

"Give it to you as a souvenir of our evening." He handed it over, a twinkle in his eye.

I fingered the blue and green and red yarn and dropped it into my purse. Even this silly gift felt like goodbye. "Gee, thanks."

"Any time. Shall we?"

The plumeria that the bar was named for were in full

bloom outside the door, bringing a hint of Hawaii to the premises. Inside, it was all dark wood and red walls and luxurious furniture, with lush photos of flowers.

The horseshoe-shaped bar faced wide windows offering a spectacular view of Bohemia's small harbor, which opened into the lagoon. The descending sun silhouetted a handful of drinkers and the bartender, who was talking closely with a tall man leaning on the bar.

Duncan took two steps inside the space and halted so fast I bumped into him.

"What —?" I asked, but he was already moving again, striding toward the man at the bar.

"What are you doing here?" Duncan asked.

As I got closer, I stifled a gasp. The man was an older version of Duncan, perhaps not as brawny, but with the same hair — shot with silver — and the same pleasing face and light eyes, if more careworn.

"Why aren't you answering your phone?" the man replied in a Scottish accent, more pronounced than Duncan's, as the woman tending bar drifted to the other end to fill an order.

"Because I didn't want to talk," Duncan said.

"To me, you mean."

"I have no problem talking to you."

The man's voice was stern. "You just don't want to talk to her, is that right? Now's the time, Duncan. You may not have another chance."

Duncan slammed a hand on the bar, and I jumped. Anger rippled out from him like a shockwave. I'd never seen him like this, didn't know he was capable of that kind of reaction.

"You shouldn't have come," Duncan said.

"She's your mother."

This had to be Duncan's father. But he lived in Austin, didn't he? Why was he here?

As if he heard me, the older Flyte turned to me and narrowed his eyes. "Another one?"

"Don't you dare," Duncan said. "Don't you fucking — "

"Hi," I said in an overloud voice, ignoring his dad's comment. For now. I held out my hand. "I'm Thea McKay."

His father stood up straight and, looking just a tad surprised, reached out his hand in return. His grip was strong and dry and brief. "Alban Flyte." He gave me a half-smile, then turned back to Duncan. "Lucky to find you here. I figured if I did the rounds, I'd find you in one of the bars eventually."

"You have my address," Duncan said with a wilting glare.

"I had to do a little brand ambassadorship, anyway," Alban said, ignoring Duncan's comment. "Can we talk?"

"I'm busy right now."

"I'm leaving tomorrow."

"You flew in for one night?" Duncan asked, incredulous.

"Two. That's all I could spare. I was in Orlando yesterday for a whiskey event. You should have been there."

"No, I shouldn't have. And I didn't know about it. I don't want to know about it. I don't want to talk. Finish pimping your whiskey and go home."

His father seemed unperturbed. "I thought you liked my whiskey."

"He does," I piped up. "So do I."

"You do?" Alban's lips curved, and I saw a flash of that charm that Duncan was so good at wielding.

I smiled and nodded. "Should we all get a drink?"

"As tempting as that offer is, I really need to speak to

Duncan — alone," Alban said, his tone pleasant but cool. As cool as the ice in a glass of Scotch.

"I have plans," Duncan said, almost as icy, but with fury burning the edges of his words.

"They can wait. You are needed at home, son."

"It's not my home anymore."

"It's the place where you were born. It will always be your home."

"Scotland?" I interrupted.

Alban laughed. "Texas."

I looked at Duncan in confusion. He'd lied about being from Scotland?

"And the only home I have is wherever I lay my head," he told his father. "So you can leave now."

"I can't. It's time for you to do the right thing."

The men stared at each other for a full minute before Duncan's resolve began to crumble. I saw it, but I didn't understand it. Some emotion ate away at his anger and turned it into something else. Something breathtakingly sad.

"Goddamn it. Give me a minute," Duncan said, and then he took my hand and led me through the door that went to the deck that overlooked the harbor. The sun was lower now, the light more magical. It should have been a perfect evening, but its perfection had been shattered. I could feel it. It was all over now.

All of it.

"I'm sorry, Thea. I don't want to talk to him, but if I don't settle this, he won't leave me be."

"Settle what?"

"Just give me a raincheck. I'll see you tomorrow. Breakfast?"

"Because this is our last night," I said, crossing my arms.

"Yes," he said with a wry smile. "I'm kind of relieved the bet is over. If you don't mind, I'll do an exit interview with you tomorrow for the vlog. Everybody wants to know what's happening with you. I get emails every day. And then I'll take you out to dinner, too. OK?"

He was *relieved?* An *exit interview?* And he wasn't even from Scotland. This was worse than I thought.

"No," I said.

Puzzlement took over his face. "No?"

"I don't want to be on camera. That's what this whole week was about, me not wanting to be on camera. I like my privacy, Duncan."

"Oh, but it's just this once."

"Yeah, because you'll have burned through the Thea clicks and moved on to something else."

"Ouch," he said, and that open sweetness I liked about him seemed to vanish from his face. His eyes shuttered. "So that's all this week was to you? A way to wrap up the bargain?"

"This was your bargain, your bet." I felt a little sick to my stomach. "And I enjoyed it. But I can't be on camera again. I can't put myself out there like that."

Duncan looked off toward the harbor, shaking his head as if he hadn't heard me right, before turning back to me. "I want to talk about this, Thea, but right now I have to deal with my father. Let's talk tomorrow."

"With your camera?"

His jaw set. Something happened in his eyes, a flicker of pain, then resolve. "Yes, with the camera."

It was my turn to shake my head. "Why can't you bend on this?"

"If I had a reason to, I would." His words were like a

smack in the face. He smiled, then, the charmer's smile, only this time, his eyes were curiously blank. No warmth. No twinkle. "I can always find someone else to film, Thea."

God, that hurt. What happened to the simple goodbye I'd planned? And what wasn't he saying? I couldn't help but feel that, somehow, I'd fucked this up. But I refused to blame myself. He was relieved it was over. He'd said so himself.

"Guess I'll see you in the elevator," I managed to say.

An ironic little smile twisted his mouth, that mouth I loved so much. *Oh, God . . .*

And then he said, "I'll take the stairs."

And he went back inside, slamming the door behind him.

I clutched my stomach and tried to breathe. I looked around for a way to escape — the deck steps. They took me to the docks, and I walked. I walked around the harbor and then on the streets of Bohemia, trying to figure out what had just happened. What I'd just done. I walked until the slanting rays of the setting sun vanished and the street lights took over. Until my sandaled feet ached. Until I ended up sitting on the edge of the fountain in Ponce De Leon Square, where I cried until I couldn't cry anymore.

I considered calling one of my friends, but I couldn't imagine how I'd describe what happened or why I was so upset. It's not like this was a surprise, losing Duncan. It was preordained. What wasn't preordained was how shitty I would feel about it. I hadn't recognized him there on the deck, the wretched, bitter person who'd blown me off. And yet — I'd seen something in his eyes that made me doubt my judgment. Had I read too much into his words? Not enough?

The gurgling of the fountain reminded me I was thirsty, but unlike Ponce de Leon, whose statue stood above me, I had no illusions about this being a fountain of youth or anything else. I dug around in my purse for my phone and Louise's card and called.

Two minutes later, she picked me up at the gate of the park. "Sit up here, honey," she said after taking one look at my face, gesturing toward the passenger seat. She reached into an insulated bag and handed me a warm chocolate-chip cookie.

I sniffled. "Thank you."

She also handed me a can of cold Coca-Cola from her cooler, wrapped in its own coozie. "We going back to those apartments?"

"Yes, please." I took a sip of the Coke and closed my eyes.

We rode without speaking until we reached my building, me sipping and nibbling, Louise humming along to the radio. I paid her, handed her the empty can and opened my door. "Great cookie. It tasted like home. Thank you so much."

Louise patted my shoulder. "He seemed like such a nice young man."

"Yeah," I said. "He sure did."

PART 3

I dragged myself into the office on Monday, mostly so I could lose myself in work. The roses Duncan had given me were still there, still pretty, the once-tight blooms now blown wide in all their brilliant orange-red glory. I almost choked when I saw them and put the whole vase, flowers and all, into the bathroom garbage can.

A couple of hours later, I saw the flowers had rematerialized on Connie's desk. I pretended not to see them and didn't say a word, just lost myself in a design job on the computer, hard rock maxed out on my earbuds.

My dad was out visiting clients most of the morning, but in the middle of the afternoon, after enduring several of my monosyllabic responses, he came out of his small office into my work area and stared at me.

"What?" I finally snapped, pulling the buds out of my ears.

"You going to tell me what's wrong? And why those flowers are on Connie's desk?"

I couldn't. I simply couldn't say anything.

My dad got a pained look on his face, pulled up a chair and sat. "Do I have to kill this boy?"

That earned a small laugh. "No need for violence," I said. "I'm not sure whose fault it was. I mean, it wasn't anything to begin with, anyway. Only it got — "

"Complicated. I know." He frowned at me. "Relationships are pretty hopeless enterprises. You know that, right?"

"Actually, yes, I do." *Because of you. You and Mom.*

"That's not to say I wouldn't do anything to go back in time and fix what happened between your mother and me. You were her priority then, and that was the way it was supposed to be. But I still have regrets."

This wasn't helping. My mom chose me over my dad, and I still didn't understand what happened. "Why did you let her go?"

"Once your mother made up her mind, that was that. It's water under the bridge now." He was silent for a moment. "I'm glad you came back to me. I missed you. If you need to talk, I'll try to be as supportive as I can."

"No offense, Dad, but this isn't really something I want to discuss with you."

"Thank God." He quirked his mouth into a wee smile and stood up. "Still — you know where to find me." And he went back into his office and closed the door, leaving me rubbing my mom's ring and wishing for time travel. Wishing I could go back in time not just to my earliest years, but to a week ago. I could have found another way out, another way to make Duncan stop the video stunt, and I'd have been left with only my fantasies about him, not the reality.

Or a day ago, when I could have found a way to change our conversation at Plumeria Bar. To make him care more. To somehow understand what had happened. Part of me still didn't believe what he'd said, didn't want to believe it. It all went out of control so fast. Duncan had seemed so different, and his mood pivoted about once a minute during that very brief chat. I also had a feeling I'd said some things I shouldn't have, but I was just protecting myself.

And despite his scorn, I missed him terribly.

I had missed the handsome prince, too, the guy who'd turned out to be a rat back in art school. Even though I knew he was a rat, I still missed him for a while. The friendship. The physicality. Or maybe I'd just missed the feeling of being with someone.

This time, even if I never really knew the real him, I missed Duncan. Maybe I missed Fake Duncan, but I still missed him.

I resisted looking at his vlog until Tuesday. When I did, it punched me in the stomach.

It was another collab — a collaboration with Lolly. And this time they were just hanging out on a couch, one I didn't recognize — her place, I guessed. They played a dumb word game, and then they started talking. Actually, she interviewed him.

"So it didn't work out with the redhead?" Lolly asked him, looking ultra-hip in her microskirt, braless tank top, dramatic makeup and jewelry.

"She broke my heart," Duncan said, but lightly, with his characteristic grin.

"Did I break your heart?"

"Of course you did."

Lolly's response was dry. "I'm assuming you say that about all the girls you sleep with." *Damn it, how could she be so casual? So frank about her life, about his, in front of hundreds of thousands of strangers? And about mine, for fuck's sake!*

Duncan shrugged. "I didn't say I slept with her. I *treasured* her for a week, and she told me to go to hell."

"Well, that was your deal," Lolly said. "You told her to tell you to go to hell."

"I did not. I told her she could tell me so at the end of the week, and I wouldn't film her anymore."

"But you're still talking about her," Lolly said.

"No, you're talking about her."

"Semantics. You're good at twisting words, I'll give you that. You're kind of an asshole."

"Ha!" he said. "Just because I don't give my heart to just anyone doesn't make me an asshole."

"So you're saying you gave your heart to that girl?"

"That's not what I'm saying." He looked up at the camera. "I'm in full possession of my heart, so if I did give it to her, she must have given it back to me."

I swallowed hard, looking into those eyes, and then he turned back to Lolly, who berated him about other women he'd *treasured*. He said he never fell short of any woman's expectations, a statement that made her accuse him of being a politician. That remark prompted him to whack her with one of the couch pillows, and a brief pillow fight followed with screeches of laughter and the end of the video.

Ugh. Duncan and Lolly and pillows. But that wasn't what bothered me. I was still hung up on that little statement about his heart.

If I did give it to her, she must have given it back to me.

What did he mean by that? And why did he say it to the camera?

Was he saying it to *me*?

For the first time, I wished I had a video recording of our final conversation so I could parse exactly what he'd said. I just remembered that he was *relieved* the week was over. He wanted an *exit interview*. He said he could always *find someone else* to film.

And then I thought about what I'd said and flashed back to my first interview with him. How I was such a bitch. How I'd gone into that last conversation fully prepared to be a bitch. Had I somehow triggered his response?

Now that was ridiculous. Nobody could blame me for his cavalier ways.

But something else was bugging me. When he came out on that deck, he was already a totally different person from the one I'd known all week. He was upset, shaken by his father's visit. He was bitter and angry. In some ways, he'd been lying to me all week, pretending that everything was all right in his life when, clearly, it wasn't.

Maybe his dishonesty was a direct product of the artifice of our arrangement, but I'd been honest with him. I'd told him things I hadn't told anyone. I'd opened up in ways I hadn't thought possible, even knowing our arrangement would end sooner rather than later.

And that had to be one reason why I was so ripped up now. I'd opened wide to him in more ways than one, and he'd plunged in his sword with a smile.

Wednesday, as I was working at home, Cali called.

"I don't want to talk about it," was how I answered the phone.

"Oh, sweetie," Cali intoned. "What happened?"

"I told you I don't . . ." I took a deep breath and caved. "Oh, shit. It just blew up, is all. It ended. That's what it was supposed to do."

"I thought you were having a wonderful time. He bought that photo and everything."

"I was. He did. I thought he was, too. Enjoying himself, I mean. It's just — he's not the guy he pretended to be. I'm still not sure what happened there at the end, but one thing I do know is that he wasn't honest with me."

"What did he lie about?"

I laughed darkly. "He's such a good liar, I can't even tell you that."

"Maybe you just don't know the whole story?"

"I definitely don't know the whole story." I sighed, and she listened as the seconds ticked by. "I let myself get way too involved," I said finally.

"This might just be a misunderstanding."

"If it is, it's a big fucking misunderstanding, and it hurts. And I don't want it to."

"I know."

"And now I can't get him out of my head. But I have to, or I'm going to go crazy. The worst part is how unresolved I feel. It feels. That, and the fact that he lives across the damn hall."

Cali groaned. "Shit. Maybe you can just go out the window on a rope."

I laughed and realized a few tears stung my eyes, too. "Thanks for calling, Cali. I didn't mean to dump on you."

"But that's why I called." I heard the smile in her voice.

"I just have to put him behind me. I mean, put last week behind me."

"I know what you mean. Look, you need to come to Alex and Sloane's party Saturday night."

"Alex is having another party?"

"It's July Fourth, dummy. You can see the Bohemia Beach fireworks from his balcony and the beach. Will you come?"

"I don't know. I have this art project to work on . . . "

"Thea, you *have* to come. Some of Wyatt's surfer friends

will be there."

I raised my eyebrows. "I do like looking at surfer boys. But I am not talking to anyone. From now on, it's looky, no touchy."

"I don't know. Touchy can be pretty nice on a surfer."

"Shut up," I said, picturing her surfer boyfriend in that photo in her gallery. "All you happy people need to shut up."

Cali laughed. "I'll see you Saturday. The fun starts at 5 so people can hang out on the beach before it gets dark."

"OK, you win," I said. And after I hung up, I murmured to myself, "Looky, no touchy."

ALL THE DELICIOUS food I'd eaten over the past week with Duncan was forgotten in the following week of no-appetite angst, so my numbers on the scale averaged out. The only good symptom of stress-related weight loss was that, for the first time in a long time, I felt comfortable in a bikini. Not a butt-floss bikini, which I saw a lot of in Cocoa Beach the last time I went up there with friends, but a cute one in water-color shades of blue and teal and green with a twisted bandeau top. Oh, and a cover-up dress with string-tie straps in a flowing, translucent fabric, with an abstract blue and green print on white that made me think of the ocean. Because there was no way I was strutting into a party in just a bikini.

I'd never been to a party at Alex and Sloane's eighth-floor condo, but I knew Alex had a reputation for having great bashes even before he met Sloane. The condo was huge — the whole top floor of the building, actually — and when I arrived at 5:30, smelling of Coppertone, caterers had already laid out delicious-looking canapés and sandwiches and a lot of red, white and blue desserts. Rock music played over the speakers, but only a few people were sitting around drinking and eating. Through the sliding doors at the far end of the great room, I could see the blue sky and sparkling ocean.

"Thea!" Sloane greeted me with a hug as I emerged from the foyer. She was in a sweet little blue dress spangled with white stars, her long, dark hair tied up with a red chiffon scarf.

"I'm not the only one in a bathing suit, am I?" I asked, handing her the six-pack of Bohemia Brewing Company beers I'd brought.

She laughed. "Of course not. I'm busy up here with Alex, but almost everyone else is down on the beach enjoying the day. And they're definitely wearing bathing suits. Or at least they are until the sun goes down. Then, I don't want to know."

I laughed nervously. "OK, then I guess I'll go down there. Unless you need help."

"No, I'm mostly ornamental at this point. Alex hires people for these parties, and I'm not complaining. But I'm putting together these strawberries with cream-cheese icing and blueberries, something my mom always makes, and I'm not letting the caterers near them."

Her mention of her mom — her parents lived in Ohio — made my heart do a little thump. My mom would have loved this place. She always had a soft spot for the ocean.

I left my bag in the guest room, grabbed my towel and sunglasses and headed down the elevator. A few minutes later, after a trek through the condo's parking garage and over the wooden steps that traversed the dunes, I was on glorious Bohemia Beach.

One thing I loved about the beaches here was that there were so few people on them. Today, of course, was an exception, but I cheered a little at the sight of people playing volleyball, grilling, grabbing refreshments and burgers and hot dogs under a white canopy, lying on the sand and frolicking in the water. There were even a few surfers riding the low waves, and I stood there for a few minutes, indulging myself in the sight of their sleek, wet bodies, graceful and muscular, as they caught some curl with their boards.

"Quit staring at my boyfriend."

"What?" I blinked, and Cali was before me, adorable and grinning in a navy one-piece suit, her blond hair wet. "Oh, I wasn't."

"It's OK. Everyone else is, too. He's gorgeous on a surf-board. And everywhere else, I might ad."

"I swear I didn't even realize he was one of them — I was pretty much taking them all in."

She looked out over the waves and nodded. "They are kind of beautiful, aren't they?"

"Speaking of," I muttered as Jace and Penelope approached. Pen, glamorous in a retro red polka-dot bikini trimmed in white, gave me a hug, and Jace smiled that devas-tating movie-star smile he had. "No play today?" I asked.

"They decided to go dark for the Fourth," Penelope said. "They figured everyone would be watching the fireworks."

"Where do they go off?" I asked.

"If you look down the beach toward the pier," Cali said, "way down near the boardwalk, you can see the barge out in the water. It should be awesome from the balcony."

Ez and Gary materialized, too, both in swimsuits, and there were more greetings. And I was suddenly overwhelmed by the couple vibe. Why was everybody paired off, all of a sudden?

"Hey, I'm going to go find a spot for my towel and maybe get wet," I said.

"Cool," Ez said. "We're over there — see the guitar on the beach towel? In case you want to join us."

"OK. Great. Thanks." I smiled with faux enthusiasm at them all and got the feeling they were trying really hard not to exchange knowing glances. It was fucking awkward when the guy you were fooling around with broadcast the demise of your non-relationship on social media.

I escaped the cluster, hearing Gary say something that started with, "Did Alex tell you . . . " as I walked away, followed by a loud "He did *not!*" from Cali. I was just glad they weren't talking about me.

I spread out my Monet "Water Lilies" beach towel, dropped the sunglasses and self-consciously pulled off the cover-up. No one seemed to notice me. We were well beyond the era of the scandalous "Itsy Bitsy Teenie Weenie Yellow Polka Dot Bikini." The only way to get noticed now on the beach would be to skip the suit and wear dabs of glitter and nipple rings.

I waded past the first few waves and half-swam, half-walked to a sandbar beyond the breakers, where the rolling surf ebbed and flowed to my shoulders, gently lifting me in the bath-warm water. I turned my face to the sky and closed my eyes, leaning back a little. There wasn't a lot of surf for the surfers today, just enough of a wave to make me feel as if I had drifted from my moorings. As the minutes went by, my tension and sadness and foolish expectations slowly dissolved in the salt water, until all I felt were the balmy waves on my body and the sun on my skin.

The sun on my skin! I tilted upright, clambering for footing on the sandbar. No matter how much sunscreen I had on, a redhead couldn't afford too much time baking. With a reluctant sigh, I turned toward the shore.

No. *No, no, no.*

Actually, yes. Just when I'd gotten him out of my mind for five minutes, there he was, Duncan Flyte. He was chatting with Cali, who shot anxious glances toward me while pretending not to. And he was shirtless, which didn't exactly help my state of mind. Had he seen me? Where could I flee? I looked around.

Alas, I saw no way to avoid him, short of swimming to the Bahamas. And, damn it, there was no reason I should. I hadn't done anything wrong. And I was tired of being a wimp.

So I made my way back through the breakers as they crashed against my back and swirled around my legs, wondering if he would even see me. Or if he would flee.

He stopped mid-conversation and turned toward me as if he could hear my thoughts. And then he just stood there, ignoring whatever Cali was saying until she winced helplessly in my direction and walked away.

Duncan didn't move as a wave washed up around his bare feet. His face didn't give away a thing. Those pale blue eyes weren't as hard as they'd been on Sunday, but they weren't warm, either. They were like glass, reflecting my own ambivalence.

Intellectually, I was ambivalent about seeing him. But my body heated at the sight of him in his swim shorts, broad-shouldered, his shapely legs set squarely in the sand, wavy hair ruffled by the breeze. Maybe my body was the cause, but my emotions were dragged into the moment, too, and my throat tightened, remembering all the crying I'd done those first couple of days while I'd processed my mistake.

This handsome, strapping mistake.

Duncan held out a hand as I reached him. "Thea."

I let him take my hand and instantly regretted his touch. It seemed to focus everything I was feeling, intensify it, like a magnifying glass held up to the sun. It burned. I let go.

"You're an angel in that swimsuit," he said.

"You don't have to compliment me."

"It's not a compliment. It's a fact. You're splendid."

"Now I know you're lying," I said.

"Why do you do that?" he asked. "I'm not lying."

"Forgive me if I find it difficult to tell."

He shook his head. "Maybe I deserve that. I don't like the way things ended on Sunday. Will you talk to me?"

I walked toward my towel, and he followed. Now I wished I'd put it far away from everyone else. I picked it up and wrapped it around my shoulders. Gary and Ez, who'd been strumming a guitar and a ukulele nearby, exchanged a couple of whispered words and took their instruments to the tent.

"I'm not sure there's anything to talk about," I told Duncan. "You said you were relieved it was over. Let's just leave it at that."

"That's not what I meant," he said, the Scottish accent getting stronger as he became more emphatic. "I was relieved the bet was over, yes. But not that my nights with you were over. I was rather looking forward to seeing you in the daytime. Like normal people. Like this." His smile was warm as he scanned my body.

Self-conscious, I dropped the towel, put on my sunglasses and slipped the cover-up dress over my head. The breeze lofted the light fabric, and I had the curious sensation of floating.

"You can't have a normal conversation without a camera," I said, "unless something like our bet keeps it turned off."

"That's not true. I left my camera at home today."

Now that was surprising. "But you didn't know I'd be here."

"Of course I did," he said. "That's why I found Alex and badgered him into inviting me."

Ah. So that's what Cali's exclamation was about earlier.

"I have to tell you something, Duncan," I said, fighting back the impulse to cry again. "I'm completely confused."

"Oh, lass," he said. "This is why I like you. You tell me the truth."

"I wouldn't mind the same from you."

He nodded. "Sunday — well, when I found out you didn't like me, I was a little bit upset. But not surprised. No one seems to like me much beyond my videos."

"I like you." *You have no idea how much.*

"You do?"

"Yes, I do. Were you not blowing me off on Sunday?"

"I — no. I mean, maybe. Because I thought that's what you were doing to me. I'm sorry if I came across as mean."

"You *were* mean," I said.

"Damn it. I'm sorry."

"What are you sorry for, exactly? I have no idea where we stand right now. And what's the truth? Where are you from? Why was your dad here?"

"That's a lot of questions," he said.

"I have all night." I bit my lip at that slip-up. Our nights were over.

"Let's walk. I'll tell you whatever you want to know."

I nodded, and we started down the beach, moving away from the crowd in front of Alex's condo building. A few other people were around, but the noise of the waves gave us enough privacy to talk.

"Let me ask you something first," Duncan said. "Were you so eager to get me out of your life?"

"That's a loaded question."

"It certainly sounded like you were. And if that's the case, that's fine," he said, a dark note in his voice. "I just want to clear the air."

"That was our deal, wasn't it? I didn't want to go on camera again."

"I wouldn't make you go on camera, though it would've been nice."

"Clicks," I said.

"Fuck the clicks," he bit out. "You shut down on me. Why?"

"You said you were happy the bet was over."

"I explained that."

"And that you wanted to do an 'exit interview.' That sounded like you were blowing me off. And let's be clear: I knew that's what you wanted from the beginning. I'll be totally honest with you, Duncan. I got involved. Too involved. That's my mistake. When you blew me off, I knew it was time to go."

"Whoa. Whoa," he said, stopping and grabbing me by the shoulders. He paused, then reached out and pushed my sunglasses onto my head and beamed those blue eyes right into my soul. "I may have been teasing you a bit when I said I wanted to spend seven nights with you, but I did want those nights. I really did. I never in my wildest dreams thought you'd go along with it or let me in the way you did."

"You're like a tornado, you know that?"

He took a step closer, grasping my shoulders again, a hint of a smile lifting one corner of his mouth. It took all of my resolve not to melt in front of him.

"Maybe I'm the tornado," he said, "but you're the lightning bolt. I knew the second I saw you that I wanted to know you better."

"Don't you feel that way about every woman you meet?"

He frowned and let go of my shoulders. "I'm guessing you saw the vlog with Lolly."

I nodded.

"But did you see all of it?" he asked.

"What do you mean?" The foolish romantic inside me wondered if he was talking about that moment when he mentioned his heart.

"I'm trying to tell you, Thea. You're not like everyone else. I want to see you again. Night or day. Whatever you want."

"Why all the secrets?" I asked, walking again.

He fell into step beside me. "The Scottish thing is a technicality. I was born in the U.S. but went to Scotland at a very young age."

"What about your dad? All the drama? Why didn't you tell me anything during the week? It's not like you didn't have a chance, while I was pouring my heart out to you."

"Shit," Duncan said. "Fuck."

A chuckle escaped me.

"Well, it's nice to hear you laugh again," he said.

I quelled my amusement. "Why are you cursing?"

"Because you are asking me to talk about something I do not talk about."

"And what are you asking of me, Duncan?"

"Your time. Another chance to see how our — friendship

develops."

"Then you have to talk to me. You have to tell me everything."

"Fuck," he said again. "Bloody hell. All right. Let's get out of the sun before I turn into a lobster, and I'll try to tell you what you want to know."

LAUGHTER FLOATED up to us from the beach. The view was stunning up here on the condo balcony, and the late afternoon sun worked its alchemy, turning the light of day into gold.

The balcony extended the length of the building on the side facing the Atlantic Ocean, and since it was shaded, it was several degrees cooler than the beach. I was grateful, since my skin radiated a low heat that told me I'd had a little too much sun. Duncan and I grabbed beers and settled into two sturdy cushioned lounge chairs at the quiet end. He pulled his chair so close to mine they were almost touching. I knew he did it for privacy as he talked, even though almost everyone was still on the beach, but as always, my body reacted, generating heat that had nothing to do with the summer day. I sipped my beer and curled up on my side, facing him, trying to put my lust on ice as I listened.

"My dad was here to convince me to see my mother," he said.

"He made it sound pretty urgent."

"That's because she's doing her best to kill herself. Has been for years. She's the worst kind of alcoholic and has advanced liver disease. She's just had another bout in the hospital."

"Oh, God, I'm so sorry."

"Don't waste your breath," he said with that edge of anger I'd seen when he'd talked with his father.

"Why did your dad come?"

"He thought he could convince me face-to-face, and since I don't go to Austin anymore, it was the only way. My father believes in always doing the right thing. For him, that's standing by my mother no matter what. He thinks I should visit her, talk to her."

"And that's out of the question?"

Duncan took a swig of beer. "I haven't talked to her in five years. Not since I left Austin and moved to Florida. I spent a couple of years in Orlando before I moved to Bohemia, and to be honest, it's been great not talking to her. Not living the lies. Not looking for a way to help. Giving up all hope is very freeing."

"Depressing," I said.

His eyes narrowed. "You have no idea what it's been like."

"Tell me."

He sighed and lay back on the lounge, staring out at the sea. "When you're a kid, you don't know how bad it is. You don't know what normal is supposed to be." He shook his head as if clearing away the cobwebs of time. "It actually all started way before me, with my mother and my father. My father was visiting his cousin, the one who wanted to start up the distillery in Austin, when he met my mother."

"She's from Texas?"

"Yeah. I guess she was very pretty, bright and vivacious. A good time," he said grimly. "He got her pregnant, and because he thought it was the right thing to do, he married her."

"Pregnant with you?"

"Yeah. I like to think she didn't drink as much then, since

it appears I came out all right. Physically, anyway."

I couldn't help an appreciative scan of his still-naked torso. "Um, yeah."

Duncan glanced at me with an amused smile, but it dissolved as he looked back at the ocean, looking into the past. "My father went back to his distillery job in Scotland and took my mother and me with him after I was born. My sister came along almost two years later. By then, my dad's cousin was talking about starting up the distillery in Austin. My father wasn't sure. I can only piece together what was going through his mind from arguments my parents had over the years, but I think he thought moving to Austin wouldn't be good for my mother. She had a wild set of friends in Texas, and she missed them. She drank some in Scotland, but he limited what was in the house, and he made it harder for her to get booze. A couple more years went by, and I guess the offer from my dad's cousin became too good to refuse. He decided he would go to Austin by himself to help the company grow and make sure it would succeed before bringing us over."

"He *left* you?"

"He didn't abandon us. Not exactly. I think, in his mind, he'd rationalized the decision to go as something that would be best for all of us, though I imagine it was also a relief. It took me a long time to realize he probably wanted to escape her, at least for a while, even if he couldn't bring himself to do it officially."

"You're angry with him."

"Only a little. And not for that. Not really. If anything, I'm angry he didn't abandon her a long time ago and get us out of her clutches. He won't acknowledge my sister's and my need to escape. He lays on the guilt thick."

"Even though he left, once."

"Again, he didn't think he was leaving us. It was . . . temporary. But terrible." He took another sip of beer, and I was struck for a second by the irony. "My mother was left in a place she didn't particularly like to raise us the best way she knew how, and she didn't know much. The drinking just got worse. Oh, she'd clean up when he came to visit, which he did fairly often. She'd get rid of the bottles and the trash and make us nice meals as if she did it all the time. But when he wasn't there, it was all about the bottle for her. My sister and I learned to make do. Make dinner. Get ourselves ready for school, clean the house and so on. Forge her signature. I took on odd jobs to help make up the budget, since she spent so much on liquor."

"Holy shit. How long did this go on?"

"Seven years," he said. "There was a particularly rotten visit when I think he realized just how far it had gone. That's when he moved us over to Texas."

"And you were twelve by then."

"Yeah. And in case you're wondering, I suppose I could've lost the accent, but it was pretty firmly ingrained by then, and living with my dad just reinforced it."

"And the girls like it," I said wryly.

"Well, yeah." He smiled and looked at me. "But the women have never meant anything to me."

"I'm not sure that's something you want to brag about," I said. "So once your family was together again in Austin, did things stabilize?"

"Yes and no. My father worked ridiculous hours, and I'd learned bad habits. I learned to hide my mother's drinking from the world, and that world included him. And she never acted like anything was wrong. When I came home from school, she'd pour me a glass of whiskey, and we'd have a drink together."

"When you were *twelve?*"

"It seemed like the thing to do to keep her calm and happy. Otherwise she'd get into a dark mood, break things or scream until she was hysterical, accuse me of judging her. Eventually I said no to her little conspiracies, but it took me a few years to wise up and get enough backbone. And then I became the rebellious teen in my dad's eyes, always running off to raise hell or make movies with my friends, anything to stay away from the house. I moved out when I was eighteen, worked some shitty jobs, took some film classes until I figured out what I wanted to do. When I turned twenty, when my sister moved to London, I moved to Florida. I haven't spoken to my mother since."

I took a sip of my beer, trying to digest the horror of his childhood.

"What if she's dying?" I asked softly.

Duncan's mouth tightened into a thin line. "She's had chances. So many chances. Nothing has changed."

"Except that she could be gone forever."

He looked as if he was swallowing an angry reply. Finally, he said, "She's been gone for years. It won't make any difference."

"I understand your need to separate yourself from her, and I'm so sorry you went through what you went through. I'm sure my own biases are at work here. But I would do anything to have just one more hour with my mother."

Duncan put down his beer on the cement floor of the balcony and looked at me, catching my eyes with a soulful gaze that almost broke my heart.

"Will you come to me, Thea? I want to hold you."

I didn't know if he wanted to hold me for his sake or mine, but I'd never wanted anything so much. I put down my bottle, clambered over and curled up against him, my head against his shoulder, my legs draped over his lap. A tear rolled down my cheek.

"*Och,* don't cry," he said, wiping it away. He kissed my wet cheek. "Please don't be angry with me. If you think I'm being an asshole, tell me, OK? Make sure I'm really being an asshole and not just a fuck-up like I was the other night."

I sucked in a few ragged breaths, overwhelmed with emotion, wondering if I was doing the right thing. "I think what we had was a failure to communicate."

He chuckled at my movie reference. "Obviously, I didn't understand what you were saying, either."

"So what is this right now?" I asked.

"I believe they call it Bohemia Beach."

I swatted his chest, and he grabbed my wrist with one hand, forcing my gaze up to his. His eyes were as intense as I'd ever seen them, dark with hunger. With his other arm around my shoulders, he pulled me closer and lowered his mouth to mine.

Crushed in his arms, I whimpered against his lips. Helplessly, I opened to him, catching fire as he licked and nibbled, entangling our tongues, his rough, stubbly beard rubbing against my cheek. My nipples hardened into sharp points, pushing out the fabric of the bikini and the thin cover-up, aching as my breasts smashed against his chest, and one of his hands strayed to them, brushing the sensitive tips in acknowledgment.

God, I've missed this, I thought. Then I told myself not to think, because I would start coming up with too many reasons to run.

When he released me, I managed to ask him again: "What is this, Duncan?"

"This is us figuring things out," he said.

I searched his eyes. "Without a deadline?"

"Without a deadline."

"Without a camera?"

"Without you on camera, if you wish," he said. "But you have to understand that the camera is part of me. It's what I do."

"That's fair. That's your passion, your livelihood. I understand that."

"I think if you really understood it, you'd want to be on camera, too. But I won't push you," he said to my frown. "I'm still not sure what your passion is. Is it your paper sculptures?"

"You make it sound like a kindergarten project. And yes. Well, it's visual art, but that's my preferred form of expression at the moment."

He pushed one of my curls back behind my ears. "I want to see it."

"It so happens that I've spent a lot of time working on it this week. Sleepless nights and not much to fill them, for some reason."

Duncan murmured in my ear. "Do you want help with your art? Or perhaps — your night?"

"Do you really think that's a good idea?" I asked, my heart beating faster as he caressed my back and kissed my neck. "I mean, we're here to see the fireworks and everything."

"I'll give you fireworks," he said, kissing me again, turning me into a puddle of melted butter. I was a goner. "Meet me at my place?"

"OK," I said breathily, not even hesitating, and he kissed

me again. It was as if his touch short-circuited all of my reasonable objections and inhibitions. When he broke the kiss, I only half-cursed myself for giving in so easily, because I wanted him so much.

We disentangled ourselves, and he helped me to my feet.

"I'll see you at home," he murmured, kissing my cheek. And then he strode down the balcony, graceful, powerful, and turned right to vanish through the sliding doors.

Home.

I stood for a moment at the railing to catch my breath, watching the happy people below, the surfers on the waves, the musicians, the volleyball players, trying to grasp my lost sense of reason.

I had about eight hundred reasons not to go to him. For instance:

1. He had a way with women that suggested hit-and-run relationships.

2. He seemed to have trouble connecting with anyone (corollary to No. 1).

3. He put his clicks first (usually).

4. He had a really fucked-up childhood.

But then again . . . my childhood wasn't going to win any awards. I was shitty at connecting with people. I was too much of a wallflower to truly understand the wild male animal. And he was so charming and sweet and sexy, I would rationalize pretty much anything to get a taste of him again.

"Thea?" I jumped at the soft voice and looked around to see Sloane. "I'm so sorry," she said. "Alex knew better than to invite that video blogger . . ."

"It's actually OK," I said. "We talked. I think we're friends again."

She looked at me with concern. "Are you sure you're OK? You look a little tired. And pink."

"Too much sun, I guess. Gets me every time."

I said my goodbyes, and she gave me a sympathetic hug. I grabbed my stuff and hastened to my car, wondering why I was in such a hurry to get burned again.

I GOT off the elevator on my floor and headed for my apartment — until Duncan opened his door and beckoned to me, stopping me in my tracks. He was still in his swim trunks. In other words, half-naked. Absolutely stunning.

"I need a shower," I protested.

"But I want you dirty. Do you know what you look like right now?"

"Sweaty and hot?"

"*Verrrra* hot," he said. *Oh, God.* It was all the charm from before, only without the rules of our seven nights. I wondered if I could handle Duncan without a few rules.

"You really don't want this," I said.

"If you could only see yourself," he said, "the light shining through that see-through little thing you have on, showing off all your curves and that goddamn bikini. Come here, wench."

Maybe I should've been offended by "wench," but instead, a laugh escaped me. He had a way of drawing laughs from my belly, where they liked to hide.

I went to him. He yanked me inside and shut the door and slammed me against it, pressing all of his body weight into me. I dropped my bag and whimpered as he crushed my mouth with his. I hung on to his hard back for dear life as he pushed one knee between my legs, pressing against the apex of my thighs. Already, need ached there, radiating out through my core. I forgot everything except the way his body felt on mine.

His mouth moved to my neck, his hands to my hips. "You taste salty," he murmured.

"All you need is tequila and a slice of lime."

Duncan chuckled into my skin, reached down, scooped me up in his arms and headed toward his bed. "Joking at a time like this!"

I just grinned, feeling free for the first time in days, kicking my sandals off as I anticipated what would come next. I didn't feel like too-tall, too-gawky Thea in his arms. He picked me up as if I were one of those princesses I liked to read about.

We were bathed in an orange glow as the sun set on the other side of the building, a beautiful ambient light that made this moment seem like a sepia-tone memory, like a loop of time in which I wanted to be caught forever.

He set me on my feet next to the bed. I slipped off a thin strap, starting to remove the diaphanous dress.

"Wait," he said, a catch in his voice, putting a hand on mine. "Wait."

He reached under the handkerchief hem, slowly lifting the garment until he touched my bikini bottoms. He dipped his thumbs in the waistband and worked them down, helping me step out of them.

And then his hands were back under the translucent fabric, gliding up my legs, over my naked hips, leaving a trail of fire. He unfastened the bandeau top of the bikini and let it fall to the floor before tracing a finger over my nipples, just long enough for them to harden under his touch. Then he took a step back, letting the dress fall into place.

"I can see every inch of you," he said in a low voice with a hint of a rumble, like distant thunder. "Your gorgeous long legs. Your round hips. That sweet little swell under your belly button. Your curls, and I don't mean the ones on your head." He gave me a half-grin as his eyes narrowed, and my breaths came short. "Your pretty little pussy, waiting for me. The curve of those breasts — fuck me, those strawberry nipples, hard for me. Are they hard for me, Thea?"

"Yes," I breathed, my eyes flicking to his shorts, tented now with his erection. I licked my lips and looked up into his face. His knowing eyes. Twinkling.

He slipped off his shorts. "Is this what you want?"

God, he was big. Thick. "Yes, please."

"It's I who should be saying please and thank you. Thank you, Thea." He stepped forward and slipped the thin straps off my shoulders. The dress pooled on the floor, and there we were, standing face to face, bare, caught up in the glow.

He cupped one breast, thumbed my nipple. I closed my eyes, breathing faster. As he rolled my pebbled peak between his fingers, he touched my open mouth with his other hand, one finger tracing my lips. I opened my eyes to see his hungry gaze. I darted out my tongue, licked his finger, and then he slid it inside and I sucked on it, lovingly, rolling my tongue around it as he pushed it in and out. He groaned, withdrew his finger and pushed me back until my legs bumped into the bed and I fell backward, my head against the soft mattress.

"Spread wide for me, darlin'," he said, the note of command so different from his usual tone and *so* fucking sexy.

Now his finger found a new place to go. He slipped it inside my cleft as I spread my legs for him. He pushed in and out, thumbing my clit.

"I might still be sandy," I managed to whisper as I started to squirm against his touch. His magical finger felt so good, sparking currents of pleasure that zipped through my limbs.

"You feel pretty wet to me, darlin', but hang on."

He withdrew his finger, and it was my turn to groan. When he came back to stand before me, he had a small bottle in his hand. He squirted the liquid onto his palm, set the bottle aside and cupped my pussy hard, grinding against me with his slick hand, sliding all the way from my crack to my clit over and over as he possessed me, teasing my anus, pressing my nub, gliding over my eager cleft.

"Oh, God," I croaked, clutching the covers.

"Does that feel good?" He was looking down at me with a kind of amused carnality that made my heart race.

"Yes. Yes. Oh, please, Duncan . . . "

"My turn to say please," he said. *"Please* come for me, darlin'. I want to see you lose yourself. I want to see you come apart, my angel. My sweet, dirty angel."

Yes. I spread my legs wider, lifting my hips, desperate for more contact. I bucked against his hand as he pushed two fingers inside me, rubbing against my sweet spot, stroking until a nimbus of electricity seemed to blossom inside and out, blooming into a crazy glow behind my eyes as I squeezed them shut, lost in the sensation of his fingers, his hand. I cried out, and he thrust harder with one hand while twisting one of my sensitive nipples with the other, exponentially expanding my orgasm until I half-shouted, half-sobbed, "Duncan, *God,* fuck me!"

He grabbed my thighs, pushing them apart even more, and he positioned himself at my entrance. His handsome face was devilish as he thrust home. I was still shaking from my last explosion, and now, tremors wracked me like an earthquake. With his hard, delicious invasion, I detonated again, crying out with each plunge. I looked into his eyes, saw the fierce desire there. It made me even higher, even more turned on, and I clenched around him hard.

Duncan rammed deep.

"Fuck," he said as he pounded me. "You're fucking me right back. Sweet angel. Sweet Venus from the sea. *Fuck*." And then he came. I felt the pulse of his seed shooting into me, triggering yet more spasms of bliss inside my body as I milked him. He made incoherent sounds, giving himself over to his release, before he collapsed against me, kissing my neck, nipping my ear.

After a few moments, he eased out of me. Somehow he swung us sideways across the end of his big bed, and I clung to him, sweaty, salty, sandy, slick with desire and come, panting still. Every molecule in my body seemed to be alive, tumbling through my blood, an effervescent circus. Again, I had the thought: *This* was great sex. I had never known great sex before Duncan — might never know it again — but this was sex I would never forget.

"Don't worry," he whispered in my ear. "It'll be better next time."

I smiled against his cheek, and then a chuckle bubbled up, and then a full blown laugh rolled out of me. And he was laughing with me, his hot breath against my ear, and we shook there on the bed, devolving into giggles, clinging to each other in mirth and satisfaction.

We dozed for a bit as it got dark, and then an explosion ripped me awake.

"What the hell?" I sat up. A glow in the room faded into darkness.

Duncan jumped out of bed. "It's the fireworks! Come over

to the window. I think we can see them from here."

I eased off the bed, and he grabbed my hand and tugged me over to his big windows, which, like mine, extended from around three feet off the floor to the high ceiling. His faced northeast. We stood there, naked, in the dark of the apartment, as a blossom of sparks erupted on the horizon over Bohemia Beach. I hadn't realized Duncan had such a good view. From here, we could see the southern edge of downtown and the causeway, along with the lagoon. Beyond it, a strip of lights marked the barrier island, where fireworks were shooting into the sky from that barge I'd seen in the ocean.

"It's beautiful," I whispered.

Duncan kissed my shoulder. "Yes, you are."

I moved to turn toward him, to kiss his mouth, but he slipped behind me. "Stay there, my sweet." He kissed my neck, and I arched against him, feeling the stirrings of his shaft against my backside. "Lean forward a bit, darlin'. Put your hands on the windowsill. Ah, that's right."

His kisses traced a path down my spine as I leaned forward. A tremble of anticipation passed through me as another cluster of fireworks burst in the distant sky. His fingers found my cleft, wet again for him, and a moment later, I felt the tip of his shaft pressing there. I braced myself, wiggling against him. He made a small, primitive noise of appreciation and slid inside me, moving slowly this time, making it last.

I moaned and sighed and pushed back, taking him deeper, hearing his growl of satisfaction as he gripped my waist. The next flower of fire bloomed in the night, and I caught a glimpse of our reflection in the window — me, with my curls wild and unruly, my breasts pendulous as I leaned against the sill, and Duncan behind me, big, dominant, his mouth slightly open, pressing his hips against me, his rock-hard cock lancing me in deliberate thrusts that made me lose my mind.

And he watched me. Watched me in our reflection with the kind of lust that can make a girl drunk on her own power, a fiery wanting I'd never felt from a man. There was the illusion of exposure as we gazed out the dark apartment's windows, and the very real vulnerability of having Duncan see me at my most raw, the wild woman who never came out to play, who caught his heated gaze and licked her lips in response and made him groan.

The fireworks sparkled. The booms echoed against the windows. And Duncan watched me and fucked me, slow and hot and deep, triggering a slow-motion orgasm that built and built until I pushed hard against him, shuddering, crying out. He shattered then, uttering a profanity that sounded sweet to my ears, knowing he'd come for me.

When he eased out of me and I stood, my arms were shaking from the strain of pushing against the sill. He turned me toward him and kissed me as the last flashes lit the night, and then all was quiet in our corner of Bohemia, except for the melancholy horn and rattle of a passing train.

Our kiss ended, and we just stood there, embracing, until I lifted my head. "I'm going to go home and get a shower now," I said.

"You could shower here," he said.

"I want my own clothes."

"I don't blame you. My laundry's a bit overdue."

I chuckled. "I'm going to slip on that dress thing, but I don't really want anyone to see me. Can you check if the coast is clear?"

"I don't want anyone to see you either," he said with dramatic propriety. "Hang on."

Duncan went to the door and, without a stitch on, opened it and poked his head into the hallway. "All clear."

With the dress on — such as it was — and my bag and bikini in my hand, I darted across and unlocked the door.

And found Duncan at my heels.

"What are you doing?" I asked as I got my semi-naked ass inside and he followed.

"I want to wake up with you, for once," he said, and my heart melted a little.

"OK," I said with a shy smile, realizing he was still nude. "Uh, didn't think to bring any clothes over?"

"Didn't see much point," he said with a grin.

He ducked into the bathroom first and took a quick shower. I let him have his privacy — because, frankly, I was sexed-out for the moment — and went in after he came out. By the time I emerged from the shower, wearing my oversized Bohemia Beach T-shirt, he was lying in my bed, pillows fluffed up under his head. I turned out the last light and slid under the covers next to him.

"Ah, you're so soft," Duncan whispered into my wet hair. "And you smell good."

"You feel good." I slipped an arm around his waist.

"Some parts of me feel better than others."

And I laughed again, into his chest, into his heat.

Within three minutes, he'd fallen into the soft breaths of sleep. I was slow to follow. With the high of our coupling fading, as was my wont, I questioned my joy. How was this really going to work? Would it work? Or would it just be another great night of sex for me to remember after this dream lay in pieces like the pop-up parts on my desk?

THE GRAY LIGHT before dawn seemed to bring out the ghosts. They moved in my dreams before I was fully awake — my mother, sometime in my childhood, teaching me to draw a barn and a windmill after a drive into the open country west of Wichita. And then I was younger and in the car with her and my father as they argued, and then I was awake, fully awake, with a warm body wrapped around mine, gentle snores making me want to laugh. More than that. Just the *idea* of Duncan in my bed, in the morning, made me want to dissolve into hysterical giggles, though I didn't, just held my breath for a few minutes as the studio slowly brightened.

Finally, urged on by my bladder, I eased out of his arms, only slightly disappointed he didn't wake with me. I was a morning person. It was wired into me, no matter how tired I was. And I had to admit, I enjoyed my solitude in the early hours before the rest of the world stirred.

Still, I couldn't help standing there for a minute, breathless with the novelty of having a man in my small bed. I watched him, his face crushed against the pillow, the muscles of his arms and chest sculpted by the ambient light creeping into the room. God, he was magnificent. And this morning — that's all I could think about for now — he was mine.

I used the bathroom, then slipped over to my work table and turned on the small lamp. My pop-ups lay there, many still in pieces. I got lost in the quiet, creating my cutouts, assembling the parts that would make up my princess' journey from her castle into the world: a colorful version of the castle, its intricate connections and cuts and folds — the white bridge — the dragon. The exploding skyline of the city, geometric and enticing but full of shadows as it unfolded.

The creatures of the alleys and the gray people of the streets. The story was taking shape, though I hadn't created a princess yet. And how would all this fit together into a work I could display in a gallery? A carousel, perhaps? My princess would have to come full circle — leaving home, learning the hard ways of the world, finding herself there and coming back. Maybe with a pet dragon?

I smiled at this idea as I delicately scored my bridge and nearly jumped out of my chair when I heard someone's throat clear behind me.

Not someone's. Duncan's.

I swiveled in the chair and faced him, noting his rumpled hair and half-smile.

"How long have you been awake, darlin'?" he asked. "I was hoping to wake *you*." The half-smile became a grin as I took in the entirety of him. Naked.

"I — uh — "

Utterly un-self-conscious, he moved closer and leaned over me, looking at my project.

"This is coming along, isn't it?" He leaned even closer, his chest in my face as he reached over me and pulled up the dragon, opening it, spreading its red wings. "Utterly fantastic. Do you have a concept yet for your piece for the show?"

I put my hands on his chest and pushed slightly to get some distance between us, get some air. My body responded as usual to the heat of his skin, but for once, I wanted to think, not feel.

He stood up straight, working the dragon's wings in fascination.

I gently took it from him, still not quite trusting something so delicate to someone so — so *imposing*. "I think I have an idea. My princess will go on a journey."

He spun my chair so I faced the table again and rubbed my shoulders through my nightshirt as he scanned my work. I struggled not to melt against him.

"But where's your princess?"

I set the dragon on the table, slipped away from him and walked toward my big windows. The mockingbird sang in the tree outside as early morning sunlight made the oak's leaves glow, suggesting layers of brightly colored paper. The images from my work danced in my head, building, expanding. But the princess eluded me.

"I haven't found her yet," I confessed.

"Found her?" He walked up behind me and put his hands on my shoulders again. His lips found my neck, and my focus wavered. "Maybe you are her."

I laughed softly. "That's silly." But there was always a little part of me in my work. Maybe a bigger part this time. "Even if I were her, I need a way to portray my princess. A series of independent pop-ups of her for each scene, maybe — like in a movie."

He stretched my shirt off one shoulder, baring it to his mouth, his tongue. A shiver skated over my skin, and in the next moment, the electricity of his touch was eclipsed by a jolt of inspiration.

"Duncan?"

"Hmmm," he murmured, licking my ear and trailing kisses across my jaw.

"Do you still want to be Steven Spielberg?"

His lips stopped their delicate journey. When he spoke, there was a different kind of interest in his voice. "What're you thinking?"

I spun to face him, feeling a rush of excitement. "A movie. With pop-ups as the background."

He smiled, indulging me, I thought. Skeptical. "With paper dolls?"

"No. Not paper dolls. Real people. We know actors. And you know your way around a green screen, right?"

He took a step back, his eyes lighting with interest. "It's technical and kind of a pain in the ass, but yeah," he mused. "You'd insert real people into your scenes?"

"Yes, for a short film."

"But what's the story? You have to have a story."

"My princess runs away from her pretty but dull castle to see the world. I was going to have her disillusioned — but there has to be hope. I want her to go back home feeling different. The ogre — she's kind to him. My paper ogre transforms into . . . "

"A handsome prince?"

"Don't laugh at me," I said to his grin. "Sure. Why not? Her kindness changes people. The city blooms wherever she steps — oh, the flowers! The lines and angles of the city try to enclose her, but then they bloom and set her free. Oh, I love this." I was babbling. I babbled for another few minutes about her journey, about how she brought light and life to the simple gray cutouts of the city, before I looked up into Duncan's face. His cheeky grin had transformed into a much warmer smile.

"You think I'm crazy, don't you?" I said. "And you're too busy, anyway."

"I live for collaborations. Keeps me from getting trapped inside an echo chamber. And I love the idea of doing one with you."

"You do?" I smiled back at him and wrapped my arms around his neck. "You would help me?"

"On one condition," he said, and dread flared in my belly before he said: "You direct."

It wasn't at all what I expected him to say. "But you're the filmmaker."

"You're the artist. It's your vision. I'll be your DP — director of photography," he said to my raised eyebrows. "But you'll have to be the producer, too. You'll need a princess and a prince."

"You?" I asked, not wanting to hurt his feelings but not sure he'd be right for the part, either.

"Best not, if I'm shooting."

"Then Penelope," I said. "She'd know about costumes, too. And Jace — God, he's almost too good-looking."

Duncan chuckled. "Thanks."

"Oh, you know what I mean," I said, grinning at him now. "Do you think they'd do it?"

"He's bloody famous," Duncan said, "but what are friends for?"

"Thank you," I said, planting a quick kiss on his lips.

"You'll have to thank me better than that," he said, crushing me to him and capturing my lips with his before scooping me up and hauling me back to the bed.

I giggled as he dropped me on the mattress and stripped off my nightshirt. The soft morning light caught every ripple of his muscles as he lowered himself over me, tonguing my ear, my neck, moving down to my breasts. He latched onto one nipple, sucking, stimulating the peak until it hardened under his little licks and nips, sending sparks skittering across my skin until I groaned and spread my legs.

"Greedy wench," he said, and I couldn't quite laugh through my exhale as he yanked off my panties and ran a finger through my cleft. "Wet and ready for me. I like that. Would you like me to fuck you now, princess?"

"I'm ready for my close-up, Mr. Flyte," I whispered, squirming against his hand.

"A girl who knows her movies. I like that, too," he murmured, supporting himself over me, pressing his erection against my clit. He slid up and down, withholding his cock, teasing me until I moaned.

I arched, coaxing him to take me. "God, I can feel how hard you are. Are you like this every morning?"

"Just wait till the matinee," came his throaty promise, and he paused at my entrance, one last tease before he drove home.

I cried out, lifting my hips to take him deep, clenching around him.

A low gasp escaped him. "Fuck, you're tight."

"Obviously, I haven't been getting enough sex," I joked, remembering last night.

"We can take care of that." He eased back, then rammed hard into me. I cried out with the exquisite agony of it.

"This is no laughing matter," he said, his voice low in my ear as he plunged again, mixing up the most outrageous cocktail of emotions inside me — the desire to laugh, to cry, to take every last inch of him, to be obliterated by him, to be lifted up by him — I had given him so much power, thrown myself wide open to him. But I loved it. I loved — *oh, God.*

I tried to crush the thought with his body as I wrapped my legs around him, meeting his thrusts with increasing speed and desperation until the sparks leapt into flames that ripped through me in a detonation worthy of any cinematic explosion. Duncan bucked and groaned as he spent himself inside me, setting off more spasms of pleasure. But the intensity of the ecstasy didn't do anything to dissipate that forbidden thought.

This was all too new, too risky. I was at such a disadvantage, an amateur sparring with a jaded champion who'd knock me out and be on to his next bout before I picked my jaw up off the mat.

I couldn't be in love with him.

I relaxed my embrace, and he eased out of me, wrapping me up in his arms, kissing my hair.

"Sleep with me a little," Duncan whispered, and like a princess under a spell, I couldn't resist. I held on to him and kissed the salty skin of his chest and drifted into hot, disturbing dreams of princes and princesses, of paper castles and lit matches.

MY FIRST CALL when I awoke and got dressed was to Penelope.

"And where did you disappear to last night?" was her first question after "Hello."

"Uh . . ."

"And was the make-up sex as good as I imagine? Because if it wasn't, you need to get rid of him right now."

"Pen!" I exclaimed. Then, more quietly: "I can't talk right now." Duncan was rummaging in the kitchen, making us a late breakfast.

"That's what I thought. If he's not good to you, your friends are going to be lining up to kick his ass."

"And this is why I shouldn't be sleeping with a video blogger."

"As long as he doesn't put the sex online, why worry?"

"Says the extrovert," I noted. "Which is one reason I'm calling. I know you've done some acting in the past . . . "

"Before I gave it up in favor of costume design," she said.

"Which you are *awesome* at."

"Uh-oh," she said, wariness in her voice.

"I have a little favor to ask."

"Does it involve the Scot?"

"Sort of," I replied, "but it's actually for me."

"That's better," Penelope said. "What's up?"

I explained to her my idea for the short film and how I needed a prince and princess, in costume. She reluctantly agreed to be my princess and asked some questions about how long the shoot would take, what I wanted the costumes to look like and when I wanted to do the filming.

"I need at least a week to get my storyboarding done," I said, "but two would be better."

"For us, too. And I say 'us,' but I really need to ask Jace if he's OK with this. He gets a lot of requests, and — "

"And he's famous and busy and has an image to protect. I totally get it. If he can't do it, let me know."

"Hang on a sec." I heard some noise on Penelope's end, low voices, and then she came back on. "He's in."

I guffawed. "That quick?"

"He's lying here naked. He's vulnerable," she joked.

"Holy shit."

"That's pretty much what I think every time I look at him."

"Oh, I didn't mean — I wasn't picturing him — "

"If you didn't, I'd assume you were dead," she said.

I laughed again. "Thanks so much, Pen. So what's a good day?"

"The play's dark on Mondays. Say, two weeks from

Monday? In a week, I'll have sketches for you to look at before I finalize the costumes. I think we have a couple of things at the Chamberlain I can adapt for our evil purposes."

"Perfect. That'll give us just enough time to edit it. Oh, thank you so much, Penelope! You're the best!"

"Sure, hon. All right, I've gotta go. Jace needs some attention before the matinee."

"Oh, lord, TMI."

Penelope laughed wickedly. "Bye, Thea. Have fun with your man."

My man, I thought when we disconnected. I rubbed my mom's ring and thought about her broken love story and tried to wrangle my little puppy of hope back into its cage.

"What did she say?" Duncan shouted from the kitchen. The heavenly aroma of pancakes wafted to me along with his voice.

"We're on!" I called back.

"Fantastic!"

Then came breakfast — and the whirlwind. My imagination was fired up, and maybe not just by art. Duncan's presence over the next several days became not just stimulating but somehow essential. He went out and produced his vlog almost every day, of course, and I designed projects for my dad, but the rest of the time, Duncan was with me, helping me work out the technical details of how we'd film each shot, kidnapping me for meals and, sometimes, just watching me work. And that was just plain strange. I was used to working in isolation. To have someone watch me design, plan, score, cut and assemble my sculptures felt like an invasion of my space at first. But then something happened. I almost began to forget he was there. Or rather, I accepted his presence. Instead of an outsider, he became part of my process. He was like a heater on a cold day, warming the hothouse of my creativity.

"Aren't you bored?" I asked one afternoon after he'd been watching me for almost two hours.

"I'm fascinated," Duncan said, leaning back in the cushy leather office chair he'd brought over from his place. "Plus, I have a beer."

I nodded at the bottle. "That looks good."

"Want one?"

"No." I shook my head. "I'm scared to death I'll spill it on something. I'm almost at a break, and then I'll have one with you."

His forehead wrinkled as he watched me for another minute. "What would you think of me filming you making one of your sculptures? A kind of behind-the-scenes video?"

"For the vlog?" I asked, already uncomfortable.

"It wouldn't have to be. They might want it as part of the art show."

"Ha. That's assuming they even accept my piece."

"Oh, darlin', they will. This is going to blow them away — the video and the carousel."

I'd decided to put my sculptures in a carousel after all. It would accompany the video, which would play on a display mounted in the center as the circle of sculptures rotated around it. I'd asked Cali's brother Damien to help me with the mechanics, since he was accomplished at multimedia art that was a lot more technical than what I was used to attempting. He'd refused a credit, saying that all he was doing was finding the right parts to support my paper merry-go-round.

"I don't know about you filming me," I told Duncan. "I'm not sure I want this to be about me."

A frown touched Duncan's lips, an expression so unfamiliar, he almost looked like a different person. "You know that art is always about you. Yes, your art has its own life, but in the end, it's about you, too. And you're putting yourself out there now. Finally. As you should. You're incredibly talented."

"Oh, stop."

He stood, placing the beer on another table so it wouldn't be in the danger zone. "Come here."

I raised my eyebrows.

"You said you can take a break. Come here."

I stood, feeling a bit nervous at the tone of his voice, at its sexy, dark roughness.

He pulled me to him and cupped my face in his hands. "You're amazing, Thea. Say it."

"What?"

"Say you're amazing."

"You're amazing."

Duncan grinned, and then he kissed me hard and deep before letting me come up for air. "You know what I mean. Say it."

I swallowed, still dizzy from his kiss, and looked into his ice-blue eyes. "I'm amazing," I whispered.

"Yes, you are." He slipped a hand to my neck and drew me in for another dazzling kiss. "Let me film you."

"I get to decide how to use it?" I managed to eke out.

"Yes. Just say yes."

"Yes," I said, and then he yanked my body against his and fucked my mouth with his tongue, and we spent the rest of the afternoon in bed.

A delay, to be sure, but totally worth it. And for the next few days, as I made the city skyline and alleys and streets from paper, he filmed the process. It was kind of fun, actually, to show how I performed certain techniques, but in the back of my mind was a nagging worry. I wasn't sure I wanted anyone to see this, to see me. To see my art.

I didn't want to fail. And at the same time, I didn't want to fail Duncan.

SOMEHOW WORD GOT out to my friends about the video shoot, maybe because I'd asked Cali if we could use her studio. She already had a green screen and good lights. Wyatt came along to help adjust them as needed.

With Jace and Penelope came Millie, who'd been acting as a costumer's assistant at the theater. Then Sloane stopped by after her class at the Bohemia School of Art and Design, just to watch. And following up on my query about where to get royalty-free music, Ez and Gary showed up with an electronic keyboard, a guitar and an original song they thought we might like to use for the soundtrack.

It was all pretty overwhelming. All of a sudden I wasn't just an artist in my little studio. I was the leader of a complex collaboration.

I was also exhausted. It had taken a lot of long hours, but I'd completed my sculptures, and Duncan and I had filmed each of them unfolding, sometimes in stop-motion to keep hands out of the picture. We chose our angles carefully, knowing we might have to film some of them again depending on what happened today. I'd storyboarded every little scene using the frames from the video so I would know where we wanted the actors to be.

Penelope had outdone herself with the costumes. Jace's princely garb was dominated by purple, reflecting the paper ogre the prince used to be, and it was trimmed in silver fur and red gems. A green and silver plume and silver cording accented his purple, Henry VIII-style hat.

Penelope, meanwhile, was a vision in a silver and light-green gown, which brought out her eyes. The green was my suggestion, not really because of her eyes, but because it symbolized the life my princess seemed to sow wherever she went. Pink tulle rosettes were scattered across the full skirt, and her shoulders were bare. A delicate tiara sparkled in her pink and blond hair, and her makeup was perfect. Then again, it always was.

Millie helped them get dressed while we set up the lights for the castle, which was the setting for the first and the last scene — the princess's flight and her return home. I'd actually made two castles for the video. The first was mostly gray and white. The second, when it popped open, was covered with green vines and surrounded by flowers. For the actual display, I'd made a third castle that was gray and white on one side and covered with vines and flowers on the other, as it would be the transitional piece in my sculpture-in-the-round.

Vines, trees and flowers were important parts of all the sculptures, not just the castle. My princess not only brought life with her, but recognized her home for its true beauty when she returned. Maybe the idea was sentimental, but as someone who didn't have much of a home to come back to, it warmed my heart.

"Thank God we don't have to deal with sound," Duncan said as he helped Wyatt set the last of the lights.

"I like the silent-movie feel of it," I said. "The music adds just the right layer of emotion." I nodded toward a shadowy corner of the studio, where Ez and Gary were tinkering with their soundtrack. It didn't have lyrics. I wanted people to experience the piece and fill in the blanks themselves.

Shooting was more difficult than I'd hoped. Framing the shots to get the right perspective, so the princess and her ogre-prince weren't absurdly out of scale, meant we shot each scene several times and from several angles to be sure we got what we needed. Penelope, to my surprise, seemed a bit nervous at first, but Jace, whose credits included TV, movies and Broadway, was a rock. His calm transmitted to her, and soon the ogre was jumping up at the princess from under the bridge (in paper form). But her scream prompted the paper ogre to flatten into the river, and she jumped in after him to save him. What she ended up rescuing was an ogre transformed into a human prince by her kindness. He pleaded to come with her on her journey (Jace's pantomime was nothing less than perfect), but she refused. She wanted to be alone and discover the world.

She narrowly escaped the dragon that followed her by entering a dark alley that led her into the gray city. Wherever she met people and gray blocks of buildings, her joy of discovery transformed the people into colorful cutouts, covered the buildings with flowering vines, and made trees bloom. The ogre-prince secretly followed her, scaring off the dragon with an enchanted paper sword. By the time the lonely princess found herself back at the bridge, with stars and moon popping out above her and no ogre in sight, she wept. She was lonely and wanted to go home. And there, on the road back to her kingdom, she found the ogre-prince, who fought off the dragon one more time to save them both. They arrived at the castle in full greenery and flower and kissed at its doorstep, on their way to happily ever after.

Then Penelope's and Jace's kiss got a little out of hand,

and to shouts and laughter, I called "Cut!" and made them do that part again.

"Is it a wrap?" Duncan asked when they'd performed a tamer kiss two or three times to get our angles and close-ups.

"Yes!" I said. "Lunch is on me. You have the trays, Cali?"

"Yep, in the fridge," she said, putting down her camera (she'd been capturing the day in stills). She headed toward the back room with Millie to get the sandwiches and drinks as Wyatt shut down the lights.

"Thank God," Jace said. "I forgot what a nuisance filming is. You have to do everything ten times."

"At least," Duncan agreed.

"But you look great in those tights," Penelope said to Jace, who smacked her butt and kissed her again before they went behind a screen to change into their civvies.

Duncan went over the video one more time, scrolling through the clips on his camera while it was still mounted to the tripod. I hovered next to him, looking over his shoulder, and he wrapped an arm around me and planted a swift, hot kiss on my mouth.

"Do you think it's OK?" I asked as he resumed paging through the clips.

"Better than OK. It's *interesting*." He looked up into my doubtful eyes and smiled. "That's a good thing."

I let out a long breath. "OK. Good. Do you think we can get it edited in time? I feel like I'm putting so much pressure on you."

"No problem. I'm a pro," he said with charming arrogance. "Compositing is going to be a bitch with all the layers of popups we're doing, but it's also going to look badass."

I laughed. "Not sure that's what I'm going for, but I'll take it."

"Oh, you're going to love it when we're done," he said as he stowed the memory cards from his camera in watertight storage cases.

I probably would love it. Almost as much as I loved him at that moment.

I walked away from the camera, grabbed my belly and closed my eyes.

"You OK?"

I opened my eyes to find Sloane watching me, her face full of concern. Her long, dark hair hung around her face today, and she wore simple capris and a T-shirt that were still spattered with clay from her pottery work.

"How do you do it?" I whispered.

She smiled at me as if I were slightly insane. "Do what?"

"The relationship thing."

Her smile broadened, and she led me farther away from the table where Cali had set up the food for the hungry cast and crew.

"I hoped you might be together," Sloane said. "I mean, I see the way he looks at you. And kisses you."

"But that's not a relationship," I murmured. "Is it?"

"Not exactly." Sloane touched the ring on her right hand.

"Alex gave you that?"

"It's a promise ring. It sort of made it official for us, but I knew long before then. Even if we had some stuff to work out. I had to be sure of him."

"What if that's impossible? What if you're just a speed bump on a guy's road to the next woman?"

"Thea." Sloane put a hand on my shoulder. "Take a deep breath. It doesn't all have to happen today. And when I see you two together, it's clear something is happening. Something important."

"But what we have, it's not a relationship. I'm not sure I even want a relationship. I mean, what you have, I admire it, but I don't even know if I'm capable of that."

"What you have is powerful. Are you worried that it's only physical?"

I nodded.

Sloane shook her head. "Trust me. There's a lot of power in the physical. I had no idea how much until I met Alex. And I can see there's more between you. I can see it in your eyes and in the way he helps you. The way he deferred to you today. Maybe all you need is a little time."

"OK," I said, trying to act as if she'd convinced me. "Thanks."

She gave me a hug and drifted back to the others, giving me a moment to myself.

Maybe what I needed wasn't time. Maybe it was time *travel.* I wanted to talk to my mom again, to see my parents when they were happy, to understand what went wrong. I rubbed my mom's ring with my thumb and watched Duncan chatting with Jace and Wyatt, completely comfortable in every situation. God, I envied that confidence. And admired it. Him. My heart about burst when I looked at him, when I thought about all we'd done together on this project — and in each other's arms.

I just wasn't sure it would ever be enough to keep him.

WE FINISHED the edit late on the night before the deadline, the day after I'd refined all the elements of my carousel and proved it could spin. Maybe "we" wasn't the right term, exactly. I relied on Duncan's skill with the video editing software, though by the time we were done, I was pretty sure I could edit a video and he could make a pop-up sculpture, not that he ever would.

The result was strangely entrancing, with our actors moving through the sculptures and layers of effects popping out, including pieces I'd made that didn't even end up in the final carousel, like bursts of flowers and the starry sky. Ez and Gary had refined their music to fit the timing of the rough edit we'd given them, and it was perfect — cinematic and quirky. Everybody got credits at the end.

"It's kind of like Charlie Chaplin doing a Disney movie on LSD," Duncan said after we'd screened the final cut on his laptop from the comfort of his couch.

I laughed. "Unfortunately, I think you may be right."

"*Fortunately,* darlin'. This is art at its most whimsical. I think they're going to love it. Do you have to bring the whole piece in person?"

"No, they want to see pictures. I called and asked if I could send a link to the video with an explanation, and they said that would be enough for them to make their decision. I'm also sending pictures of the carousel."

"So that means we have to upload the video. I'll make it unlisted on my channel." He opened a web page, clicked around and typed in a few words as the upload began.

My stomach tightened with sudden nervousness. "Does that mean your fans will see it?"

"No, only the people with the link can see it," Duncan said. "But I can't wait to make it live later. You're going to get a zillion hits on this thing."

I stared at him. "Make it live?"

"Yeah," he said, a puzzled look on his face. "You know, put it on the vlog."

"But we never talked about putting it on the vlog." Tendrils of panic wove themselves through my insides, jagged and constricting, like the thorny thicket that trapped Sleeping Beauty.

"Thea." Duncan put the laptop on the coffee table as the upload progress bar advanced. He sat back and wrapped an arm around my shoulders, pulling me closer. "You said you wanted to do a collaboration. A collab means posting it online, doesn't it?"

"I — I don't want to."

A shadow of impatience crossed his face. "Well, why in the hell not? We can wait till after the exhibit so we don't take any gas out of the gallery show. But the world needs to see this. It's brilliant."

I was in full panic mode now, and I didn't know exactly why. I shrugged off his arm and sat straight up, at the edge of the cushion, staring at the laptop with dread as the upload neared its completion.

"I don't want to," I said again. "I don't want all those people looking at it."

"This is what art is about," Duncan said. "What are you afraid of?"

"I'm not afraid."

"You're petrified. Look at you." Was that disgust or concern in his voice?

"I'm not," I said, tears coming to my eyes as I stood and took a few steps away from him, trying to control my rapid breathing.

"My God, Thea. What's wrong?"

"You just want the clicks," I snapped — a reaction that I knew was, at some level, more defensive than reasonable — but I couldn't stop myself.

"You really are insane, do you know that?" He stood, too, but I took a step away before he could touch me. I totally lost my mind when he touched me.

"Maybe I am insane," I said. "This is what I was afraid of."

"What?" Duncan asked in exasperation. "What are you really afraid of?"

I honestly couldn't answer his question, because I didn't know. Or maybe I did. I was afraid of people seeing me. Knowing me. Rejecting me. Of . . .

"Are you afraid of me?" he asked, more quietly this time. "Have I once chased you with a camera? Pressured you in any way?"

I turned to face him. "You — you *are* pressure," I said. "I can't think around you."

His answering smile had a touch of worry to it. "Isn't that a good thing?"

"I don't know what I'm doing here. I can't do this!" I moved toward the door.

"Thea? Thea! Don't go. Don't go!"

But I did go, slamming the door, running across the hall, locking my door behind me.

I was sucking in air. My chest hurt. I felt cold and clammy, and I was trembling. The apartment was dark except for the glow of my computer monitor. I didn't want any more light. I wanted to hide in the shadows.

I had no idea what had happened in there. Duncan's world was so different from mine. I wanted him so much, but I just couldn't put myself out there the way he did. Why would he ever want to spend time with me, anyway? My mind was spinning in ridiculous circles, and I was sobbing.

Somewhere inside, I knew my thoughts were not a little absurd, but the darkness was so strong, so convincing. The darkness that had visited me over the years, all too often. I could get lost in it. I was lost in it now.

What had I done? Thrown away a chance at — at love?

But no. He'd never said he loved me. He was playing with me. Playing with my soul. I was another collab, another Lolly, only not as delectable.

And I should be angry, shouldn't I? Wasn't it all about the clicks with him?

But what he'd said came back to me. He was right. He hadn't pressured me once about going on camera. He hadn't talked me up to amuse his fans. And he'd given me so much of his time for the past few weeks — so much he seemed like a comfortable habit. A bad habit, maybe. Or a really good one.

But how could he pressure me when he knew how I felt about this? How could he?

The darkness was talking again, but I couldn't argue with it. It made me want to run. And so I did.

"What's wrong?" my father said as he answered the door in striped pajama bottoms and a white T-shirt. His thinning, silvered hair stuck up, and his glasses were askew. "Are you OK?"

"Oh, Dad," I said, and I threw myself in his arms.

"There, there," he said, patting my back. "Why don't you come in and tell me all about it?"

But I didn't want to tell him anything, not really, so I just cried for a while at the kitchen table while my dad made tea. I sipped it as he stared at me, and then he started reading one of the magazines that were stacked there as if I hadn't shown up hysterical at his house while that annoying old Irish clock in the foyer was bonging midnight.

His lack of reaction was just what I needed, I think. Eventually, the panic dissipated under the calming influence of Earl Grey. After I exhaled a long, noisy sigh, my dad pushed his glasses down his nose and looked at me.

"I suppose I have to ask again if I have to kill the young man?"

I sort of laughed, though a little bit of a sob tried to get out. "No. It's not his fault."

"Are you sure? Because usually it's the guy's fault. It was mine, anyway."

"Oh, Dad," I said, though his comment made me curious. "Whatever happened with you and Mom was a long time ago."

"The past is always with us." He took a sip of his tea. "When I think how many times I could have tried and didn't — could have tried to make things right —"

"When I was little," I said, "I used to ask Mom if we were ever going back to Bohemia, but she said that bridge was long burnt."

"She burned it, but I can't blame her. Thank God I got to see her one more time."

"What?" I sat up straight, confused.

"About a year ago," he said matter-of-factly. "When she came to town."

"She what? She — she came to Bohemia?"

Now it was his turn to look puzzled. "She never told you?"

"No. No!" I sifted through my memories, trying to remember when she could have come without me knowing about it.

"I think she said you were on a business trip. Some kind of training?"

Oh, shit. There had been a few days when I was at a course in Kansas City for the ad agency. I'd talked to my mom on the phone while I was there, and she'd never said anything about being in Florida. And she certainly didn't say anything when I came back.

"She came for a few days. She didn't stay here," Dad said regretfully, "though she did come by to talk. She was taking care of some last-minute things, she said. Consolidating bank accounts and paperwork and such. I told her she shouldn't worry, that she was going to get better, but she said she wanted to plan. Honestly, she didn't look well."

"I think we knew by that point that it was only a matter of time," I said softly, wondering at this last secret she'd kept from me. "Why — what did you talk about?"

He smiled ruefully. "You, mostly. She wanted me to look out for you."

I nodded. She loved me that much. But I was hurt a little, too, that my Dad had reached out to me only because of her. "I thought you really needed me to work for you. I thought that's why you offered me the job."

"I did. I *do.* I would have asked you to come home even if Liz hadn't said anything. I want you to take over the business, sweetheart. You know that."

"I don't think I can," I said. "I want to do my own thing." But what was my own thing? My art that no one would ever see? How ridiculous was that? How ridiculous was I?

"You have to work it out for yourself," he said. "I know enough in my advanced middle age that you can never make anybody do something they don't want to do."

For a moment, images of Duncan crossed my mind,

Duncan enthusiastically helping me with my art project — cooking me breakfast — making sex so hot it burned. I hadn't made him do any of that. Maybe he *had* wanted to.

But all the old insecurities nibbled at me, all too real. For so long, I'd felt awkward and inadequate, still the girl being pushed against the lockers and mocked in the halls. Pretending to have a boyfriend didn't change any of that.

"Listen," Dad said, "I've got a meeting in the morning. Feel free to stay here. Your old room is made up. Are you going to be OK?"

"Yeah, I guess so. I'm sorry I woke you."

"I wasn't really asleep. I don't sleep much anymore."

"You taking your medicine?"

He looked at me strangely for a minute. "Yes. Don't worry about your old man. Get some rest, and we'll have breakfast in the morning before I go in."

"OK." He left, and I heard his bedroom door shut behind him just as the clock bonged one. It had been marking every fifteen minutes; the top of the hour was always a production, as the full Westminster Quarters were followed by a clang for every hour. How could anybody sleep with that thing in the house? Though I had as a kid, somehow, before my parents' fights became louder and longer.

I tried lying down on the couch in the cluttered living room, not wanting to muss the guest bed, but the caffeinated tea and my busy brain conspired against me. I thought about my mother and the last few months of her life, about her coming to Bohemia and not telling me. Did she think I'd reject my dad if he reached out to me? I'd never resented him. If anything, I'd missed him, and the short visits with him over the years only made me wish even more that our family had never dissolved.

Giving up on sleep, I sifted through the overflowing book-shelves in the living room until I found the photo albums. True to form, my father had thrown nothing away, and there was still one with photos of all of us: my mom holding me at the beach. My dad and mom holding hands on the tiny Bohemia Beach boardwalk. All three of us in a Christmas portrait, and another I'd taken of them on their anniversary, badly framed. One shot showed us hugging Mickey Mouse at Disney World. Well, I was the only one hugging the mouse. My dad looked annoyed, and my mother was gazing at me indulgently. They must have handed the camera to some tourist who didn't want to wait for us all to smile. At least we were together. That wasn't long before Mom and I left for Wichita.

The clock chimed 2 a.m. Damn it, I was never going to get any sleep here, but the idea of going back to my place — which was also essentially Duncan's place — was still upset-ting, partly because now that my panic had subsided, I was embarrassed at how I'd acted. Anxiety had betrayed me again. If I couldn't control it, I had to break things off. How much worse would it be when he broke my heart?

I wandered into the foyer as the last notes cleaved the air. The clock really was lovely, even if it was annoying. I supposed I should appreciate it more, but it was made for a house where it could bong away on one floor while the family slept on another. It was made by one of Mom's ances-tors and was one of the few things that had come over with them from Ireland.

Its silvered face had dulled with time, but the brass orna-mentation was still exquisite. The hands were dark, delicate wonders that complemented the ornate black numbers on the face. I ran a finger over the dusty wooden scrollwork of the case. It was familiar, somehow.

Oh, my God.

It wasn't just familiar. It was intimately known to me. The heart of the carved pattern was the triskele, the three connected spirals. Spirals like the ones in my ring. In fact, around the face, it seemed the triskele pattern was repeated several times, in different sizes, nestled one within the other. It was a master-piece of art and geometry that culminated in a tiny triskele carved within a larger one above the round clock face.

It's the key to time travel, my mother had said.

My heart beat faster. This wasn't a time machine, surely. But maybe — just maybe — could there be a connection to my ring? My mother's ring, and her grandmother's before her?

I slid the ring off my finger and examined it closely, then held it up to the pattern carved into the clock. It was the same — but different. But what was different about it?

Of course!

As soon as I knew how it was different, I had a feeling I knew why. It was a mirror image. And that meant . . .

I held the face of the ring, the deep grooves of its pattern, up to the tiny carving at the clock's apex. I turned it slowly against the wood, testing the fit. And then it happened.

It clicked into place, perfectly notched into the grooves. I sucked in a breath, but nothing happened.

I pressed. I jiggled. Disappointed, I pulled the ring away and looked at the wood carving on the clock more closely.

Was that — could that be a thin line around the inner-most triskele? A circle?

An almost invisible groove in the wood?

And if it was circular, could it turn?

Hands shaking, I set the ring against the grooves again and oriented it until it clicked into place. And then, pressing firmly, I twisted the ring.

And it turned.

THERE WAS A *SNICK,* a satisfying sound that seemed to evoke a tiny sigh from the clock, as if it was letting out a breath of air. Something had unlocked, I was sure of it. But what?

I slipped the ring back on and examined the clock. Finally, I picked it up and turned it around. On the back, a long, narrow panel that ran along the lower half of the clock had revealed itself, tilting open just enough to expose a chamber inside.

"Holy shit," I said aloud, sticking my fingers in the slot, opening the hinged panel all the way, hoping no spiders waited inside. I touched something both rough and smooth and managed to get enough of a purchase on it to slide it out.

"A book?" The slim, leather-bound tome emerged in my hand. I shoved the clock back on the table and turned the book over. The brown leather binding was tooled with Celtic knots. I gingerly opened it, expecting ancient magic.

Instead, I got my mother's elegant, concise handwriting. A different kind of magic altogether.

My eyes blurred for a moment, so much so that I couldn't read the words. The very fact that she was speaking to me from across that bourne from which no traveler returns — it would have been enough to shatter me any other time. But I'd had enough crying for tonight, and now that I'd opened Mom's time machine, I wanted to see what was inside.

The diary began a month before my mother married my father. It was strange and wondrous to read it. Once I began, I almost put it back, because it was so personal. But I figured my mother wouldn't have planted those dreams of time machines in my head, telling me my ring was the key to time travel, if she hadn't wanted me to unlock her treasure.

I sat at the kitchen table with another cup of tea and read about her giddy preparations for their wedding on the beach, about their honeymoon in the Keys (she left out the most personal details, to my relief), about the first months and years of their life together. About how much they were in love.

As I read, I also dreaded learning about when it all changed — dreaded it but needed to know. And the beginning of the end went like this:

I confirmed it today — the doctor tells me I'm definitely pregnant. I can't wait to have this baby. I have such high hopes for her. I hope she has Milt's brains and talent and my imagination. I hope she will be happy. I know it's a girl. Somehow, I just know. I love her already. She's going to be amazing.

Amazing. Duncan's word. Duncan's word for me.

I swallowed and kept on reading, unveiling, page by page, a childhood I didn't even remember. In those first few years of my life, when I thought my parents were fighting about me, there was another story being written.

Milt was at the track again. He gets so high and excited. That's how I remember him from when I first fell in love with him. So full of life and energy. But it's different now. It's worst when he starts gambling. He loses, and then he gets angry. Dark. He neglects his work. He neglects everything. He accuses me of things sometimes, things that make no sense. He drinks so much. One day I came home and found him drunk on the front porch. Thea was in her crib crying. It's like he forgot she was there.

He scares me sometimes. We fight. And then on the good days, the good weeks, when he acts like he could capture the moon and hang it in our living room, it's easy to get sucked into hope. But I see something in his eyes that never used to be there, a disconnect. It worries me. Something's wrong. Really wrong. I've asked him to see someone. He won't do it. I don't know what to do. I have to protect the baby. But I love him so much.

My father? She was writing about *my father?* How could I not remember any of this?

But I did, sort of. I remember him being angry. I remember their fights and, rarely, his exhilarating energy. But I was so wrapped up in myself, a child at the center of my own universe, worrying when I heard them shout my name. I thought it had been about me.

How naive I'd been.

The unraveling of my parents' marriage was revealed in page after painful page as I skipped through the diary. But so was the love. My mother loved so much about my father. They shared a passion for art, among other things. And it was clear that, when he wasn't possessed by his illness — there was no doubt that he suffered — he loved her, too.

Thea and I celebrated her fifth birthday today. Milt spent the day at the bar. She asked where he was, and it just about broke my heart. I can't put off my decision any longer. He won't get help, and I can't put Thea through this hell. She deserves calm

*and love and safety and a father who puts her first. I've done
everything I can. I have to walk away for both our sakes. I hope
she understands someday that I'm doing this because I love her,
and I love him, too. I don't think he will ever get help until he
understands how much he's lost.*

The horrible thing is, I've lost him, too.

I was out of tears, but my throat was scratchy as I read
more about her plans. Her heartbreak. Her goodbyes. And
then a brief, final entry that said she was consigning the diary
to the clock.

And then another entry, dated a year ago, when she
visited Bohemia.

My dear Thea,

*I hope you are the one who finds this diary. I couldn't bring
myself to give it you. Not yet. I think time will reveal it to you
when you're ready. I want you to know how precious you are to
me and to your father. He has changed so much. We both have. I
left him for your sake, but I hope you understand now that I did
it for myself, too. And he let us go because he loved us. I know
that now.*

*You are a wonderful young woman. I don't think I told you
that enough. You are beautiful and talented and precious to me. I
love you, sweetheart. Know always that you are worthy of that
love. I see the shadows in your eyes sometimes, and I worry. But
I know that you will grow your wings and fly.*

With all my love,
Mom

I had a few tears left after all. I lay my head on my arms
on the table and wept again, silently, missing her voice and

her kindness and her humor. Her cookies and her art lessons. Walks with Pookie, his soft ears flapping as he padded along the sidewalk between us. The home she made for me in a world where I was so often lost.

The smell of coffee and the popping of the toaster woke me.

"I thought you were a morning person," my dad said as he buttered his English muffin and I rubbed my eyes and stretched my stiff muscles. "Did you sleep here all night?"

I didn't answer right away, but I accepted a cup of coffee from him and eyed him as he sat across from me with his mug and muffin.

"Don't look at me like that," he said. "The next muffin is yours."

"Why didn't you tell me you were sick?"

His brow creased. "I'm not sick."

"When I was a little girl. What was it, Dad? That isn't blood-pressure medicine you take, is it?"

My father studied the English muffin in his hand and took a big bite of it, chewed and swallowed.

"How do you know?"

"I found mom's diary. She hid it in the clock."

His eyebrows lifted. "That's what she was doing with that damn clock. I tried to get her to take it."

"You're not answering the question."

"You didn't need to know." His forehead was creased with pain.

"I want to know now."

"All right," he said. "I was — I am bipolar."

"You are?" I asked, though it made sense now, all of it. And the news was, strangely, a relief to hear. To know there'd been a terrible but real reason for the end of my parents' marriage. I felt like an idiot for not recognizing his disease sooner, but my brief times with him as I grew up held no clues, and now he seemed as solid as a rock.

"I've been on medication for a long time," he said. "There have been ups and downs, but nothing like I was when you were young. I feel OK. I needed to get better after what I went through with your mother. I'm just sorry it took losing you both to get my life together."

"Oh, Dad," I said. "I'm sorry, too." I took a sip of my coffee and got up to butter the muffin halves that had just popped out of the toaster, the normality of the task grounding me as he spoke.

"I should have told you, maybe, but what would have been the point?" he said. "I control it with medication. I gave up alcohol years ago. And once she started allowing you to visit me, after she knew I was all right, I didn't want to ruin what little relationship we had."

"By not telling me what you were struggling with? I would have understood."

"I'm not so sure. Your mother never told you?"

"Maybe she thought it wasn't her secret to tell. Not that it should have been anyone's secret."

"You're right," he said as I sat again at the table. "But it was easier to pretend things were OK. And they are OK, now, if I don't think too much about what I lost." He looked up at me, and his eyes were watery. "I'm so sorry."

I got up and went to him and hugged him, and he patted my back, saying, "I'm sorry. I'm sorry."

After a minute, I sat back down and ate my muffin. What the hell else do you say after that?

"Will I see you at work later?" he asked as he wrapped up his breakfast.

"Not today. I have other stuff to do."

A few minutes later, we both left the house. I took the diary with me.

"We're OK, then?" he asked me on the front step, looking worried.

"Yes, Dad. Of course we are. I'm sorry I didn't ask more questions."

"I'm sorry I didn't tell you more. Anyway, you were a child," he said. "We wanted to protect you. I love you, you know."

"I know." I smiled. "Thanks for putting up with me."

He gave me a brief, wordless hug and went on his way.

I drove home to my apartment, my mind full of everything I'd learned. In the back of it all, I wondered how I was going to talk to Duncan again. I still hadn't figured out what to do, but I loved him. As irrational as I'd been, as much as my heart was at risk, I loved him anyway. I just didn't know how many levels of brave I could be, even with my mom's last message to me ringing in my mind. Maybe I was worthy of love, but the truth was, I didn't know *how* to be worthy.

And I still questioned Duncan's motives. I was sure he wanted clicks and money and fame. And he wanted at least some of me; there was no denying our physical connection. Could he want the rest of me, too? I didn't know if there was any room for me and my insecurities in his on-air world, but for the first time, I saw a path to obliterating my fears. I would do it because I had to.

I pulled into our parking lot, under the big oak tree, and almost ran into Duncan coming out the front door of our building.

I halted, not sure what to say, dying to say something. His

face was haggard, and he was hauling a backpack and a roller suitcase.

"Thea. Fancy meeting you here."

"Hi, Duncan." My voice was scratchy from the long night, and he looked at me with a dark expression.

"Where were you?" he asked, his voice rough, his gaze roving the parking lot. Did I hear jealousy in his question? Worry? Or simple anger? "I knocked on your door. I wanted to tell you I sent you the link to the video. You didn't answer."

"I went to my dad's."

He nodded, looking down at his sneakers, and we stood there, at an impasse. Suddenly, I wanted to hold him, not just out of need — though being near him inevitably ignited something primal inside me — but because I wanted to connect with him. To tell him everything I'd learned. I took a step forward, but something in his rigid posture stopped me, and I paused.

"Going on a shoot?" I asked.

"To the airport."

"The airport!"

"To Texas."

"Oh, no. Is it your mom?"

"She's very ill. My father called in the wee hours. I thought about what you said. I thought I should do the right thing, whatever that is." He tone was bitter.

"You know what it is," I said softly. *Duncan wants to do the right thing. Why have I had so much trouble believing that?* My heart swelled with sympathy, and I moved to hug him, but he sidestepped me. *Damn.* "Let me come with you."

"No," Duncan said brusquely. "You don't want to come."

"Yes, I do."

"Thea," he said, looking me straight in the eye for the first time. "I don't think you know what you want. Goodbye."

He pushed past me, heading to his car, leaving me reeling. Is this the answer I got when I tried to reach out? Maybe it was the answer I deserved.

"Wait! Duncan!" I called out, starting to run toward his car. But he was already revving the engine, pulling out and away. Had he seen me?

I was a fool. I helplessly watched him drive down the street, wondering if I'd lost him forever. It had been a wrenching night, but I was out of tears.

Goddamn it.

A train rocketed through downtown and roared past the other side of our building, rattling the tracks, blasting its loud, lonely horn. In its wake, the mockingbird sang from the oak tree. No matter what happened, that mockingbird kept singing.

A fresh morning breeze carried the tune and the scent of the ocean, and I took a deep breath.

I had one more thing to do before I got some sleep: Submit my work to the art gallery. I headed into the building, ready to take a chance.

I TRIED to call Duncan over the next few days, but he didn't answer. Maybe he was with his mother in the hospital, where they didn't like cell phones, I thought. But I knew the more likely truth was that he wasn't ready to talk to me. I'd pissed him off, or maybe I'd hurt his feelings. Probably both. After all, I'd basically told him I didn't trust him. That's what it came down to. And perhaps I didn't — or hadn't. But as I relived our confused conversation — well, *my* confused conversation — and recalled his pain the next morning as he left for the airport, I realized that I *wanted* to trust him.

I resorted to texts, next. Simple ones, like: *Can we talk?*

And then: *I'm sorry about the other night.*

And finally, I made a pop-up sculpture of a Scottish thistle and shot a video with my phone of me opening it. I sent him the clip with this caption: *I miss you. I'm ready to talk when you are. I hope everything is OK.*

It was the closest I'd gotten to admitting any kind of emotion, though I was feeling so much, I thought I would burst. In Duncan's absence, I relived my parents' past, reading and rereading my mother's diary. In the meantime, I worried that Duncan would never talk to me again.

I teetered on the raw edge of despair for a week. I even contemplated flying to Austin and trying to find him, but since I knew so little about the situation with his mother, I chose to wait it out.

His video blog also was silent for seven days. On the eighth, on a quiet Friday afternoon in my dad's office, I got a notification of a new video. It was all I could do to wait until I got home to watch it, since I didn't want my dad to see me break down again anytime soon.

As soon as I got to my place, I sat at my desktop computer and navigated to Duncan's channel to play it.

The video didn't start with the usual *Flyte Night* opener. In fact, it was just Duncan sitting on an ugly sofa in what had to be a hospital waiting room. He looked tired, but his voice was clear and calm and intimate. Hearing it was like a kick to my stomach. I missed him so much. And as I listened to what he said, I longed to hold him tight.

"Hello, friends," Duncan said to the camera. "*Flyte Night* has had a bit of a rest this week because I've been dealing with life off camera. I know, it's hard to believe, but there *is* life off camera. That fact has only recently come to my attention.

"You all know I usually share my life directly with you, as it tends more toward comedy than drama, as a rule. It's a little different this time, and for once, I don't feel like I can tell you everything. I'm hoping it's enough for you to know there's been a death in the family.

"It's hard to lose people," he continued, his pale blue eyes preternaturally clear. "I've made it a habit to lose anyone I got close to simply by moving on. This time, I didn't have a choice, but it wasn't so hard to lose my mother. It was a relief, really. It was the end of a struggle — hers and, I'll admit, mine, too. That's all between me and her and the angels, but I wanted to share a kind of revelation that hit me when I saw her pass, and that is: I'm going to have to rethink how I deal with the world. You wouldn't think one second of one minute of one day would change anyone all that much. Sometimes you think you've already put the past behind you, and then suddenly you're tripping over it, and it's messy and painful and in your face. And then it's gone, all the reasons you are the way you are. All the excuses.

"That's all," he added. "It's not a revelation that is easy for me to lay out in front of you like a hand of cards. A lot of answers are still in the deck, and I'm still looking for the aces. I guess I'll be looking from now on with totally different glasses." He pulled a pair of sunglasses from off camera and slipped them over his eyes. "I'll see you lads and lasses soon. Flyte out."

And the video ended with a fade to back. No credits, no music, no copyright. Just — nothing.

A blank slate. An end. A beginning, maybe.

I felt Duncan's message in my bones. It wasn't directed at me, I knew that — except maybe that bit about living life off camera — but given all I'd just learned about my family, his words seemed to apply. The world looked different now.

Duncan looked different.

I needed to go to Austin, be with him for the funeral. It would squeeze my budget, but I'd find a way. I needed him, and I liked to think he needed me. I needed to convince him that he did.

I was the one who always told my friends to go with their feelings. All along, I'd been going with the wrong feelings, the suspicious ones, the scared ones. They'd crowded out the important ones: respect. Confidence. Love.

I went to a travel site to search for flights and heard a noise in the hallway.

There was something about the sound that made me wonder — made me think — hope — it might be him.

A door closed. His, I was sure of it. Could he be home? Or was it just one of his friends crashing on his couch again?

I had to find out. I stood, then almost jumped right out of my skirt when a loud knock sounded on my door.

About eighteen emotions careened through my body all at once, though there was no guarantee it was him.

God, I hope it's him.

"Thea?"

It was him.

I threw open my door and threw my arms around his neck.

"I'm so sorry, Duncan. I'm sorry about your mom and about being weird," I said into his ear as I damn near smothered him. "I'm so sorry."

"Darlin', darlin'," he said, sounding just a wee bit amused.

He pushed me inside the apartment and shut the door behind him, even as I still clung to him. "Don't be sorry, love." He let me squeeze him for a minute. "Does this mean you don't think I'm here for the clicks?"

My face flushed hot as I released him. "I don't know why you're here after all the stupid things I said, but I'm glad you are. I'm sorry I said that."

He smiled, but his eyes looked tired. His shorts and T-shirt were rumpled, and there was something about his bearing that seemed different. Ordinary. Not the larger-than-life superstar who'd interviewed me at the theater.

I reached out and touched his cheek. "I missed you. I have a lot to tell you."

"Uh-oh." He was only half-joking, I thought.

"I was worried about you."

"I got your messages. I just — there's no excuse for not responding, but I just wasn't up for it. I already had one drama to deal with . . . not that you're a drama."

I sighed. "I *am* a drama. You don't have to explain. I was having a weird night, and it got even weirder, and then you left. I want to tell you about it, but it can wait. Did you come straight from the airport?"

"Yeah, just dropped my bags across the hall."

"Want a beer?"

"Please," he said. He followed me to the kitchen and watched as I popped the cap off a bottle of Bohemia Brewing Company Red. I handed it to him and grabbed one for myself.

"Are you OK? Did you already have the funeral?" I asked as we made our way to the couch.

"We're going to have something later, the next time my sister comes home from London," he said. "My father has the ashes. But I don't really need the closure. It's over. It's so strange that it's over."

"Your mother may be gone, but she'll be with you for a long time, I think," I said as his brow creased. "I know that's probably not what you want to hear.

He fell into the cushions with a sigh, and I sat a few inches away, one leg tucked under me so I could face him, watch him breathe. The glow of early evening lit up the room, gilded his hair, as he sipped his beer and looked off into space. With him there, my apartment suddenly felt like home. Maybe absence made the heart grow smarter. I only wish it made mine a little braver. Now that he was here, fear muted my planned declarations. But he was here, wasn't he? He came back to me. I had hope, now.

"Did you enter your piece in the show?" Duncan asked.

"I sent them the photos and the video. I haven't heard yet."

"I'm glad," he said. "It's really good, you know."

"Thanks. That's mostly because of you."

"No, it's not! Don't believe it for a minute."

I shrugged. "Well, there's a lot of you in it."

"The handsome prince, you mean?" he teased, his dimple showing for the first time this evening.

"No!" I smiled and smacked his arm. "The photography."

"Oh, that." He grinned.

"It was a collaboration," I said, "and I want you to put it on the vlog after the exhibit. I mean, if it's accepted into the exhibit."

Duncan's eyebrows rose as he sipped his beer. "Are you sure? You really don't have to. I didn't mean to pressure you. It's yours, and you can do whatever you want with it."

I shook my head. "You were right. What's the point of art

if no one sees it? Maybe a philosopher has an answer to that, but I don't want my work to be like a tree that falls in the forest with no one to hear it. I want it to be seen. Even if no one likes it, the important thing is to make it and share it. And I'll make more. I'll make it to please myself, but I'm also going to put it out there. It's time."

Duncan smiled and took my hand, tugging me closer.

"It's time," he repeated. "Absolutely." He leaned in and kissed me lightly on the mouth.

It was brief. Sweet. Almost chaste. And yet the kiss kindled a fire in my blood.

I tried to quench the flames. As much as I needed him physically, we needed to talk.

"What changed your mind?" he asked. The question was simple, but I sensed a weight behind it.

"I think I knew when you asked me that I was being irrational. I just needed to work out some things."

He nodded. Wary.

I quelled my anxiety and changed the subject. "I saw your vlog. You had a hard week."

"Ha. You could say that. It wasn't so much watching my mother fade away that was hard. I mean, it was, but it wasn't unexpected, and it was a blessing to end her suffering. She had a bleeding ulcer. She'd been slowly killing herself for years. The worst thing was watching my father try to deal with it. He still loves her, in spite of everything."

"And you?"

"I loved her once. I still do, I suppose, or some memory of her. Maybe it's biological. We had a bond, as twisted as it was. She said she was sorry." Duncan looked surprised, reliving the moment. "That was a novelty."

I reached over and squeezed his hand, let it go. "She never

said she was sorry before?"

"Noooo," Duncan said. He took another sip of beer. "I've been angry with her for a long time, but watching her die — " He finished off his beer and set the bottle on the coffee table. "It was like letting all the air out of a balloon. I just didn't have the outrage anymore. It all dissipated, almost all at once. It was an odd sensation."

"How do you feel now?"

"Still pretty strange. But glad to see you." He caught my gaze and held it. "Are you OK? Really?"

"I am. I mean, I've had some doubts, especially since I've learned about my dad."

"Learned what?" he asked, sounding concerned.

"Oh, it's OK. He's OK. It's just — it's kind of a long story, but I learned that he's bipolar. Has been for a long time. His problems are what broke up my parents all those years ago. I have to admit, there were a couple of times this week when I wondered if I should be worried about inheriting his mental illness. But I think I'm OK." I took a deep breath, admitting something to myself, to him. "It's pretty clear I've fought with depression and anxiety over the years, but it's nothing like what he went through. And I'm going to see someone, get some counseling. I — I'm sorry if I took it out on you. I'm sorry I got so crazy the other night."

"You weren't crazy. I shouldn't have said that. A bloody poor choice of words, given what you just told me. I like all of you, you know."

This time Duncan took my hand as I pondered his choice of words: *I like you.*

"You don't have to be happy all the time," he went on. "God knows I'm not."

"No one would guess," I said.

"Unless you really know me." There was the slightest hint of a smile in his eyes.

"You know," he continued, "I wondered about your dad when I saw what he was taking, when we went over there for dinner. My mother was on at least one of those drugs at one time."

I looked at him in shock. "You knew they weren't blood-pressure meds?"

"I guessed. I didn't realize you didn't know."

"Wow." I was silent for a minute.

"How did you find out about your dad?" he asked.

I explained about the diary. Duncan seemed fascinated.

"So the ring really did have a secret." His eyes got that twinkly, mischievous look, and he began to rub the back of my hand, the ring, with his thumb. "That's *verrra* cool."

"Those rolled 'R's' aren't going to work on me anymore," I said, but I couldn't repress a smile.

And, damn it, they *were* working. He inched closer until his body pressed against mine, strong and warm and real. His touch reminded me how terribly I'd missed him. Heat built in my core, even as I tried to stay focused on what I wanted to tell him. Needed to tell him.

But he leaned over me, grabbed the beer out of my hand and put it on the coffee table, reminding me of the first time we'd kissed on this couch. He pressed his lips to my neck, to the sensitive spot just below my ear. The kiss was whisper-light, as was the next and the next, traveling down to my shoulder, where my boat-neck top revealed just a hint of skin. His free hand moved to my knee and slid up under my skirt, trailing fire along my legs, and then I had all the cool discipline of an erupting volcano as his mouth claimed mine.

I whimpered as he pushed me backward against the cushions, his tongue driving between my lips, sliding against mine, penetrating my mouth, making me wild. His intensity was electrifying. Maybe he needed to burn away his fatigue, his sadness. I knew something had changed between us, but this had not, this molten physical connection that made me want to give him everything.

And this time, I felt not just the fire, but joy in the fact that he wanted me. *Me.* He hadn't dropped me at the first (or second or third) sign of trouble. He was kissing me. *Me.* And I loved it.

Loved *him.*

But this was no time to tell him, not when his mouth was ravening mine. I didn't want anything to interrupt his kisses, his touch, the finger he slid under my panties and slipped inside my creamy cleft. He *hmmm'd* in appreciation when he felt how wet I was.

"Duncan," I groaned.

"Yes, wench?" he teased as he stroked my inner walls with his clever finger, melting away my last resistance.

"I — I've missed you so much."

"The feeling is mutual," he said gruffly, grabbing my panties and pulling them down my legs, knocking my sandals off in the process. He flipped up my skirt and ducked his head between my thighs, and then his tongue was invading my most intimate place, teasing my clit, flicking and sucking that little bundle of nerves until it throbbed, until my sex clenched with need.

I threaded my fingers into his thick hair and uttered nearly incoherent sounds of pleasure and pleading as he licked and sucked and teased, as his rough beard scraped my tender inner thighs and labia, as his hands clasped my ass, lifting me toward his hungry mouth.

The explosion, when it came, was in slow motion, blossoms of fire rippling through me, a seemingly never-ending orgasm that had me groaning his name. When he finally released me and I opened my eyes, gasping for breath, I marveled at the way the amber light caught his pale eyes and his smile. He licked his lips and leaned in to kiss me, making me taste myself as he plunged his tongue into my mouth again. It was so naughty, so good, as tremors of ecstasy still rippled outward from my pussy.

God, he made me feel empowered. Pretty. Sexy, even.

"I want you to fuck me," I whispered as he ended the kiss. "Fuck me hard, Duncan. Own me. Tear me apart."

"*Fuck,* I like it when you talk dirty," he said, yanking off his shirt and pants and Batman boxers, which made me smile. As he stripped, I pulled off my shirt, my bra, and then I took in the breathtaking sight of him, naked and gorgeous and —

"Oh, God," I moaned as he flipped me over and positioned me so I knelt at the edge of the couch.

"Hold on to the back of the couch," he ordered as he pushed up my skirt. "I going to fuck you this way, and I'm going to fuck you deep."

His big hands cupped my buttocks, gliding along my smooth skin, squeezing my flesh, spreading my cheeks to let his hot, hard cock slide against my crack. Teasing. Dominating.

I sucked in a breath, for a second not sure what he would do. Willing to do anything. And then his shaft notched itself in my drenched cleft, and he plunged.

I cried out. It had been over a week since I'd had him inside me, a week when I thought I might never have him again. Now he possessed me, driving hard into my wet passage, slamming into my depths. With one thumb, he brushed my anus, a sensation so wrong, so delicious, it sent a shudder through my loins. I moaned, and he grasped my hips and shifted angles, his cock probing depths I didn't know I had.

One of his hands crept around my front, cupping a pendulous breast, manipulating the fleshy globe until my nipples hardened to sharp points. He flicked the one he was playing with, and I lost my mind.

With another cry, I convulsed hard around him, and in the next second he shattered me again as he shot his seed inside me. He came with me like a supernova, with a shout, yanking me against him. It was pain and pleasure all at once as I shook with him, every nerve ending alive and snapping with fire.

He bent low over my back as our bodies slowly calmed, his hot breath at my ear, and kissed my neck, my spine. He gently withdrew, and I sighed at the loss of him. He rolled me into him, spooning my body against his, working my skirt off so I could feel his cock against my naked behind. We were all slick skin and heat, yet I shivered to feel him, still half-erect, settling against me.

We fit. *Damn,* we fit so well.

It was a long moment before I realized Duncan had fallen asleep.

I couldn't help it. I giggled softly as he exhaled into my hair, an adorable beast, rutting one moment, unconscious the next.

This is happiness, I thought. *Fuck all my insecurities. This is happiness. This moment. This minute.*

When I awoke, I was in my bed, and I was alone, and the pink light outside suggested that it was dawn. I'd slept straight through — gone to bed without supper, apparently

— and I started to wonder if it had all been a dream. But then I stretched and felt the evidence of the night before. I hugged myself. The week had drained me, and I'd needed the sleep. My worries were gone this morning. Gone for now. Worries would never go away forever, but Duncan was back, and I'd held him close. Held him inside me.

I hadn't told him yet. And he had told me he . . . liked me. Liked me.

He wasn't here, but I wasn't worried.

Not much.

"REMEMBER WHAT THE ASTRONOMER SAID?"

Duncan had knocked on my door just after noon. He'd already gone out, shot a video with some surfers and posted it to his channel, "feeding the beast," as he liked to say. Now we sat at my retro dining table, eating a pizza he'd brought over.

"Refresh my memory," I said.

"The Perseids meteor shower is happening now. It peaks next week, but we might have a shot at some tonight. Want to go to the beach?"

"Are you going to wear your Darth Vader boxers?"

"I don't have to wear anything at all," he said impishly.

"I am not bailing you out of jail. Better wear something."

"I'm also OK with you being naked," he said.

I couldn't help but smile. "OK. I mean, I'll go with you. I'll reserve judgment on being naked."

"Tease," he said.

"So I got an email this morning from the gallery. I got into the 'Three-Dimensional' show!"

"Fantastic!" He grinned. "When's the opening?"

"In a couple of weeks, during one of Bohemia's street parties. I almost can't believe it. I mean, I know it's small-time, but it's my first show."

"And it won't be the last," he said.

"Here's something interesting. The gallery owners actually asked if they could put the video on their website to promote the show."

"Really?" Duncan frowned. "So they get all the clicks?"

I was starting to hate that word. But I got it, now. I wanted Duncan to get the clicks, too.

"Actually, they said they can embed it from where you uploaded it. You get the traffic then, right? I asked if it would be OK to put it on your vlog at the same time, and they were really excited about the publicity. Apparently they'd heard of you."

A smile overtook his face again. "You're enabling my clicks, lass? Do you know what this means?"

"No, what?"

"You've accepted me for what I am."

"What?" I asked.

"A click whore."

I giggled. "I thought you were going to say 'man-whore.' " And then I bit my lip, regretting uttering the term I'd tagged him with that night in the theater.

Duncan put down the piece of pizza he was holding and looked closely at me. "You really think that about me?"

I squirmed in my chair. "Well, of course, not now, but when I met you . . ."

"I see," he said.

"It's not like it's a bad thing," I said. "Well, it does sound kind of bad. But you're such a charmer, and the women seem to melt all over you, and there was your little band of friends, and Lolly, and all those fans drooling over you online."

He cocked his head. "Been paying attention, have you?" he asked, his tone arch.

"Oh, Duncan."

"So you still think I'm a man-whore?" He came around to my chair and pulled me out of it, yanking his body close to mine. "Just using my body to get what I want?" There was an edge to his teasing that worried me. Thrilled me.

"It is a pretty nice body," I eked out.

One of his hands slipped to my butt, and he pressed me against him. *Shit.* I could feel his erection through his shorts, prodding through my clothes, against my pussy.

"I'm glad you think I'm such a chick magnet," he said.

"You mean you aren't?"

He nipped my earlobe, and I jumped, but I was still trapped in his arms. "I've had my share of women, but I wasn't cutting the swath you seem to think. They were using me, darlin'."

I whimpered as he grazed my neck with his teeth, a big Scottish vampire.

"Are you sure they looked at it that way?" I whispered.

He pushed me toward the bed. "I ran into a lot of women at conventions and meetups when I moved to Florida. Groupies and ambitious blogger starlets and con sluts. They wanted a little taste of what they saw online, but they moved on faster than I could blink. I gave them up. They wore me out. They bored me."

"Do — do all women bore you eventually?" I asked as he lowered me to the bed.

"I don't know yet," he murmured, an edge to his voice, as he slipped a hand under my T-shirt and squeezed one breast.

He'd caught me by surprise when he showed up with lunch, so I wore no bra, and he took full advantage, kneading me, skimming my nipples.

"I'm not using you, Duncan," I said softly, wondering at how this strange conversation had gotten turned around.

"Do you want me to use you?" His voice was rough as he pulled my T-shirt off over my head.

I gasped as he renewed his attentions to my breasts, squeezing and pinching so hard it hurt. Pain. Pleasure.

God, I was wet.

"Let's use each other," I said, my voice husky, and he fell on top of me, crushing my mouth with his, unbuttoning my shorts and yanking them down.

I did the same with his, and we got them down and off and he was slamming into me, no preamble, no words. Just primitive, raw fucking. I didn't know what this was. Goodbye? Resolution? All I knew was that it was fucking hot, and I wanted more of it. I wanted all of him.

My climax roared through me like a roller coaster, and as the last waves of pleasure rattled through me, he pulled out and grabbed his cock and spilled his come onto my breasts in hot spurts. When he stopped, he was breathing hard. I lay there in shock, sated, turned on, feeling dirty. Delicious.

Thrilled to see him lose control.

The hard lines of his face relaxed, as if he were coming out of a dark dream. "Thea," he breathed.

He stepped away to the bathroom and came back with a towel and tenderly wiped me off, and then he lay down next to me and kissed me.

Wrapped up together, we didn't say anything for a long, long time.

When he did get up, he put on his clothes silently. Then

he looked at me still lying naked on the bed, exposed to him and, to be honest, still turned on.

"I'll pick you up at 8," he told me, his crystal-blue eyes sharp and unreadable.

And then he left.

I HAD to masturbate in the shower after Duncan left. I'd never been broken down to my component parts like that, transformed into a hot live wire of raw physical need. I should have been appalled, maybe, or frightened, but there was something about his intensity — something so forthright in his desire — that I felt strangely reassured.

For our outing, I put on light, linen tan pants to help keep the mosquitoes away and a white tank top with a built-in shelf bra and a gauzy button-up blouse over it. And flip-flops, because it was the beach.

I opened my door before he even knocked, and he smiled at me and dropped a light kiss on my cheek. And then we were off, with a stop for a burrito and a beer before heading to the beach, chatting about meteors and Austin and anything except what had happened today.

It was well and truly dark when we parked on a quiet street by the ocean in Bohemia Beach. We had a couple of hours until moonrise, and today storms had fired early and stayed on the western side of the state. In short, it was perfect viewing for meteors, and Duncan set up his camera on a tripod out on the sand to capture the stars and whatever meteors might streak across the sky over the glinting waves. He was shooting long exposures on an automatic time-lapse, so there wasn't much to do but relax and wait.

The ocean breeze helped take the edge off the heat of the day, and the beach was deserted. Duncan had brought a blanket from his car and spread it out on the sand. He sat on it, cross-legged, while I lay on my side, leaning on one elbow, listening to the camera click.

"Which direction should we look?" I asked.

"I think roughly northeast will work. It might be better if you lie on your back."

"I'm sure you say that to all the girls," I quipped, but I lay flat, letting my hair spread out under my head, and looked up.

"There you go again," Duncan said wryly, still sitting next to me.

"Were you actually hurt by me calling you a man-whore? I mean, you've never heard that before?"

"Ouch."

"That came out wrong. I didn't mean — I know you're not — oh, hell. I'm sorry." I tried to read his face, but it was impossible in the darkness.

"You know what made me talk you into our seven nights?" he finally asked. "You say what you think. You're honest. You show your feelings, or at least you have trouble hiding them. You aren't like the other women I know."

"Your groupies? That's a poor sample. Most women aren't the users you describe. And maybe your hookups thought you wanted the same things they did." I paused. "It's not like you said 'no.' You must have gotten something out of them."

"Only a few moments to forget I was alone."

"At least they were evidence that you're famous," I said philosophically, surprised that I was no longer bothered by the thought of his past relationships, such as they were. "That had to feel pretty good."

"Cold comfort, and I'm not very famous."

"Famous enough," I said. "Famous in your circles. And kind of irresistible."

"Oh, am I?" Now there was a smile in his tone. He lay down next to me, his elbow just brushing mine.

"You know you are, you devil," I said.

"No, I don't know that at all. Tell me all about it."

I giggled. "I love you, Duncan."

Oh, shit. It slipped out. Just like that.

And he didn't say a damned thing. I tried to keep my breathing under control and focus on the stars, the faint ones more visible as my eyes adjusted. A tiny bright streak whipped across a corner of the sky and was gone.

I jumped as he touched me. His fingers intertwined with mine.

"Do you love me, lass?" he asked softly. "Or are you just plying me with your wiles?"

"You know I don't have any wiles, you big jerk."

He let out a low laugh. "I've never met anyone like you. Anyone who confounds me as much." That didn't sound like a compliment. "Why do you think I can't stay away from you?"

I didn't know what to say, what he was trying to say. My heart was so full, one little push from him might make it spill over.

"Do you know what kind of name 'Flyte' is?" he asked.

"Completely made up?"

"Ha, no. But it's English, not Scottish. My father is descended from an Englishman who moved to Scotland because he fell in love with a woman there, rather inconveniently, about the time the English crushed the clans in the rebellion. You know what I'm talking about?"

"I've read *Outlander*," I said irritably. What was he getting at? And did he forget the fact that I'd told him I loved him?

"Well, then you know they both had a tough time of it," he said, "but he stuck it out. Went native. Sometimes I think when my father fell in love with an American, it was history repeating itself."

"What's your point?"

"Love is hard. Life hasn't given me much reason to believe in it."

"Me either," I said.

"So you've had a change of heart?" He rolled toward me, and I could see his eyes glittering in the scant starlight.

"About love? Or about loving you?"

He leaned over me, pressed into my body and kissed me. Oh, it was lush, this kiss, his tongue lazy and lascivious as it slipped inside my mouth, as he moved his lips over mine, feasting. When he pulled away, I was breathless.

"I love you, Duncan," I said again, rolling to face him, resting a hand on his hip. "You've made me change my mind about love. And I'm not going to change my mind about you, even if you do get bored with me."

"Thea," he murmured, cupping my cheek. "I will never, ever get bored with you, my Irish redhead. *And I will luve thee still my dear, till a' the seas gang dry.*"

Tears came to my eyes as he kissed me again. I wrapped my arms around him as he rolled on top of me, and I reveled in the weight of him, the reality of him.

When we came up for air, he caressed my cheek, ran a hand over my hair and looked into my eyes.

"And here I was afraid you didn't like me," he said, and I could tell he was only half-teasing. "I didn't think it was possible for me to fall in love, for someone to really love me.

But from the moment I met you, I think I knew. It took me a week to be sure."

"Only a week?" I gazed up at him in wonder, remembering all of my doubts.

"Half a week, really, because it was only the nights."

He lowered his mouth to mine, and joy rushed through me like the waves sliding up the beach. Unfolded by his candor and his kisses, my heart opened up like one of my pop-ups, only pulsing and alive, ever flowering, unlimited by cuts and creases. It became its own starry universe, expanding from the Big Bang that was Duncan Flyte.

That silly double entendre, if only a stray thought in my meandering mind, made me smile against his lips, then giggle.

"You are not laughing at me at a time like this," he said with mock umbrage, breaking off the kiss.

"Oh, no," I said, the giggles uncontrollable now. "I'm laughing with you. Always with you."

"You'd better, wench," he growled, stopping my laughter with kisses, caressing me, loving me.

We broke off our embrace after several minutes — by mutual agreement, I think — given the unforgiving sand under the blanket and the warm night. He rolled onto his back again, but this time he stayed close, hip to hip, his hand holding mine.

A bright, fast-moving orb of light ripped across the sky above us, trailing sparks, and after a second, it was gone.

"Fireball!" Duncan shouted.

I laughed again. "Yes, you are."

∼

WAKING up the morning of the gallery show felt just a little bit like Christmas. My work was going to be in a real art show. I had a great dress for the occasion. And I had Duncan.

Only when I woke up, he wasn't in my bed, and these days, he usually was. Or I was in his, depending.

It was strange that he was missing, given he'd definitely been there last night — I felt hot just thinking about last night — and he wasn't the morning person that I was. But Duncan moved in mysterious ways, and I was content to catch up with him later when he escorted me to the show.

I needn't have worried. When I got out of the shower and was toweling myself off in the bathroom, I heard his voice in the apartment. Which was also kind of weird, since he wasn't talking to me.

Wearing just my towel, I poked my head out the door to make sure he was alone.

"Hello, darlin.' " Duncan was sitting on my bed, and he had a big gift box wrapped in silver paper on his lap.

I looked around. "Who were you talking to?"

"Me?" He looked like the cat who'd eaten the canary. "No one."

I narrowed my eyes at him and walked out to kiss him on the lips. Instead of tugging on my towel and enfolding me in his arms, as I fully expected, he clutched the box and barely responded.

I stood up straight and crossed my arms. "What's going on?"

He grinned.

I could have sworn the box moved, and he sat there frozen, with that silly smile on his face.

"Is there something in that box, or are you just happy to see me?"

"Oh, all right," he said, plopping the box on the bed. Before I could move to open it, the lid nudged on its own, then popped straight off, and a small furry head poked out of the top.

I gasped.

"I want you to meet Fergus," Duncan said.

As if he knew his name, the little dog, an adorable terrier mix in white and brown and black with rumpled fur and perky ears, leaped out of the box and stood on the edge of the bed, gazing at me with glistening brown eyes, a lolling tongue and a vigorously wagging tail.

Who knew I could fall in love twice in one summer?

"Fergus?" I took a step closer, and he barked with enthusiasm. "Oh, my God, he's so freaking cute." I held out my hand for Fergus to sniff, and he licked it. A good sign. I sat on the bed next to Duncan, scooped up the dog and cradled him in my arms. Memories of Pookie came back, and my mom, and all the sweet, loyal love that dog gave us.

"Oh, shit, you're crying," Duncan said. "You weren't supposed to cry!"

"It's because I'm happy," I said as I petted the little dog, who squirmed and licked the tears off my face. "What is he? Where'd you get him?"

"Remember Holly?"

"From the jewelry store?"

"Her sister Molly —"

"Just stop it. You're kidding, right? Molly?"

"No, seriously," Duncan said, but he was trying not to laugh. "She volunteers at a shelter, and I've had her keeping an eye out for the right dog. And little Fergus came along. He had an older owner who died. He's just a year old. House-trained. I thought he'd be perfect for you."

"For us," I whispered, smiling at Duncan.

"Yes, for us," he said more softly, rubbing my shoulder and then scratching behind Fergus' ears. I let the dog down, and the little scamp romped around the bed, pouncing toward Duncan, hopping backward as Duncan reached for him, letting himself be rolled over and happily offering his belly up for a thorough rub.

"He's adorable!" I got in on the playing and petting as Fergus pawed at us in a totally YouTube-ready way. "You didn't get him just for the clicks, did you?"

"Noooo," Duncan said, but he bit his lip through his smile. "Though you have to admit, he's total clickbait."

"As long as he's having fun, it's OK," I said, scooping up the dog again and giving him a hug. "Geez, I don't have any dog stuff. Food, bowls, bed . . . "

"All taken care of."

"I love you," I said, leaning over to kiss Duncan again, half-squishing Fergus between us.

"And I am extremely confident in that fact," he said, "given that I brought this handsome creature into the house. Most men wouldn't be able to compete with a rival like this."

I laughed. "That reminds me. I have something for you." I handed him the dog and retrieved an envelope from my work table.

Duncan put Fergus on the floor so he could explore and took the envelope from me, tearing it open. He opened the card within and laughed out loud.

"Do I really look like this? And how did you know about the dog?"

"I didn't," I said, grinning at his reaction to the paper pop-up of Duncan holding a camera, framed by a TV screen, the words "Thank you, Love, Thea" scrawled next to the sculpture. "The 'thank-you' is for everything else. For everything. Thank you."

His eyes shone as he looked up at me. He set aside the card, pulled me onto his lap and kissed me until Fergus tugged at the corner of my towel and pulled it off, making us both dissolve into giggles.

We lost the next couple of hours to playing with Fergus, setting up his crate and supplies in my apartment, and going for a nice walk with him down to the harbor and back.

The whole day was a beautiful blur, and then, with an exhausted Fergus settled in his crate, we headed for the opening exhibit for Gallery Zora. It was a hip new space in the Bohemia arts district with rough brick walls, movable partitions, a painted concrete floor and a sign on the window painted by my dad, who'd promised to see the show "when there aren't so many damn people there."

The "Three-Dimensional" show was full of fascinating pieces. Some actually did hang on the wall, but they expressed the idea of three dimensions in some way. One huge piece required 3D glasses for viewing. A mind-bending sculpture played with the idea of parallel universes with mirrors and iterations on a scene; another consisted of a head sporting three faces.

Mine was set up at the center of the space, with the video monitor mounted in the middle of the slowly rotating carousel of pop-ups. The film of my colorful fairy tale played on a loop, alternating with Duncan's behind-the-scenes short featuring me. I thought I'd feel sick seeing myself like that, but instead, to my surprise, I felt something strangely close to pleasure.

"Nice placement," said Duncan, camera in hand.

Though the art deserved my attention, I'd had trouble

taking my eyes off him since we'd left our building. He wore a stunning, slightly outrageous blue and green tartan suit that brought out the blue of his eyes and was sleekly tailored to his fetching form.

I hadn't known he was wearing it, so my choice of dresses was an eerily perfect complement: a 1950s-style strapless dark blue gown with an organza overlay and sheer tartan accents in similar colors — a plaid piece swooping diagonally over the breasts and two more draping down the sides of the skirt. I swore Duncan's grin when he saw me wearing it almost broke his face.

Of course, Duncan's suit looked a lot less outrageous when we saw what Damien was wearing.

"No black tonight?" I asked nonchalantly as Cali's brother sauntered over to us in his bright white, blue, pink and green flamingo-patterned suit.

"Hell, man, that thing is a marvel," Duncan said. "Where can I get one?"

I suppressed a laugh, but Damien knew he was being kidded. "Off the rack, actually," he said. "Wait till you see the one in the jaguar print."

"Thanks for your expertise on the carousel," I told Damien.

"No problem. Your piece is cool, if a little too life-affirming for me," he said drily. "Next time, apply for a grant, and maybe you can get a cylindrical LED monitor. I told you — if you're ever in doubt, add multimedia."

"That's exactly what I did," I said, looking up at Duncan with a smile. Duncan swooped in and kissed me, hard and fast.

Damien rolled his eyes. "Want to interview me?" he asked Duncan, gesturing to the camera.

"Might as well. Have to feed the beast, and my fans are going to love that suit." I nodded at him, and off he went.

I walked up to Penelope and Jace, both dressed to the nines, and gave them each a hug.

"Thank you so much for being in the film," I said.

"It's wild," Penelope said. "I never thought I'd see myself in a storybook."

"It was my pleasure," Jace said. "It's got me thinking, actually, about a new play. Would you be interested in consulting on the sets if we were to go with a pop-up theme?"

Jace Edison was asking *me* to consult on one of *his* plays?

"Hell, yeah," I said, and they laughed.

Ez and Gary were circulating, too, and I thanked them for their music on their way out the door — Ez had to get over to the Junction Box for a gig with her band.

Maybe Cali's Goth brother had gone to Florida pastels with his flamingo suit, but Cali wore atypical black that contrasted elegantly with her blond hair. She tapped Duncan and brought him over to me so she could get a shot of us together with the sculpture in the background.

"Where's Wyatt?" I asked.

"On a surf trip to Costa Rica with friends."

"And you didn't go?"

"I've got to let the boy wander a little without me. It's in his blood. He'll be back." She winked. "Hey, Sloane, get over here!"

Duncan escaped again to catch an interview with the gallery owners while Sloane came over to talk with us.

"Hi, cuz," she said to Cali. Then to me: "I love the show. There are a couple of great ceramic pieces, and yours is absolutely captivating. People can't stop looking at it."

"I'm happily surprised," I said, glancing at the patrons

examining the carousel and watching the videos. "You look delectable, as usual."

"Oh, this thing," Sloane said, twirling in one of her cute little dresses.

"And where's Alex?" Cali asked.

"Planting a bottle of good wine on the wine table so he can drink without wincing," Sloane said. "He's such a wine snob."

We laughed, and then a sparkle on Sloane's hand caught my eye.

"Hey," I said, pointing. "Didn't that ring used to be on your right hand?"

She looked up at both of us with a sly smile.

Cali gaped. Then shrieked. Heads turned, and Sloane hushed her.

"You're getting married!" I exclaimed, although more quietly than Cali.

"You — Alex — oh my God. I'm shooting the wedding," Cali declared. "Sloane! Why didn't you tell me? I can't believe this is happening. You have a date set?"

"We're thinking a Christmas wedding. Won't that be pretty?"

Not a little stunned, I left her and Cali as they chatted about the details. I was almost dizzy with the happiness around me, the excitement, the creativity. Coming back to Bohemia really had been coming home for me. I just hadn't realized in how many ways: Family. Friends. Art. My past. My future.

I smiled as Duncan walked toward me, ridiculously handsome in his tartan suit, his eyes sparkling, his reddish-brown hair irresistibly ruffled.

"Something just occurred to me," I said.

"And what's that?" He draped an arm around my shoulders.

I leaned into his muscled body, tingling with the current that flowed between us. "The last time we were at a gallery show, you bought a piece of art, I believe. What did you do with it?"

Duncan looked down at me with a mischievous smile. "Because you haven't seen it in my apartment? And you're wondering if a giant portrait of you in your underwear is in a rubbish bin or hanging over some stranger's sofa, am I right?"

"I — oh, no. You wouldn't give it away, would you? It's not in your friend Pete's place or something, is it?"

Duncan laughed. "It's leaning against the back wall of my walk-in closet."

"Your *closet?*"

"That way I can give you a kiss every morning when I get dressed, even if you're not there. Though you're going to be there on a permanent basis soon, so I think it's safe to find a wall for it now."

I shook my head, but I was smiling. "Maybe you should leave it in the closet."

"Not on your life! And I'm going to have Cali shoot a matching portrait of me to hang next to it. Maybe wearing a kilt and nothing else. Would an upskirt shot be too gauche?"

"You're incorrigible," I said, laughing. I tilted my face toward his in invitation, and Duncan slid his mouth over mine, sweet and hot, loopy and lovely, solid and sure, until I got lost in his limitless kiss.

Lost — and found.

∽

AFTERWORD

Thanks for reading! Sign up for my newsletter to get fun original content, giveaways, news and cocktail recipes, and I'll send you a free story. I also have a Facebook group where readers can hang out and chat about books and life — please join us in Lucy's Lounge.

More online:

LucyLakestone.com
Facebook.com/LucyLakestone
Twitter.com/LucyLakestone
Bookbub.com/authors/lucy-lakestone
Pinterest.com/lucylakestone/
Amazon
Goodreads
YouTube

ACKNOWLEDGMENTS

I appreciate all the support I had while writing *Bohemia Nights* during a difficult time. It was especially nice to meet my fellow scribes at the coffee shop for motivational and writing sessions, including Alethea Kontis, Jax Cassidy and Naomi Bellina. Naomi also kindly agreed to be the "hands" for the book trailer so the pop-ups could magically open.

Speaking of the pop-ups, I'm especially grateful to Lovepop (lovepopcards.com), which makes incredible pop-cards and gave me permission to use a few of their wonderful designs in the trailer.

Thanks to readers Crystal, Christina and Karen for their great ideas for puppy names. I used Karen's adorable suggestion, Fergus. Karen also consulted her Scottish relatives to confirm that Scottish men do say *baws* when they mean "balls," *and* she shared an inspiring GIF involving kilts.

Thank you also to author Whitley Cox for her advice, for sharing her hot books, and for her promotional savvy.

Thanks, as always, to the members of Spacecoast Authors of Romance for their support and inspiration.

I'm very grateful to editor and friend Holly Martin for her feedback — Holly, I told you I would name a character after you!

Mr. Lakestone deserves my heartfelt thanks for his continuing tolerance of my writing obsession and the piles of books that sprout around the house.

And, finally, thank *you* for reading!

ABOUT THE AUTHOR

Lucy Lakestone is an award-winning author who lives on Florida's east central coast, among the towns that serve as an inspiration for the hot romances of her Bohemia Beach Series, including *Bohemia Beach, Bohemia Light, Bohemia Blues* (winner of the Golden Quill), *Bohemia Heat, Bohemia Nights* and *Bohemia Bells*. She's been a journalist, photographer, editor and video producer but prefers living in her imagination, where the moon is full and the cocktails are divine. She is also the author of a novel of romantic suspense, *Desire on Deadline.*

BOHEMIA BELLS

The sixth BOHEMIA BEACH book

A HOT ROMANTIC COMEDY

∽∂℮℘

Merry mayhem at a Christmas wedding!

When hyper-organized Millie Romano is drafted to plan her friends' Christmas wedding in Bohemia Beach, she knows it needs a spectacular centerpiece. Why not hire a world-renowned sand sculptor? Soon she realizes that no matter how talented Bennett Westyn is, he's also a troublemaker, stirring up spats with the snooty caterer and driving Millie crazy. Worse, she can't resist him, even as his merrymaking steers her toward a wedding-day disaster. As her Christmas Eve deadline nears, there are two things she can't figure out: why her orderly life has become so muddled, and how she's lost her heart in the mayhem.

LEARN MORE AT

LucyLakestone.com